LOCKED IN DEATH

By the same author

LOCKED IN DEATH

A Penny Lane Mystery

John Paxton Sheriff

ROBERT HALE · LONDON

© John Paxton Sheriff 2009
First published in Great Britain 2009

ISBN 978-0-7090-8762-5

Robert Hale Limited
Clerkenwell House
Clerkenwell Green
London EC1R 0HT

www.halebooks.com

2 4 6 8 10 9 7 5 3 1

Typeset in 11/13½pt Plantin.
Printed by the MPG Books Group
in the UK

For my niece, Belinda Devery,
with love and appreciation.

Author's Note

As always, I have tinkered with geography and locations. The Dee Bar Lighthouse does not exist. There are newspaper offices in Old Hall Street, Liverpool, but the one mentioned in this novel is a figment of my imagination, as are the people working there. I have been as accurate as possible with details of Rhodes town: the hotels and restaurants are real, the Tourist Police HQ is on the corner of Papagou and Makariou streets, and Rhodes National Bank is in Museum Square. However, all characters in or near those establishments are fictitious and, as I did the research, any mistakes are mine.

The gravel car-park in front of the tall office block was almost empty. Sodium street lighting and the lights from the windows of offices still occupied by workaholics turned shallow potholes brimming with dirty rainwater into pools of liquid silver and gold. The weather gave an elderly black BMW parked close to a high, crumbling breeze-block wall the illusory gloss of a vehicle driven straight out of the dealer's showroom. Affixed to its roof by a tubular metal rack, a dull silver luggage box was a curvaceous fibreglass capsule glistening with droplets of recent rain.

At 7.30 that cold, damp evening, a black Jeep SUV with dark tinted windows turned out of the main road traffic and slipped silently down the slope into the walled enclosure. Its lights winked out. Tyres crunching, it executed a wide, leisurely half circle that brought it to a halt alongside the BMW. The sound of the engine was an expensive murmur. Other than a faint cloud of white vapour drifting from the chrome exhaust, there was nothing to advertise the vehicle's presence.

Five minutes after the SUV had parked, a tall man emerged from the office-block's swing doors and jogged towards the car-park. His approach was noted in the SUV's mirrors. Doors clicked open on both sides of the vehicle. Two men stepped out. They were dressed in black polo-necked sweaters and black jeans, and carried the bulk of men who habitually pumped iron but trod with the weightlessness of ballet dancers on expensive training shoes.

One of them walked around the vehicle, then both stood

waiting. The tall man jogged to join them. The three men came together in the shadows between the two vehicles.

The man from the office wore faded blue jeans and a blue-and-white hooped rugby shirt. He had hastily thrown on a dark fleece. Now he zipped it up to the neck, huddling into it as if chilled. When he spoke, he was breathing more heavily than might have been expected from such a short run. His voice was low, tense, a little unsteady.

'Got him?'

'In the back,' one of the other men said. 'Dead to the world.'

'So let's get it over with.'

The taller of the two men from the Jeep stepped silently around the vehicle and swung open the back door. He bent to reach deep inside, clutched something with both hands, and heaved. A heavy weight slid towards him. A pair of trainers came into view, then stone-washed jeans. There was a soft snicking sound as cloth caught on metal. He straightened. His eyes glittered in the street lighting as he looked around and waited.

His companion joined him. He, too, stood waiting.

The man from the office turned away. In the mixture of fluorescent and sodium lighting his face had taken on a pale-green sheen. There was a faint jingling as he reached into his pocket and pulled out a bunch of keys. He turned to the BMW and looked up at the luggage box on the roof. After a moment's hesitation he reached up and used one of the keys to open the box's two locks. Stretching, straining, he pushed the box's lid and let it fall open.

'OK, get him up there.'

The two men from the Jeep dragged the man out of the back by his feet, face down. They dragged him all the way, without pause, keeping hold of his ankles. The upper body dropped limply, heavily. His face and chest smacked into a pool in the gravel. Water splashed. One of the men holding him chuckled.

'The budgie has landed.'

The man in the fleece said, 'Is he dead?'

That brought a broad grin. 'What is it they say about bears and woods?'

'For Christ's sake get on with it.'

And now the man in the fleece was looking about him nerv-

ously. He watched one of the men walk backwards between the
two vehicles, dragging the limp body. The watcher's eyes
narrowed and his mouth twisted in a grimace as the face scraped
across the rough ground. Then both the big men bent to the
body. They clamped their hands on the clothing and effortlessly
heaved the man to chest height, held him against the wet, slippery
side of the BMW. The car rocked, creaked. One man grinned.

'So this is what they call a dead weight,' he said.

'Dead easy,' the other man said, and together they pushed
upwards, then turned the body and slid it head first until the
torso was in the box, the legs dangling.

'Hold him there,' one of them said.

He jogged to the front of the BMW, and vaulted on to the
bonnet which crackled beneath his weight. Luggage boxes take
up most of a car's roof. This was a big one, so there was nowhere
for him to go. He leaned forward, braced knees and thighs against
the windscreen, his chest against the front of the box. Then he
used both hands to drag the body all the way up.

His watching companion grinned, clapped slowly, mockingly.

Still braced, the man on the BMW's bonnet again grasped the
body with both hands and tried to fit it into the box so that the
lid could be closed. But he quickly discovered that a body, unconscious or dead, tends to flop: try to position it one way, and it will
go the other. After a few minutes he cursed softly, let the body sag
loosely and stood up straight on the bonnet, arching his back.

'Bastard's too big, too heavy, and the container's too small.'

'Bend him the other way,' the man from the office said. 'On his
side, foetal position.'

'Back to the womb,' the other watching man said.

'Let there be darkness,' said the man on the bonnet. He leaned
forward again and flopped the torso on to its side in the box, used
his strength to hold it there while he adjusted its position: arms
folded across the chest, thighs up against arms, feet against
buttocks. Then, breathing hard, he drew back and slammed down
the lid.

The man from the office tossed up the keys. The man on the
roof locked the luggage box, then jumped down to join the
others.

'*Finito.*'

'Thank Christ,' the man from the office said. He took the keys, slipped them into his pocket. 'Get out of here, but don't look as if you're in a race.'

Without another word he turned up the collar of his fleece and jogged back towards the office block. The two men in black climbed into the Jeep, slammed the doors. It drove away, crunched across the car-park, pulled up the exit ramp.

The gaunt Liverpool scally in the brown hoodie had been leaning against the wall close to the car-park entrance, bent over with bony hands cupped around the warmth of a match flame as he lit a cigarette, when his eyes were drawn to the movement down in the car-park. He'd finished lighting the cigarette, then straightened up and watched the Jeep park alongside BMW; waited, lifted his gaze as yellow light flooded from the office block's door and the man in the dark fleece emerged and ran down to the two cars. He watched the three men come together, huddle, talk, and his first thought had been the obvious one: drugs. His teeth had glistened as he grinned.

But the smile had been wiped out when he saw the limp figure pulled from the back of the Jeep, watched as it flopped on to the gravel and was dragged between the two cars. Still watching intently, he'd tossed away the cigarette, reached into his jacket and pulled out an expensive mobile phone. Then, after looking around to make sure he wasn't being watched, he'd held it out in front of him and begun using the phone's camera. He took several shots, zooming in very close when the man's dead weight was heaved up on to the BMW's roof and folded into the luggage box like a life-sized rag doll.

The luggage box was locked. The man in the dark fleece jogged back to the office block and pushed his way in through the glass doors. And now the two big men climbed into the Jeep and drove up to the car-park's exit. The black SUV stopped close to the skinny youth in the hooded jacket. Despite the tinted windows, he saw light reflected in the driver's eyes as he turned to look for a gap in the traffic. Cheekily, he raised the hand holding the phone to warn the driver to wait, and when a gap finally appeared he stood close and waved the Jeep forward like a bullfighter making a graceful pass with the cape.

At the last second, before completion of that sweeping movement, he turned his face away and lifted his hand to pull the side of his hood forward so that his face was hidden. The driver had again glanced his way. This time the scally saw him clearly and recognized the man, his shaven head, the scarred eyebrows, the badly set broken nose – and suddenly he was frightened.

He kept his face averted, looking down the street with his lips pursed in a silent whistle as he listened to the tone of the Jeep's engine and the faint squeal of its tyres as it joined the road and accelerated away.

Then, softly, fiercely, he said, 'Right, you bastard', as he lifted the phone and took one last photograph of the SUV's rear end and registration number.

He watched the Jeep turn right at the traffic lights, waited until it was out of sight, then slipped the phone into his pocket and jogged down into the car-park. He ran to the high side wall, paused long enough to grind the cigarette under the heel of his grubby trainers, then slowly worked his way towards the BMW with his jacket's shoulder rasping on the breeze blocks.

He heard the first hollow sound as he drew near to the old car. His hair prickled. He stopped, his heart pounding; replayed the sound in his mind, recognized it and felt sick. Frightened, fighting the curiosity that frequently got him into trouble, he stood with his back to the wall and his hands flat against the cold blocks. Then, as he tightened his lips, shook his head and turned to run for the exit, the sound came again.

'Shit, shit, *shit*,' the youth whispered, and he squeezed his eyes shut and counted slowly to ten.

Then he opened his eyes, took a deep breath and ran the other way – towards the BMW. He ran with his heart racing, intent on looking and listening but with no intention of hanging about. When he reached the car he stopped his rush by slamming his palms high on the cold metal. He shut his eyes and rested his forehead between his hands, tried to calm his breathing, block out the hum of traffic and the even, too-fast hissing of his pulse.

In that false, unnatural silence, he thought he could hear the muffled rasp of someone else's laboured breathing. He waited. And then, definitely, no question, dead bloody certain, against his cold forehead he felt the car rock. His eyes flicked open. He lifted his head, again felt the rocking, this time detecting the faint movement through his palms.

He stepped back. His hands came off the car, peeling away from the metal with the sticky sound of plaster tearing off skin. When he looked at his palms, they were dark with fresh wet blood.

'Jesus,' he whispered.

The man in the luggage box must have heard him.

He groaned. Said something. A word ... a gargle.

The groan was the same ghostly, disembodied moan of pain, terror and despair that had drawn the youth reluctantly to the BMW and was now turning his legs into two thin lengths of wet string that refused to hold his weight. He bit his lip, reached out to cling to the tubular metal framework holding the luggage box; remembered the blood on his hands, the man doubled up in that tiny space, and shuddered as he took an involuntary step back.

He looked up at the box that would, he guessed, soon become a coffin. Then he reached up and slapped it twice with his palm to let the man inside know he was not alone.

'Hang on,' he said hoarsely and then, again, 'hang on in there, I'm callin' police an' ambulance, all right?'

Then he hurried away, trembling fingers fumbling for his mobile phone.

As he hurried up the ramp, it began to rain. Behind him, in the car-park, the light droplets spattered the BMW. They splashed on the scratched roof, on the luggage box where, incredibly, they began to dry as the heat generated from within warmed the shiny surface. Then the rain became heavier. The warmth – minimal at best – began to lose the battle. A light breeze came in behind the rain, carrying with it the salt smell of the River Mersey. The box cooled. Car and box glistened in the street lighting. And, as the minutes passed, the blood that had leaked from the box was first thinned, then washed away by the rain until no sign of it remained.

chapter one

Monday

I was at the breakfast bar in the kitchen drinking Kenyan coffee and watching the rain dancing on the conservatory when Josh came through from the bedroom. Good job I was sitting down. We've been married twelve years and the sight of him still makes my knees go weak. Tonight even more so, because he was all togged up in a way that would slay the *señoritas*. Not that there were any where he was going. It was 7.30 on Monday evening and he was off to the writers' group he'd recently formed with Steve Easter. Sozzled Scribblers I think it's called. Something like that. And mostly male, which is unusual because haven't women taken over the writing game? Anyway, thick, stylishly untidy grey hair was making my fingers ache with the urge to run through it. A charcoal-grey shirt worn under a slightly darker suit was open at the neck exposing his tanned throat, and the thought of planting a kiss in that tantalizing vee was doing strange things to my pulse.

He was grinning. The sparkle in his blue eyes told me he knew exactly what I was thinking, and was deciding on a suitable riposte.

'Perhaps later,' he said, as he hoisted his lanky frame on to a stool and reached for his coffee. 'If you're very good.'

'Now there's a *double entendre* if ever I heard one. I'm always very good, whichever way you take it. But what if it's a case of now or never?'

'If it's now you know you'll get all steamed up. A flushed and breathless Penny Lane will disconcert our stamp collector, and that's before he discovers you were once Penny Black.'

'Stamp collectors are kids using glue to stick British colonial and eastern bloc pictorials in notebooks. Galleywood's a philatelist, and I'm not going to tell him.'

'That he's a philatelist?'

I glowered fiercely. 'That I was once Penny Black.'

'Why not? Could be a useful ploy to get him talking, the metaphorical bottle-opener that opens the Buck's Fizz of useless information.'

'Doesn't that have a cork? Anyway, Penny Black's about me, and I'm interested in him.'

'Mm. Like, finding out why a philatelist turned numismatist for a day. And what he's going to do with a coin collection of one.' He looked at me steadily over the rim of his mug. 'I know an intriguing newspaper article's drawn you out to charm the socks off this Larry Galleywood, but I still don't know which hat you're wearing. What are you tonight, journalist or private eye? And do please say it's journalist. I don't think my nerves could take it if you go back to consorting with criminals.'

'Nonsense. Anyway, it depends on whether there's a crime involved, so I'll decide as the evening progresses. And, talking of which …'

I glanced hastily at my watch, slid from the stool and gave my full skirt a twitch so the right bits pointed fore and aft.

'Yes, and talking of which, me too,' Josh said. 'Time's creeping on and the Seasoned Scribblers await my presence.'

'I thought it was the Salty Scribes. Will Steve be there?'

'No, he's working late. But our esteemed co-founder has definitely invited us round to his place for a latish drink and a nibble.'

I was at the mirror, fluffing grey hair that didn't want to fluff. Over my shoulder I could see Josh watching me with a certain something in his eyes. I bit my lip, willed my knees to behave, then turned round and covered my confusion by scouting around for my tote bag.

'Steve will be there if he makes it home,' I said.

'Doesn't matter. Sheila's in all evening. She'll take pity, let us in if it's raining.'

'Of course, but my point still stands. The chances of Steve arriving *anywhere* are slim, unless he's finally dumped that awful car.'

'Nope, still driving the ancient black beemer.'

'Not black, rusty. And isn't beemer an Americanism? Shouldn't it be BMW?'

'Ah, but I am a writer of crime novels.'

'Yes, and as the latest is set in America, you're ensuring realism by adopting the speech and mannerisms of your main character?'

I shook my head as he grinned and spread his hands in a what-can-I-say sort of gesture.

'Well, at least I know what I'm in for,' I growled, at last locating my bag and slinging it over my shoulder. 'Come here, you silly old fool. If you promise not to get all steamed up I'll give you – in the parlance, of course – a juicy parting smacker.'

In the fine cold rain sweeping across the Wirral from the Irish sea the big red-brick house set back in the trees close to The Beacons in Heswall was a cross between Poe's House of Usher and the Bates Motel from *Psycho*. At eight in the evening the wan street lighting struggled to reach it through clattering wet branches, leaving its windows like flat dead eyes. Falling autumn leaves were lost bats fluttering around the tall building's sagging slate roof. It was three storeys high – four if you counted the basement, the tops of whose dark and dusty windows peeped at me over a stone parapet as my little red Ka crunched up the drive and on to the rectangular forecourt. And somehow I knew that when I climbed the steps and announced my presence at the massive oak front door I would do so by pulling on a rope that would set a distant brass bell mournfully clanking in the servants' quarters.

Was this what I had been expecting?

I knew something of the man I was visiting, most of what he did, and from that information I'd tried to guess what his house would look like. Well, now I knew, but as I climbed out of the car, slammed the door and ran through icy rain towards the creepy, crumbling pile, I realized the question that had been answered raised another that was still more intriguing.

A philatelist sitting at a dusty desk using tweezers to pick up scraps of coloured paper might have chosen such a residence and failed to notice as it came tumbling down around his ears. An estate agent sitting in a modern office, on the other hand, would surely have chosen a luxurious house acquired at knock-down price as one of the semi-legal perks, or this house, but restored it to its former Victorian glory.

The Larry Galleywood I was calling on, unannounced, was both an old-fashioned philatelist and a modern estate agent making use of a website, databases and digital cameras. Understandably, my guess about the house had been miles out because vocation and hobby came together in a whopping mismatch, a head-on collision of the old and the new.

The question intriguing me was what kind of a man would live in a house like this? What did Larry Galleywood look like?

When I pressed the modern bell push and got not a clank but the kind of musical tones that usually announce Avon I knew at once that this was one of those nights when I'd get everything wrong. And when the heavy door was opened on soundless hinges, not by maid or doddering butler but by a slim grey-haired woman in a white blouse and saffron-yellow skirt that together probably cost as much as my car, I almost sighed in disappointment. Her face and bare arms were tanned to perfection, and I thought sun beds and holidays in the Med or further afield and decided it was a lot of time spent on both. As if sensing my gaze she swept back an errant wisp of hair that was being toyed with by the wind. As she did so her other hand seemed to slip from the door handle and she tilted sideways in slow motion with a dreamy smile of surprise. Well oiled, seemed an apt description of the hinges and the woman. I was forced to suppress a giggle.

'Oops,' I said, as she settled lightly against the door jamb. 'Long day, or several short drinks?'

She lifted one generous eyebrow in a manner that might have been expressing amusement or bemusement. But her eyes had turned as cold as wet Welsh slate and I took a half step backwards and lifted a placating hand.

'Sorry. Bad weather, house not as expected, door answered by elegant apparition – my aplomb's been badly shaken and I'm not

myself. Well, actually I am, of course, if you know what I mean.'
I closed my eyes and took a deep breath. 'Hang on. Let's start
again. My name's Penny Lane. I'm a freelance photographer, and
I write magazine articles. I haven't got an appointment, but I
wonder if Mr Galleywood could spare me a few minutes?'

The second eyebrow rose to join the first.

'At this time of night?'

The voice was educated, the tone one of disbelief, the eyes now
suspicious. I wondered what she didn't like? Photographer?
Scribbler? Or perhaps she recognized the name and was reacting
to my other more recent occupation. Private investigators arouse
the same reaction as police officers: one turns up on your
doorstep and at once you start worrying about the car's road tax.

'Well,' I said, as she eased away from the door jamb and stood
swaying gently in the breeze, 'one way of finding out is to ask him.
Would you do that for me?'

'He's in his office. The door's locked. If I knock he won't
answer. Do not disturb.' She risked losing her balance completely
by lifting both hands close to her ears then wiggling her forefin-
gers to sketch airy quotation marks around the last three words.

I rolled my eyes. 'Oh dear. How long's that likely to go on for?'

'Christ knows.'

'That sounds promising: at least somebody does.'

She'd gone from refined to coarse in two words and hadn't
even blinked, and I began to look at her with fresh interest. Then,
realizing I had my back to the fierce weather, rain was dripping
from my light-blue waterproof jacket and I still hadn't gained
entry I said, 'You know, the wind's in the wrong direction and the
backs of my legs are getting cold and wet. If you let me in perhaps
we could share a long drink while I'm waiting.'

That got me a calculating look. Then she sighed, turned with
great concentration and walked into the gloomy interior.

I stepped in out of the wet and closed the door. I'd grabbed my
bag as I got out of the car and had been fiddling with it from time
to time as we talked. It's a voluminous canvas tote-bag thing I
chose for its size and the neutral colour that doesn't attract attention, and because it's so secure when in position around my body
that if a bag snatcher did try his luck he'd discover he was

dragging me with him. Or should that be her and she? Which would then be PC but discriminatory – wouldn't it?

I almost giggled as, with my bag slung from my shoulder – containing, amongst other items, a dinky little Fujifilm FinePix F30 camera which is ideal for low-light work – I followed prissy Miss yellow skirt down a panelled passageway that was as musty as a mushroom cellar and as dark as the *Lusitania*'s hold. I guessed she was in her mid-fifties. Around my age. Tall and lissom in that expensive outfit, she walked as if she had a basket of washing balanced on straight grey hair with the sheen of silk, and managed to tread silently on brown lino that squeaked like mice beneath my wet shoes.

Clichés, I thought, listening to myself with a touch of disdain, and I couldn't help imagining what Josh would say if he was privy to my thoughts. The truth was the house had spooked me and I was doing a bit of mental babbling to keep my spirits up – and even that choice of words threatened to raise a shiver.

My tall, tanned and ever-so-slightly inebriated hostess led me into a huge kitchen that reminded me I was in a house of contradictions. The exterior and entrance hall were dilapidated Victorian. Here, in a room as hot as a sauna, modern pine units lined the walls and a red oil-fired Aga gleamed as if wet. There was a distinct smell of newness. I changed course to a granite double sink where a wide window with a rotting wooden frame – another contradiction – looked out over a long garden as impenetrable as a tropical rain forest. Yellow light shone on trees and shrubs that tossed madly in the wind. The rain was a rapidly shifting veil blurring the distance.

'The light's from his office,' said the woman in the yellow skirt. She was standing behind me, very close, and pointing towards the ceiling. I could just smell drink on her breath, and gave myself a mental tick for keen perception.

'Like this room, then,' I said, 'it looks out over a jungle.'

'That's not what interests him. There's a grassy track on the other side of the gate. It leads to a private health club. In the summer he likes to watch the young ladies jogging to the gym in their skimpy gear.'

When I turned around, her face told me nothing, but there was a glimmer of amusement in her grey eyes. Safe on her own territory, she seemed to be thawing. She held out her hand.

'I'm Melanie Wigg.'

'Housekeeper or secretary?'

'Oh, very much more than either of those, but the actual job description escapes me.' She cocked her head as she thought, then her lips curved in another of those dreamy smiles. 'I work with him in his estate agency, of course, have done for years. Here I suppose you could call me a domestic without portfolio. Live in.'

'Nice place. Been here long?'

'I moved in at Easter, this year ... perhaps just before ...' her words trailed off, and again there was the hint of a smile, this one clearly expressing a secret amusement. Then a frown wiped out the smile and she said, 'Of course, if you're thinking what I think you're thinking – you're wrong; it's not like that.'

'What I was thinking was that it all adds up to a lot of hard work. Do I detect a tendency to down tools at day's end and recover with a drop of the hard stuff?'

'I like that detect bit,' she said, turning away and walking without a hint of a wobble to the solid oak table where a half-full bottle of Calvados and a half-empty glass stood waiting. 'I'm sure it was you did some clever detecting in a recent murder case. Didn't you lead the police to that Welsh lawyer who'd been washing his hands in other people's blood?'

'Ah. I had a feeling you'd recognized my name.'

'Well, I did and, despite the risk to reputations, I let you in. Now you can sit down and tell me why you're here.'

She'd drifted past the table and gone to a high cupboard. She reached inside, waggled a crystal wine glass at me. Fleeting thought: was *everything* new in here? I shook my head. She shrugged and replaced the glass. When she sat down at the table she pushed her half-finished drink away with a thoughtful frown.

The heat from the Aga was already drying and tightening the skin on my wet legs. I pulled out a chair and sat down opposite Melanie. She was watching me with a look I'd seen when one of Josh's mates was sitting in his corner waiting for the bell announcing the first round of a boxing match he'd been conned into. If I was looking for a label, I think I'd call it apprehension mixed with defiance. And quite a bit of smouldering aggression waiting to be fanned into flame.

'I told you I take photographs and write articles,' I said. 'Well, characters help sell both, and Larry Galleywood is an interesting man – not least because he recently got his name splashed all over the local paper.'

'So what is it you want to talk to him about? The rare coin?'

'Er, yes – isn't that what I just said? What you were expecting?'

'All you did was mention the newspapers.'

'What I mean is, once I rang the bell and you let me in you must have realized it was the newspaper article that brought me here.'

There was a lengthy pause which, if I'd stuck with my clichés, I'd have called pregnant. It was one of those moments when the person looking at you seems unable to drag their eyes away, while being frighteningly aware that if they keep looking they'll give the game away – whatever that might be. And as she pursed her lips and continued to stare, her gaze apparently locked on mine – I realized she'd said newspapers in the plural and it suddenly occurred to me what was wrong.

'There was more than one article, wasn't there?' I said.

'You said it yourself: he's an interesting man.'

'Indeed. So what was this second article about?'

'There were lots of them.'

'And all suggesting, er, inappropriate behaviour for a reputable businessman?'

'Buying that coin at auction from under the nose of a dipstick doctor like Malcolm Moneydie,' she said haughtily, 'was not a scam.'

'Scam is your word, Melanie, not mine. Where'd that come from?'

A faint flush spread from her throat to her cheeks, neatly complementing the bright yellow of her skirt. She looked in a speculative sort of way at the glass she'd pushed away, ran the tip of her tongue gently along her lips then took a deep breath that finished up as a sigh.

'Yes, well … that's something else you'll have to take up with Larry.'

'When I can. I know you said he doesn't like being disturbed, but how long's he likely to be?'

'It's hard to say. His routine's been disrupted. He's been getting chest pains. On the way home from Liverpool and the local library he called in at the doctor's.'

'Not this Moneydie, by any chance?'

'Yes.'

'I think I know the library, but where's the surgery?'

'Not far from here.'

She named a road I was familiar with, completed the address – in case I wanted his side of the story, she added, her face sour – and I nodded, my mind busy.

'Wasn't going to Moneydie with his health problem a bit risky? I mean, Galleywood had snatched a coin from under his nose.'

'*Bought* a coin.'

'Yes, all right, but even *buying* a coin coveted by a keen collector who happens to be the family GP is surely inviting a prescription for … I don't know, strychnine suppositories, arsenic lozenges?'

'That's silly. Or are you joking? Besides, it's been diagnosed as reasonably mild angina, and Moneydie sensibly prescribed moderate exercise and plenty of fresh air—'

She broke off as a sharp crack from somewhere overhead made her start. It was followed by a faint thump, then a second much heavier thud.

'Dropped his pen, then his book,' I said helpfully, as she looked up at the ceiling. 'Now he's down on one knee, picking them up.'

'Some bloody pen, and you're some bloody private investigator,' Melanie said. 'The first crack sounded much more like a shot.'

The inebriated woman who had answered the door to me was long gone. Now the woman who scraped back her chair and headed for the door was the model of high speed efficiency, her chin thrust out and lips pressed into a thin line as she pitter-pattered down the passage with hair flying and me in hot pursuit.

I'd gone several feet before I remembered my handbag, and the little Fuji camera. I dashed back into the kitchen. By the time I'd scooped up the bag by its strap and flown back to the passage I could hear Melanie's footsteps ascending the stairs. I ran after her. It was back to the dark ages or I'd never have heard her, brown linoleum covering wooden treads so that her feet slapped noisily, and a lofty stair well at the top of which – as I craned my neck to look – I could see a frosted-glass skylight and what appeared to be a couple of pigeons huddled miserably outside in the rain.

We didn't climb that far. The first-floor passage went in both directions and Melanie had scooted right. I glimpsed the open door of a bathroom, caught up with her as she pressed her ear to a solid oak door leading into the next room and tapped gently on the panel.

'Lex?'

First name terms, nicknames, didn't quite go with domestic without portfolio, and as we both waited for a sign from within I began to wonder about the relationship and how it began.

'Lex, are you all right?'

She'd tapped for a second time and was becoming anxious. Her eyes, when she glanced at me, were strained and also puzzled.

'Mild angina's not usually fatal,' I said, 'especially if he was sitting at his desk.'

'If he was sitting at his desk, what the hell were all those bangs and bumps?'

She turned away with a fierce shake of the head. Quickly she tried the brass doorknob. When it turned, but the door refused to open, her clenched fist came up and she hammered on the panels.

'Lex, if you're all right, answer me now, or open the door. If not I'll—'

She hesitated, looking at me as if waiting for words of wisdom.

'Have you got another key?'

She nodded, then bent down, squinted through the keyhole.

'Won't work. He's left his in the lock.'

'There are ways. For a start, we might be able to poke it out with a skewer or something.'

She shook her head irritably, then again pounded on the door.
'Lex, this is getting silly; for God's sake open up.'

She waited, listening hard as her eyes focused on lurid images flickering in her imagination.

Nothing. Not a sound from inside the room.

Melanie grimaced.

'Lex,' she said, 'I'm going to have to call the police.'

Did I detect a hesitancy in her voice? I thought I did, but if so, why? What was making her wary? Was it an anticipated angry reaction from the man, Larry Galleywood, if the call was unnecessary? Or was it the police she feared?

I watched as she waited. She tried again, banging on the door, repeatedly calling his name. Then she looked at me, her lips tight. I took out my mobile phone, waggled it. She nodded.

I dialled 999.

chapter two

The two uniformed officers who answered the call had damp shirts, belts loaded with tackle and were clearly excited by the mere idea of doing something different. The tall young man and much smaller blonde woman introduced themselves as PCs Faraday and Kirk. They exchanged glances as Melanie explained who she was and what was wrong – introducing me as an afterthought – and, as they clattered up the stairs after her with me again taking up the rear, I could hear PC Faraday whispering into his radio and wondered if he was calling up the lads with raucous voices and one of those ugly battering rams.

We formed a half-circle in front of the locked study door. PC Faraday asked Melanie if she was sure Galleywood wasn't answering. She glowered at him.

'Positive. If you don't believe me, you have a go.'

He did. His voice was loud, his fist much heavier than Melanie's, but the result was the same: the room remained silent. *As the grave* was the thought that entered my mind. I quickly banished it to the dark recesses, knowing from recent experience that it would almost certainly claw its way out.

The young PC had stopped pounding and was now looking with misgivings at the heavy oak door.

'Can't see us getting through that without help,' he said.

'A door's only as strong as the fittings,' Melanie said. 'These are brass and a hundred and fifty years old and they were rattling when you knocked.'

'You reckon the lock will give way?'

'Lock or hinges.' She smiled sweetly. 'The choice is yours, but try something pretty quick because a man could be dying.'

I'd taken a few steps away from them. I turned my back as the young constable debated which side of the door to kick and, sensing drama, took the little Fuji camera out of my bag. Remembering an incident from the Gareth Owen case, I also found a spare memory card and palmed that in my left hand.

When I turned to face the group, the young police officer was leaning with his back against the wall opposite the door. He took two fast steps, raised his bent right leg in front of him, straightened it so that the knee locked then rammed the door with the flat of his foot. The impact was alongside the lock. The door burst open. The old brass lock had held, but the jamb had split. Splinters of white wood stuck out like a carnivore's broken teeth.

Every action has its own reaction. As the door swung into the room and slammed against the interior wall, the tall constable recoiled and almost flattened his blonde colleague. PC Kirk squeaked a protest. For an instant, my view into the study was unobstructed. I raised the camera to my eye. Without bothering to look at details I took three shots in rapid succession, without flash, then let my hand drop naturally to my side.

Melanie, her knuckles pressed against her teeth, was staring into the room. Her eyes had widened in horror. Suddenly she gasped something unintelligible and ran towards the open doorway. PC Kirk recovered her balance and stepped in front of her.

'Wait, there may be someone else in there—'

Melanie's bony elbow whacked her on the breastbone. For a second time the blonde constable was swept aside. Her head banged against the door jamb and I saw her blue eyes cross. Yellow skirt flying, Melanie entered the room at a canter and, without pausing, went down on both knees alongside the man who was lying on his back on an expensive Chinese rug. She had gone down like a football striker celebrating a goal and, as growing excitement and the increasing tension made me feel oddly giggly, I half expected her to pull her blouse up over her face.

Faraday was watching me. I could see a flicker of amusement in his eyes, and sensed a kindred spirit. I gave him a knowing wink, then pulled a face in mock disgust at our behaviour.

Then the two constables followed Melanie into the study. Craftily, I hung just a little way back so that inquisitive eyes were looking the wrong way to notice my camera.

The ceiling light was off. The only illumination came from one of those green banker's lamps. After a swift, searching sweep of the room that must have told him there was nowhere for anyone to hide, PC Faraday nodded to his colleague. PC Kirk gingerly lowered herself alongside Melanie, keeping well clear of her elbows, and reached out a hand to check for a pulse in the man's carotid artery.

She looked up, and shook her head.

'Christ almighty,' Melanie said, 'he's bloody well gone and died on me.'

Stone-faced, PC Faraday backed away and began whispering into his radio. Kirk rested a comforting hand on Melanie's shoulder. She shook it off – almost angrily, I thought – and stood up using her hands on the dead man's chest to push herself up. She looked across at me. I don't think I've ever seen such an expression, such a reaction to the death of someone close. But had they been close? – or was there something else that was bothering Melanie Wigg, something that for the moment I was unable to understand?

I grimaced at her in what was meant to be a sympathetic way, then deliberately dismissed imponderables from my mind and looked about me. With both constables now occupied, I had time to take in the scene. I moved silently through the door and stood, unnoticed, just inside the study.

The room was smaller than I'd expected. Faded red velvet curtains hung on either side of a huge old sash window. I could see the rain still sweeping across the tossing trees, but the window panes were dry and I remembered that the wind was driving against the front of the house and this was the back. A leather-inlaid desk stood near the window, with a swivel chair behind it where Galleywood must have swung to and fro as he watched lissom young ladies heading for the gym. The Chinese rug on which he was now stretched out was in front of the desk. Bookshelves lined the walls, and I could see one complete shelf of leather stamp-albums, another of catalogues and so on. A huge wooden filing cabinet that might have come from a police station was against the wall near the door.

But what about the dead man?

I edged further into the room, circling closer so that I could see around Melanie who was standing grim-faced, her arms folded across her chest as she stared down in an abstracted kind of way at her dead employer. The Chinese rug was thick and oblong, and he spanned the length of it: he had been tall, and from what I could see there wasn't a trace of fat on the long frame inside the crumpled black suit. His tan equalled Melanie's, which led to the possibility of his having been abroad for some time. With her, I wondered and, if so, doing what? Holiday? Business?

As for cause of death, well, without looking too closely – which my sensitive stomach told me would be a bad idea – he appeared to have been shot in the eye. The right socket was a pool of blood that had welled and trickled darkly down one hollow cheek.

PC Faraday had drifted towards the open door, head still bent to his radio. I saw him pull the heavy oak panel away from the wall and reach out to touch the key that was still in the lock. On the inside of the door. He lifted his head and frowned. When he glanced towards the window I knew he was thinking what I was thinking: that old sash window hadn't been opened in years, and in any case we were on the first floor. In buildings such as this, with a sort of half sunken basement that meant stone steps were needed just to get to the front door, the first-floor windows were unreachable from the outside without a very tall ladder.

Kirk was talking to Melanie. They'd moved away from the body. Melanie was now dabbing her eyes with a tissue in what, to me, seemed to be an appalling demonstration of false grief. The blonde constable had hold of her other arm and was half watching the sniffling Wigg, half watching her colleague.

For the moment, I was invisible. The way was clear.

I backed off, lifted the little camera and took a shot of the dead man. There was a thick book lying close to the body. It looked like a Stanley Gibbons catalogue, and I remembered that Galleywood had been to the library. The book was closed, and there was a deep scar across the cover. I took another shot, again thankful for the camera's low-light capabilities that meant I could manage without flash.

Not that it made much difference. Faraday had finished with the radio, and suddenly realized what I was doing.

'Hang on a minute,' he said, coming over. 'This is a crime scene, you can't take photographs.'

'I am sorry, I really wasn't thinking.'

'Nonsense. You're a journalist, here to interview him.'

'Well, I was hoping too.' I shrugged, glanced at Galleywood and pulled a rueful face.

He was looking at the camera. 'That's digital, isn't it? You'd better give me the memory card.'

'It's all right, you can watch me erase the images,' I said, knowing that he wouldn't agree.

'No. Give me the card. DI Dancer will want to see what else you've got on there.'

'Dancer knows me from the Gareth Owen case,' I said. 'The Welsh serial killer, remember? I was instrumental in his apprehension.'

Faraday was unimpressed. He held out his hand.

'The card, please.'

All my talk was for camouflage, of course, as was the deep sigh as I turned my body a little, fiddled with feigned awkwardness at the camera's little flap, took out the memory card so that he couldn't quite see what I was doing and handed him the card I had cunningly palmed.

He took it, and grinned knowingly.

'All right, now the camera.'

Meekly, I gave it to him. As he examined it to make sure the card slot was empty, I slipped the card I'd removed from the camera into my skirt pocket. My mind was racing. Adrenaline was making me light-headed. I was Penny Lane, again changing hats and slipping into exhilarating PI mode.

Faraday had finished his examination and was proffering the camera. I didn't take it.

'Problem is,' I pointed out airily, 'some little digital cameras have internal memories.'

He frowned. 'What's that mean?'

'That card I gave you could be blank. The pics of Galleywood's body might have been recorded on the internal memory.'

'Well, were they or weren't they?'

'I'm no expert,' I lied, 'so I can't be sure. You'd better keep the camera. Give it to DI Dancer to play with.'

'Right,' he said. He tapped the camera against his palm, still frowning as he nodded slowly, probably wondering what I was up to.

What I was up to was planning ahead. Somehow I'd once again got involved in murder and, if by chance I wasn't invited in to answer more questions, I now had my own valid reason for calling on DI Billy Dancer at the police station in Queen's Road, Hoylake.

But while I mentally patted myself on the back, I was also wondering what had made Melanie Wigg, in a voice that revealed not shock or grief but something close to indignation, blurt out, 'Christ almighty, he's bloody well gone and died on me.'

It was almost as if she had been expecting something like that to happen. No, I thought, that wasn't quite accurate. Melanie Wigg *had* been perhaps half expecting Larry Galleywood to come to a violent end but, more than anything, it was clearly something she had been dreading.

It was still raining when I left the Galleywood house, and my hair was wet and clinging by the time I'd run thirty yards and climbed into the Ka. Dashing the hair out of my eyes and wiping my hand on my skirt, I checked my mobile in case I'd missed anything, then started up and drove out on to the main road. As I turned right and prepared to accelerate, the howl of approaching sirens came to my ears and I pulled a face, slowed to a crawl and hugged the kerb. Headlights on full-beam hit the windscreen like distress flares and two police cars flooded the wet road with blue light as they raced by. They were closely followed by an ambulance in which I could see the pale faces and green-clad figures of para-medics. In the mirror I watched with blotchy vision as all three vehicles swing into the Galleywood drive.

Easing back into the road, still watching the mirror as the sirens wailed into silence like the plaintive moans of exhausted alley cats, I saw a big car pull away from the kerb some fifty yards behind me. It had been parked under the trees close to the Galleywood entrance. The driver switched on blinding halogen headlights and I raised a hand to cut off the glare from the wing mirror as the big vehicle raced by so fast that my poor little Ka seemed to tremble. I made a mental note of the incident (if that's what it was), decided after a quick instant replay in my mind that the car had been a big old Volvo with two dark figures indistinct shapes behind tinted windows. I recalled the pale blurs of their faces and an impression of what I like to call mafia shades, then forgot about them.

Because of the article I was writing I had half-decided to call on Dr Malcolm Moneydie when his name came up in connection with the rare coin. After the discovery of Galleywood's murder I had an altogether different and more pressing reason for talking to the doctor. The philatelist had paid him a visit only hours before his death, and gratefully accepting the first lead to come my way I now drove for a quarter of a mile and turned into the road Melanie Wigg had named.

It was tree-lined, and subdued street lighting filtering through almost bare branches lit rugged stone walls and uneven pavements attractively strewn with soggy autumn leaves. I had driven down it several times, the last occasion being when I'd needed something done to an in-growing toenail and had been visiting a chiropodist wearing a slipper on my left foot. So, if I say Harley Street but rural rather than urban, you'll get the idea. Brass plates alongside front doors set in rustic brick walls half-hidden by Virginia creeper glinted in the discreet lighting. Mercedes and Jaguars were parked on horseshoe-shaped drives with a gate at each end, a touch of grandeur that eliminated the annoying need to reverse.

The number Melanie had given me was eighteen. Most of the houses had adopted names like Greenmantle or Badger's Drift, which were embarrassingly pretentious and made finding Moneydie's place difficult. However, I'd spotted a thirty-four carved into a slate plaque as I turned into the road, and by counting backwards in twos on my fingers I decided that a low-slung dormer-type house with a tiled roof sweeping in wondrous curves over the upper windows had to be the doctor's.

I drove in, parked my little red car behind a white Toyota, slid out into the rain and ran for the front door. Soft yellow lighting gleamed through frosted glass. A shadowy figure appeared shortly after my ring, and the door opened to reveal a tall man with close-clipped white hair who was wearing one of those aprons designed to look like women's underwear. The bra was drooping on one side, and the black panties appeared to be splashed with fat. He must have come straight from the kitchen, for I could hear the sizzle of something frying. From the aroma I guessed steak and onions, and the background scent of coffee percolating almost finished me off. My mouth began to water. I swallowed noisily, swept rain and damp hair from my forehead with the back of a forefinger, and tried to look assertive.

'Doctor Moneydie?

'Yes.'

'I've come from Larry Galleywood's house. I'd like to talk to you. Can you spare a few minutes?'

'This is about Galleywood? I saw him on a medical matter just a few hours ago. What are you, some sort of health visitor?'

'No, I'm a photographer. I also dabble in criminal investigation.'

'Dabble.' The ascetic face that had been wearing a smugly superior expression I guessed was a permanent fixture, now managed to add contempt that was revealed in the curl of thin lips. I couldn't really blame him, couldn't believe how foolish I'd sounded.

'More than dabble, actually,' I said, hastily mending fences. 'I'm quite good. The police describe me as helpful.'

'References?'

'DI Dancer will recommend me,' I said. My face felt pink as I added untruths to continuing foolishness. Behind my back, my fingers were tightly crossed.

'What's Galleywood done now, been caught in more dodgy dealings? Wouldn't surprise me one bit—'

'He's died,' I said, and saw the shock register in the widening of his pale-blue eyes.

Moneydie actually rocked backwards. His shoulder hit the door. It shuddered all the way open and banged against the wall.

Instinctively I stepped forward. He frowned and shook his head, waved me away, then glanced behind him as a feminine voice called anxiously from the kitchen.

'It's all right, Jessica,' he called. His thin lips had tightened. He took a deep breath through flared nostrils, seemed to get a grip of himself in an almost physical sense and said, 'You'd better come in.'

His manners matched his charisma. He left me to deal with the front door, and I shut out the damp and the cold with a carefully controlled slam and followed him across the carpeted hallway into a front room that must have been decorated and furnished by his wife when she was still dazed after watching a documentary on Barbara Cartland.

A big bay window was spattered with rain. Moneydie was staring out across the garden with his hands thrust into his pockets. He heard the whisper of my wet shoes on the carpet and swung to face me.

'I don't understand what you want. You say you're a photographer and you play at detective. So what have you brought with you, camera or handcuffs? What am I supposed to have done?'

'As far as I know you're the last person outside his household to have spoken to Larry Galleywood. You might be able to help in some way. You see, I went to his house to interview him, and while I was there he died in unusual circumstances.'

He waved me to a seat. I sat down on a chair that was so squashy at the edges it threatened to dump me on the carpet. Moneydie moved away from the window and sat down in the chair opposite, using his stiff legs like pit props to hold his position.

'What d'you mean,' he said, 'by unusual?'

'He died from a bullet wound while inside his locked study.'

'Ah, you mean it was suicide? He shot himself?'

'No, somebody shot him.'

His eyes told me he wasn't sure if I was joking. His elbow was resting on the waistband of the apron's black lace panties, the side of his hooked forefinger pressing on his upper lip as he nodded slowly in thought. I was trying to concentrate, but this arrogant man's apparel and the strong smell of cooking was making me giddy. I'd looked at my watch just before I walked in, and I wondered what time he and Jessica ate, and if I'd be invited to the feast. At that errant thought the little imp that torments me decided to prod me into a giggle. Valiantly I tightened my lips into a tiny puckered purse, and concentrated on Moneydie.

'I still don't understand why you're here,' he said. 'Galleywood obviously told you he'd been to see me, but—'

'Afraid not; he died before I could talk to him. But Melanie Wigg knew he'd visited you, and she knew it was to do with his angina. What I'd like to know is if Galleywood said anything to you during that consultation? Did he look worried, did he say he was in danger – did he say *anything* that might explain what happened to him so soon after he left here?'

'I asked him if he'd been overdoing it. He said he hadn't, but I knew he'd been in Greece on business for most of the summer. As I've served in hot climates, I know what that can do to a man. He'd had too much sun, and was exhausted.'

'Yet you recommended exercise.'

'Mollycoddling soldiers gets you nowhere; I don't see why civilians should be treated differently.'

'You're an ex-army doctor?'

'RAMC for thirty-five years. Major. Been out for ten, and I'm not impressed.'

'As a travelling man,' I said, 'you must have handled lots of foreign currency prior to the Euro. Is that what started you on coin collecting?'

'Of course.' He took his finger away from his lip, and stabbed it at me accusingly. 'You're on a different tack now, aren't you? I suppose you've heard the story of the rare coin he bought, but what is it you're after? Proof that I'm angry at that Galleywood twerp's chicanery? Or are you actually still on the same tack and slyly insinuating I might have done something about it, gone over there and … and…?' He spread his hands, apparently at a loss for words.'

'If you did,' I said, 'you're an exceedingly clever man.'

That really did please him. His form was as lean as a greyhound's, but his chest swelled visibly and the impression that created under the ridiculous apron was the final straw. I fought my way out of the chair's soft embrace and bid him a mumbled farewell before beating a hasty retreat with laughter bubbling.

chapter three

Because Josh finds it difficult to stretch out his long legs in the Ka's passenger seat we'd agreed that I'd return home after the interview with Galleywood and we'd use the Range Rover to get to Steve Easter's house. I knew Josh's meeting with the Seasoned Scribblers was going to be short – something to do with arranging a Christmas dinner – so I wasn't surprised to see the big 4 x 4 already in the drive when I got back to Heswall.

Josh and I work from our bungalow home in which two of the three bedrooms have been converted into offices. My delicious husband lap-tops his mysteries; I sell prints of landscapes on fine art paper and panoramic abstracts to private buyers and multi-national corporations through a website called *Penny Lane Panoramas* – Penny Lane being me, not a street in Liverpool.

A month or so ago I found a body on the beach, made a terrible mistake and became a sort of bumbling amateur private investigator in my efforts to put things right. A delightful young woman called Annabel Lee was also involved and, when every-thing had been sorted out, she came to work for me.

Annabel has a photographic studio in her terraced cottage in Parkgate, a small town on the silted-up River Dee. Before she arrived on the scene I wouldn't touch wedding photography. Scared stiff, actually. Anyway, to test her ability with a modern digital SLR camera, we took on a wedding shoot at a church near Chester. That turned out to be a disaster – yes, another dead body was discovered – but since then everything has run smoothly. We're now averaging one wedding a week, and Annabel is deservedly building up a solid reputation for high quality work which is also imaginatively artistic.

What this rambling is leading to is my constant amazement at the way coincidences crop up. Annabel is covering a wedding on Saturday. The man getting married is Andy Galleywood. He's a member of the Seasoned Scribblers; he's written a couple of thrillers still doing the rounds of publishers, and he just happens to be the son of the estate agent I had left sprawled on a Chinese rug after apparently being shot through the eye. In mysterious circumstances.

That last, by the way, was not just my snap judgment after the brief glimpse I had of the body. During the short questioning session with Faraday and Kirk that followed the confiscation of my camera I'd had time to take a *really* good look around. I'd noticed several things about the killing of Larry Galleywood that were both puzzling and exciting, and I was looking forward to discussing details of the crime scene with the man who likes nothing better than to dream up the impossible crime.

'There was no weapon to be found anywhere in the room.'

'He took it with him,' Josh said.

'Impossible.'

'But if it's not there in the study—'

'It's not. But that's not the point: how did the *killer* get out of the room, then lock the door from the inside?'

'Good point,' Josh said, nodding approval. 'But there's another: how did he get in? This – what's her name, Melanie Wigg? – she didn't say anything about Galleywood having a visitor up there, did she?'

'She did *not*,' I said firmly, 'and I know from experience how difficult it would be to get past her.'

We were in Steve Easter's front room, toasting ourselves before the living-flame gas fire set into the wall and waiting for Sheila, who had disappeared into the kitchen to pour the coffee. We'd already downed one or two tiny liqueur glasses of Cointreau – well, I had, my driver was making do with fruit juice – and I was deep into the tantalizing tale I'd dangled before Josh on the way over in the Range Rover. After the bit about Faraday and Kirk arriving on Larry Galleywood's doorstep and the young PC's efficient demolition of the study door, I'd moved swiftly on to describe the body. Now I was well into the interesting bit; the irregularities, as the police might call them, that made Larry Galleywood's murder a perplexing locked room mystery.

Shelia came through while I was smugly watching a crime writer chew, without much hope, over the information I'd given him and probe for non-existent weaknesses in the case I'd made for an impossible crime.

'Suicide's out,' I added casually, 'for the same reason: no weapon – certainly not a pistol.'

'Ah,' Josh said, pouncing on that. 'You saw blood in the … what was it, right eye?'

'The right eye socket, yes.'

'OK, so you saw a pool of blood and assumed that was the wound that caused his death – but, of course, it might not have been a bullet wound and, yes, it could have been suicide. What if he'd stabbed himself in the eye with a paper knife?'

Cups rattled as Sheila advanced into the room – have you noticed how modern ones never fit properly in those circular recesses in the saucers? – and, as she placed them on the occasional table with a sigh of relief, she looked at both of us with a bright smile.

'Up to your usual, from what I could overhear. What's this you're discussing, the plot of your new book, Josh?'

'Nope, this is real life,' he said.

Sheila's eyes widened. I carefully brought her up to date with my experiences in the Galleywood house, using the exercise as an opportunity to go over the material again in my mind.

'Larry Galleywood,' she said softly when I'd finished, looking slightly stunned as she sat down with her coffee. 'Surely his son's a member of your writers' group, Josh?'

Josh nodded. 'Andy. He's been in it from the beginning – though he wasn't there tonight.'

'So, with Steve, that was two people missing. But you and the others still managed to arrange the Christmas party?'

'Provisionally, yes. The Golden Fleece is pencilled in.'

'Then Steve *will* be pleased. It's his favourite … what shall I call it, hostelry?'

'How about gin mill?' I said.

Sheila smiled and sat back, crossing long slim legs in stone-washed jeans. She was sitting on the settee facing the window, and I knew she was watching the rain dancing down on the rockeries flanking their front drive and waiting for Steve to roll up in what Josh called the beemer.

'Gin mill,' she said appreciatively, absently toying with glossy fair hair that just touched the shoulders of her white T-shirt. 'That comes straight out of Lawrence Block's Matt Scudder novels. And with that racy terminology, I think we're right back with the real-life murder mystery you've stumbled into. Again. You're beginning to make it a habit, aren't you, Penny?'

'Twice in, what, a couple of months? Not exactly a habit – and I'm not actually involved at all until I make the decision.'

'Ha bloody ha,' Josh said drily. 'Take a look at her sparkling eyes, the attractive flush colouring her cheeks, the—'

'That's the Cointreau,' I said hastily, nevertheless patting my face delicately with my fingertips to feel the heat.

Sheila grinned. 'So what about this knife Galleywood used to stab himself in the eye?'

'And *that* was Josh's clever idea. Problem is the only blade of any kind in the room was a genuine antique paper knife with a lion's head on the brass hilt. It was lying on the desk, unstained by blood. In its usual convenient position so he could slice open envelopes, by the look of it, not dropped by the dying Galleywood as he sank on to the rug.'

'So let me get this straight,' Josh said. 'The study's on the first floor, overlooking the back garden. When the door was broken open the key was in the lock, on the inside. There's no other way into or out of the room other than through the window, and that window is one of those ancient, heavy sash affairs that takes an Arnie Schwarzenegger to open or close.'

'When it was in working order. Its rotted cords probably snapped years ago,' I said.

'Right, and both you and PC Faraday, young bobby and inexperienced amateur private eye—'

'*Female* private eye,' I put in sweetly.

'—both came to the conclusion that the window hadn't been opened for years.'

'Decades.'

'And anyway, that window is at least fifteen feet above the back garden.'

'Not only that,' I said, 'but it was raining heavily as it has been all evening, there's a wide herbaceous border beneath the study window, and in that soggy soil the only footprints the police could find had been made by a blackbird poking about for worms.'

'You're sure of that?'

'Could've been a starling.'

PC Faraday had given me the information, reluctantly, when he came back into the Galleywood house with soaking wet hair, muddy boots and an aggrieved expression after a quick scout around the garden. By then, Melanie and I had been kicked out of the study that had become a crime scene, and banished to the warm kitchen. Shortly after I'd learned about the herbaceous border and the industrious blackbird, I'd been allowed to leave, but with instructions to present myself at the Queen's Road Police Station at ten o'clock the next morning.

'One thing that struck me as odd,' I said after a long silence, 'was the way Melanie seemed immediately to recognize the crack we heard from the kitchen as a gunshot. The second odd thing is that she was right. Now, why would that be? Why would a ... I don't know, secretary, housekeeper ... why would such a person recognize that sound?'

'Doesn't have to be sinister,' Sheila said. 'Maybe she goes clay pigeon shooting. A gunshot's a gunshot, after all. She didn't actually say it sounded like a pistol – did she?'

'Well, no, and we don't know that it was. About all I can say is it wasn't a shotgun, or there wouldn't have been much left of Galleywood's face.'

'Interesting, though,' Josh said. 'It couldn't have been the first time she'd heard Galleywood up in his study. There must have been lots of bumps and thumps and bangs before today. So why was this one a shot?'

I pursed my lips. 'I also wondered about their relationship.

First when she stood outside the study door calling him Lex, then later when I noticed their matching tans.'

Sheila was shaking her head in disbelief.

'I'm beginning to think crime writing and crime investigation is turning you two into know alls, or addling your brains. Dump that nonsense about her recognizing the sound for what it was. A perfectly reasonable explanation is that Melanie Wigg is an avid *reader* of crime stories. As for the rest, why don't you look for the simple answer instead of over-complicating? Or ask me?'

Josh and I exchanged glances.

'They'd worked together for years,' Sheila went on smugly. 'They had matching tans because one of the perks of being an estate agent is you get free trips overseas – their most recent was to the Greek Islands. They were gone for some time. Galleywood's son ran the business in their absence.'

Josh nodded, pulling a face. 'Yes, I remember that,' he said. 'Andy Galleywood mentioned it during casual conversation at the writers' group, told us how he was run off his feet with extra work.'

'But, gone for some time,' I said. 'What does that mean, how long are we talking about?'

Sheila shrugged. 'Six months, I think.'

'Doesn't make sense, does it?' I said. 'Estate agents go on trips to look at locations and accommodation, or to exotic locations selected by travel companies for seminars. Seven days there and back, fourteen at the most.'

'I know,' Sheila said. 'There was talk, gossip, about something fishy going on. Naturally enough, I suppose, because what could they be doing in the Greek Islands for all that time? In fact,' she said, 'Steve's doing some investigating. I think he's got wind of property fraud of some kind.'

I pursed my lips. 'Good for him. But what put him on to that?'

'Don't know,' Sheila said. 'All I do know is that Steve did an exposé article about a successful property fraud a couple of years ago, and he got very interested. The whole idea caught his imagination, in much the same way as he always gets fired up over Las Vegas gambling scams and such; he loved that book by

Michael Connelly, *Void Moon* I think it was, d'you remember it, Josh?' She caught his nod and smiled. 'Anyway, getting back to reality, Steve said the only other reason for Galleywood and Melanie to stay abroad for so long would be the usual boy-girl stuff' – she grinned – 'but neither of them are or were spring chickens, and six months of energetic lovemaking is stretching it a bit in that heat.'

'So assuming there was something going on, had he got any details?'

'Well, he hasn't told me much, let's put it that way. He does know they were using Rhodes as a base – that's Rhodes town – but a base for what is still anybody's guess.'

'Their absence explains the tans, but leaves a lot unanswered. For instance, back here, what's Melanie Wigg doing *living* with Galleywood?'

'She's not, not exactly, or at least not in the sense you mean,' Sheila said. 'It's a big house and she's had a couple of rooms there since soon after Galleywood's wife died. . . That was something like eight months ago. He got over her death very quickly – according to rumour, the marriage was as good as over when she was alive – then Melanie moved in and stayed on.'

'If they spent six months abroad,' I said, 'she must have moved in then straight out again and on to the plane for Greece.'

'With Galleywood. Yes. But when they got back she was still with him and I believe she acts as, well, not a housekeeper, more a sort of live-in companion who shares the cooking and cleaning and so on.'

'Best of both worlds,' I said, but Sheila was no longer listening. Her eyes were on the window, and suddenly she sprang from the settee.

'You two amateurs are in luck. Steve's here, so now you can get help from a genuine, working journalist.'

As she left the room, Josh frowned, stood up and crossed quickly to the big bay window.

'Well, well, well,' he said, and there was sudden concern in his quiet voice as he stared out at the slackening rain. 'I hate to put a damper on Sheila's delight, but Steve's got company he could do without. A car with nasty flashing blue lights has turned in after

43

him. For the second time this evening, you're going to be uncomfortably close to officers of the Merseyside Police.'

'Never mind me,' I said. 'What the hell has Steve done to put
the police on his tail?'

Josh stayed in the front room, lurking like an apprentice spy alongside the heavy curtains. Blatantly nosy, I crept into the hall and tiptoed across the parquet flooring to the open front door. There, like Josh, I stood to one side and peeped out.

The door was half glazed and Sheila must have seen the flashing blue lights through the glass before she opened it. Without hesitation she'd dashed out into the chill November night, T-shirt bright in the glare from the security light alongside the door, and was now standing waiting for Steve.

He climbed out of the car without hurrying. In his mid-forties, tall, broad and comfortably well padded, thick fair hair streaked with grey, he was dressed in faded jeans and a dark fleece over a blue and white rugby shirt. There was a frown on his face as he slammed the door and looked towards the road. Distracted, puzzled, his hand lifted to brush back a floppy forelock, an unconscious act he must have performed countless times – without success – each and every day.

The police car had stopped at an angle across the drive, blocking the exit. Two police officers got out. One was tall, one short and thickset, both looked grim. Doors slammed. Without hurrying, they approached the black BMW.

'Steve Easter?'

Steve nodded. 'What's the problem?'

'This your car, sir?'

'If you tell me what's—'

'Yes or no. Is this your car?'

'Yes, it's my car.'

The tall officer not doing the talking was walking around the BMW, peering in through the windows, touching rust spots and scratches, looking up at the dull silver luggage box. Steve was caught between watching him and paying attention to the officer doing the questioning. He looked one way, then the other, and noticed Sheila. She was standing there, looking nervous, getting wet. Steve grimaced and shook his head.

'Go inside, love. I'll see to this.'

'I'll wait.' She looked at the police. 'It can't be serious, so it won't take long.'

Steve spoke to the stocky constable.

'Can we deal with this inside?'

'Your wife can go into the house.'

Steve took a deep breath, quickly slipped out of his dark fleece and draped it over Sheila's shoulders, then returned his gaze to the constable.

'Mr Easter,' the constable said, 'can you tell me where you were at seven-thirty this evening?'

'I was … in my office – I think. I can't be sure of the time, but I think I'd just returned from a meeting. Or I was about to return. From an editorial meeting.'

'So at that time, seven-thirty, you were in your office?'

'Yes. As I say, if I've got the time right. I could be out by, oh, a quarter of an hour either way. Maybe a bit more.' He shook his head. 'I'm sorry. All I can be sure of is after the meeting I was in my office filing papers, tidying up, preparing to come home.'

'I think you're wrong. About the time. Think carefully. Go back over what you've just said. Now, would you care to change that story—?'

'It's not a bloody story—'

'At a little after seven-thirty this evening,' the stocky constable went on inexorably, 'a 999 call reported a man in the car-park outside the office building in Old Hall Street, Liverpool, where you work as a journalist. He was seen coming out of that building. He was seen from a distance, but we know he was tall and dressed in a dark fleece over a rugby shirt, jeans and trainers.'

The constable paused and looked Steve up and down.

'Half the people in Liverpool,' Steve said, 'dress like this. A lot of them are tall.'

'So you're sticking to your story?'

'I'm waiting to hear what this man was doing. Why someone would see him, and call the police.'

'You. They saw you.'

'No.'

I felt a hand on my hip. Josh was behind me. He rested his chin on my shoulder. I could smell his after-shave, feel his warm breath on my neck, and I shivered and reached back for his hand. He gave mine a reassuring squeeze.

Outside, in what was now a mist of fine rain, the tall constable had finished his perfunctory inspection of the BMW and was standing alongside his colleague. He smiled at Steve.

'It was this car, this BMW. The caller gave us the registration number. We checked it on the PNC. You're the registered owner.'

'I've already told you it's my—'

'A man answering to your description was seen alongside this car, your car, watching two other men with a heavy – object – that had been off-loaded from a Jeep SUV with tinted windows. The object was lifted on to the BMW's roof and put inside the luggage box.' He used a thumb to point over his shoulder. 'That one. Yours.'

Steve shook his head. 'No. That's impossible. It's always locked. And it's empty.'

'You were seen opening it.'

'I told you I wasn't *there*,' Steve said fiercely. 'It's a clear case of mistaken identity—'

'Your car, your luggage box, a man answering your description,' the stocky constable said. And then he grinned. 'The 999 call came from a mobile. Now, there's a surprise. The point is, the caller said he'd not only seen what was going on, he'd photographed it. On that very same mobile, he said. Not top of the range, but good enough. Apparently it's got a hell of a zoom. Took him in nice and close.'

'Excellent,' Steve said. 'If you've seen the pictures—'

'We haven't. He's bringing the phone over from Liverpool as we speak. But, getting back to this luggage box, if you *are* telling the truth about it being empty then you won't mind unlocking it for us.'

'Bloody right I won't,' Steve said through his teeth.

Halfway through the questioning he'd begun tossing his car keys from hand to hand as he grew increasingly angry and frustrated. Now he dangled them in front of the constables, reached across with his other hand and with finger and thumb seized two small keys. He held them by those two keys. The bunch jingled as he walked across to the BMW. The constables followed.

'Notice they're now either side of him,' Josh murmured. 'What the hell's going on, are they expecting him to bolt at the sight of what's in there?'

'There's nothing in there, it's all a big mistake,' I said. My eyes were on Sheila. Even from several yards away I could see her shivering. 'You'll see,' I said. 'Ten minutes from now we'll be back in the front room laughing and joking about this over drinks.'

Steve had turned the key in one lock. Now he did the same with the second. Then he rammed the bunch in his pocket and stood back. He looked at the constables.

'It's all yours.'

'Open it, please, sir.'

Steve shook his head.

'No. I've gone far enough with this, done all I'm going to do. I've told you the box is empty. If you want to look inside, go ahead.'

Without hesitation, the leaner of the two constables walked to the side of the BMW, reached up and flipped open the luggage box's lid.

It flew up with a rush, almost as if pushed from inside. Fleetingly, in a moment of pure horror, I thought of a jack-in-the-box and those colourful clowns that leap out wearing an insane grin and flop about atop a glittering coil spring.

But what came out of Steve's luggage box was not colourful, and the grin on the face of the man who had been folded inside was a ghastly rictus of terror frozen in death.

My grip tightened on Josh's hand. I heard him grunt with shock. I bit my lip, half turned away from the scene in front of me, tried in vain to avert my gaze as the body inside the box seemed to unfold in slow motion. The man had been placed in the box on his side. Somehow – I thought of pressure and bodily gasses and had to clench my teeth – the head and torso reared up, right shoulder first, then twisting as if wriggling desperately to get free. As it came upright the chin dropped slackly, exposing gleaming white teeth smeared with wet blood. Then the body tilted. The small of the back came down hard on the sharp edges of the box. Both arms flopped sideways, wide and loose, as if in a desperate appeal for help. Then upper-body weight took over, dragging the corpse backwards and down. Dark hair dangled lankly as it slid down the side of the BMW and hit the gravel with an almost soggy thud.

The watchers seemed frozen.

The constable at the side of the car was still holding the box's lid like a conjurer who couldn't believe what had popped out of the hat. Steve was standing with his keys dangling from his hand, forgotten. As the body fell, the stocky constable had taken a fast step backwards. He'd tripped, and was sitting on his backside in a puddle.

Sheila Easter was the first to move. Delicately, she pressed her hand to her heart and sighed. Then, as if the bones had been spirited away, her legs refused to hold her and she slumped to the gravel in a crumpled heap.

'Jesus Christ,' Josh said softly, as I turned and buried my face against his chest. 'That was Andy Galleywood in there, Pen. I *wondered* where he'd got to.'

I was beginning to feel like one of those potent liquid accelerators arsonists splash around when they're starting their terrible fires. I'd strolled into two houses in the past few of hours. In each – and within what seemed like minutes – a gruesome corpse had popped up and police and ambulances were converging on the premises with sirens screaming.

As soon as the bruised and bloodied body of Andy Galleywood flopped on to the wet gravel drive, the police had arrested Steve Easter. We were paying little attention, as Josh and I had rushed to help Sheila when she fell to the ground in a dead faint.

She recovered quickly, but was not allowed anywhere near her husband, and we knew that we would be looked on as unwanted impediments interfering with police procedure. So we stayed at the Easter house just long enough to help Sheila into the front room, where she had settled on the settee with a large brandy and telephoned her married son, Mark, with the bad news. By then, an ambulance and more police cars had arrived, and warm light was flooding into the road as doors opened and curious residents poked their heads out to see what was going on. What they saw was the Easters' front drive, where lazily rotating blue lights cast an eerie illumination over swarms of paramedics and uniformed and plain-clothes police officers.

A senior officer in baggy plain clothes had informed Sheila that her husband was being taken in for questioning, and would certainly be held overnight. Sheila gave him her new address and telephone number: she would, she said, be staying with her son in

Chester – certainly overnight, she added, with a token smile faltering beneath a baleful glare.

Of course, the senior officer was DI Billy Dancer, the policeman I had got to know well during the Gareth Owen case. The tall, gaunt detective with a liking for alpaca suits that hang on him like a becalmed schooner's sails – my simile, that one, so I'm sticking to it – cast an eye in my direction, then got on with the job he had to do. I was content. I like the man; he was kind to me when I was an excellent photographer who was floundering out of her depth in strange murky waters, and I was looking forward to talking to him in Hoylake the next day.

Thankful that we had parked the Range Rover in the road and not deep in the drive which was now clogged with official vehicles, we said our farewells and slipped away into the damp night. The interior of the car was cold. Our breath clouded the windscreen. Both of us felt chilled by events. Doors slammed, seat-belts were fastened, and we drove off leaving behind us a white cloud of condensation that was a ghostly mist adding to the ghoulish atmosphere.

On the drive home to Heswall there was no talk at all, and I knew why. I thought I'd given an excellent example of mouth galloping out of control ahead of brain when Melanie Wigg opened the front door to the Galleywood residence, but Josh's remark when Andy Galleywood made his dramatic appearance was a classic.

The silence was uncomfortable, and I guessed Josh was furiously berating himself for that awful gaffe. If he'd looked to me for comfort I'd have told him that shock had caused him to blurt the first thought that came into his head, it hadn't been overheard, and his secret was safe with me. But he didn't, and in any case my mind was working overtime. I had been shocked, then intrigued, by an impossible crime at the Galleywood residence. Now there was a dead body that had been squashed into a luggage box mounted on top of a very familiar BMW. According to what must have been a reliable witness, it had been put there by the car's owner.

Well, that witness was wrong, and the police were wasting time. Somebody had murdered Andy Galleywood; *somebody* had

stuffed him in that box, but that person was *not* Steve Easter.
And, I thought miserably, this latest trouble couldn't have come
at a worse time.

Sheila and Steve had been struggling to get their marriage back
on track. Steve had seriously strayed – mid-life crisis or some
such nonsense – and had spent a lot of time with Another Woman
with whom he had become infatuated but who had never been
identified. Sheila quickly became aware that something was going
on, of course. When she was absolutely certain, she had coura-
geously tackled Steve about it and, during a furious row, she had
given him the usual ultimatum: her or me, your choice. Well,
Steve made the right choice (my opinion) and in the eight months
since he walked away from the mystery woman both Josh and I
had watched two adults apply temporary patches that became
permanent, put their troubles behind them and begin to enjoy life
together. And now this. More trouble, coming out of the blue –
no pun intended. What is it they say? I'm not quite sure, but if I
was to paraphrase what I think it might be I'd end up with something like 'when one door opens, another closes' …

Once inside the bungalow with the front door closed to shut
out the night and its secrets we shed damp clothes, slipped
dressing gowns on over cosy night wear, and moved – still without
speaking – into the kitchen. There, subdued lighting under wall
units illuminated familiar surroundings, the rain pattering on the
conservatory and trying to fill the pond that Josh had never
finished was suddenly a joy rather than a misery and, as I
switched on the electric kettle and Josh clinked mugs and jars and
spooned instant coffee, pulses that had been pattering away in the
hundreds at last returned to normal.

At least, mine did. A couple of hours ago my story of stumbling
on an impossible crime in a crumbling Victorian house had
certainly interested Josh Lane, the crime writer. Josh Lane the
husband, on the other hand, wouldn't have been relishing the
thought of his wife embarking on another risky investigation.

Now there had been another murder, just as puzzling, much
more brutal, and quite possibly linked to the first because the two
dead men were father and son. Not only that, one of our close
friends seemed to be implicated. He would by now have been

taken in for questioning, and might have great difficulty in discrediting the eyewitness.

The Gareth Owen case had been my first outing as an amateur PI, and I'd been sucked into it by the silly mistake I'd made on Hoylake beach: discovered a body, snatched a clue from under the noses of the police, immediately filled with regret and determined not only to make amends but find the killer. At the time, Josh had said he didn't feel that a female photographer of advanced years was cut out for PI work, and I'd responded by calling him a conceited, patronizing prick who writes third-rate books and lives on his wife's earnings. He'd said the work was dangerous – his, not mine. I'd scoffed at the idea, while admitting I felt scared.

Nevertheless, from that point on I'd come to like what I was doing. All right, I'd been beaten up and had my face pushed in cold vomit in a Liverpool back entry, been outwitted at almost every turn and escaped being shot more by sheer bloody good luck than Rambo-style heroism. And, I must admit, without the help of Josh himself and a dashing hero from the heart of Liverpool's renovated dockland by the name of Ryan Sharkey, I might have failed miserably. But I didn't. In the end, muddling through, three amateurs had got what football coaches might call a result, even if that too involved a huge chunk of good luck.

The trouble is, a criminal investigator of any kind must get those results consistently, and neither Josh nor I is equipped to do that.

Josh is fifty-eight, and has no close relatives. He joined the army as a boy soldier in 1965, and left the Royal Engineers with the rank of sergeant-major in 1989. Late in life. He was then forty, and getting his first real taste of civilian life at that age was one hell of a shock. We've been together for almost eighteen years, married for fifteen and I know my big, strong soldier inside out. He plays blues guitar, until recently ran marathons with Liverpool Harriers, goes to the local gym every morning where he swims twenty lengths and on Wednesdays works out on the nautilus equipment. But – and this is a big but - I know damn well he's never fully adjusted to civilian life, and probably never will.

My own background is different, but in its own way just as ... well, unsettling ... and certainly the wrong training for tracking and collaring dangerous criminals. I left university with a good degree, moved into teaching when I was twenty-one and for the next thirty years lived in a closed world populated by young teenagers. When, disillusioned with my profession, I walked out in 2003 – ten years after marrying Josh – I found myself, *like* Josh, splashing about in the deep end of a world I soon realized was as familiar to me as the bottom of the deep blue sea. Both of us had been cocooned in our careers, then abruptly dumped naked into the cruel world. We'd been on the cosy inside, looking out without really seeing. Gazing back the other way, with wistful longing for what we had been, left both of us with a dull ache.

Now, as we sipped coffee on stools at the breakfast bar while the rain whispered on glass and in some bare, smelly little inter-view-room Steve Easter was undoubtedly enduring the first minutes of intense grilling, Josh was watching me with what was already weary resignation.

'Your first steps into criminal investigation were taken in an attempt to put things right: you'd made a mistake that could have cost a man his life. What's your excuse this time?'

'Steve Easter not only writes excellent short fiction, he a fine journalist. Sheila telling us about the story he's working on leads to the possibility that he's stumbled on something important. If he's been digging, he might have been treading on the toes of violent men. But, over and above all his work achievements or problems, he helped you found the Sozzled Scribblers – and he's a close friend.'

'*Seasoned* Scribblers.'

'Yes. Silly me.'

'It's a silly time,' Josh said softly. 'Both of us are acting daft.'

'Mm. When you had that slip of the tongue, you said you wondered where Andy Galleywood had been. Well, now you know. He'd been out somewhere getting beaten to death and squashed into a luggage box. And for that, Steve Easter's going to be accused of murder, Josh.'

'Not surprising, if the police eyewitness is reliable.'

'He can't be. He's got it wrong, you *know* he has.'

'He had a mobile phone with a camera. He took pictures, Pen. Quite soon they'll be viewed by the police.'

'I still say there's something wrong. I've seen two dead men tonight, two murdered men. I'm convinced those killings are linked. Father and son. What are you going to say? That Steve was behind both? Or that both men getting murdered within hours of each other is coincidence?'

'I'm not commenting. But surely you can see that whether there's one murder or ten, linked or not, Steve's position is unchanged. He's been photographed at the scene of a crime. A dead man was found in the locked luggage box mounted on the BMW he was driving.'

I pulled a face, looked angrily into my coffee. Suddenly remembered how I'd carefully switched memory cards in the Galleywood house.

I smiled with relief.

'Remember the Gareth Owen case, Josh? How my memory card was switched so that photographs taken by someone else, somewhere else, were in my camera? I did the same tonight at the Galleywood house: switched cards. That's obviously what happened with Steve.'

'Except that a mobile's SIM card is not that easy to get at. Besides, this is an eyewitness who happened on the scene by the purest accident and used his own mobile-phone camera to take pictures of a crime. Switching memory cards of any kind just doesn't come into it.'

'It could. This eyewitness could have been paid. Someone gave him fifty quid, the card to put in his phone and instructions to call the police and tell a totally false story.'

Josh was looking at me with one eyebrow raised and a crooked smile on his face.

'Do you really think that's what happened?'

I sighed and shook my head, realizing that he was right and I was creating a complicated scenario where none existed simply because I was clutching at straws.

'So Steve's guilty?'

Josh has this mannerism that makes me love him to bits. When he's deep in thought he rests his elbows somewhere handy – his ribs, if there's nowhere else – then steeples his fingers. The tips touch his chin. Sometimes he nods very slowly, sometimes he closes his eyes, but it's his mouth I watch most of all. If he's merely pensive, he'll purse his lips. If he's disturbed, those lips will become a firm line, while anger will tighten them into a thin droopy line – I call it his moody mouth – and cause the big muscles at the angle of his jaw to bulge.

At the moment he had nowhere to rest his elbows, but he was nodding slowly, and he was pursing his lips. Deep in thought, then. Pensive. Giving my question careful consideration. And not, after all, about to warn me off the case. Or cases.

'All I know,' he said, 'is that the most likeable and harmless-looking chaps have turned out to be killers.'

'Fine, Josh; one out of ten for loyalty.'

'Loyalty doesn't come into it, if it's misplaced. What we've got to do – what *you've* got to do if you're about to saddle that gallant white charger – is work out how to proceed. And be honest with yourself: this is not about Steve. You were itching to get your teeth into an investigation when you found yourself embroiled in the Larry Galleywood murder.'

'Embroiled?' I grinned. 'Hardly, not yet, but I will be, because you're right and I've been getting bored and then this cropped up and …' I spread my hands. 'And it's not *just* about me. Poor old Joanna's got nothing to gossip about, and I know Ryan Sharkey's up there in his penthouse drinking that coffee and vanilla-layered liqueur—'

'Sheridans. I thought that was reserved for your visits? Or for other young ladies.'

'Could well be, but I know it's *my* phone call he'll be eagerly awaiting.'

Josh rolled his eyes.

'Also,' I said, 'I *am* a little more embroiled than I've admitted, because I've already been to see Dr Malcolm Moneydie.'

Josh frowned. 'Who's he?'

'Come on, Josh, try to keep up. I went to see Galleywood because of that newspaper article. Remember? Galleywood was the philatelist who'd bought a rare coin from under the nose of a keen numismatist. There was something in the article about the stamp feller collecting for love, the coin feller for profit – and Galleywood couldn't stand the thought of this particularly beautiful old coin being locked away in a drawer lined with velvet. I suppose, to his way of thinking, it'd be like putting it in a coin coffin or crypt; burying it for all time.'

'So Moneydie is the coin collector?'

'And Galleywood's doctor. Galleywood visited him an hour or so before he was shot. He had chest pains. Moneydie recommended fresh air and plenty of exercise.'

'Sounds a bit severe.'

'Yes, well, Moneydie's ex-army and doesn't think much of us namby-pamby civilians.'

Josh glared, sat upright on the stool and turned pink as he expanded his chest.

It was my turn to roll my eyes.

'Yes, all right, so he hasn't seen you,' I said, 'but as he *had* seen Galleywood and had a reason for, well, getting his own back—'

'But not necessarily for killing him – and even if he did fancy bumping him off, there was no possible way of doing it if the crime scene's as you described it.' He hesitated. 'But that's why you went there, to weigh him up? So what was your impression? Hard enough, crazy enough … daft enough?'

'Yes.'

'Which?'

'All three.'

'The visit gave you something then, if only a meeting with a genuine weirdo.' He grinned fleetingly, then turned serious. 'All right. So, if these murders are connected, you've got to find some kind of a chain and possibly, just possibly, Dr Moneydie is one tiny link. But what else have you got to go on?'

I frowned, sipped my coffee, then slid off the stool and carried the mug with me as I went to stare through the conservatory to the flagged patio and the glistening wet grass that trailed away into the darkness at the bottom of the garden.

'Now that's *not* a jungle,' I said softly.

'Come again?'

I swung around, frowning thoughtfully.

'I looked out just now and was taken straight back to Larry

Galleywood's house. We were in his kitchen, Melanie Wigg and I. The light from his study was shining down on his overgrown garden and, shortly afterwards, she let slip something that's the only thing I've got go on in both murders.'

'Which is?'

'I thought there was just one newspaper article, the one about the rare coin he bought from under the nose of the keen collector, but, according to Melanie, there were others.'

'About?'

'I don't know. She used the word scam when I challenged her, and that rang alarm bells. And now Sheila's really set them jangling because she mentioned … what was it, talk of something fishy going on when those two were in Greece?'

I marched across, planted my empty mug on the counter and wrapped my arms around my big hunk of a husband. My mouth was close to his ear, my warm breath tickling him until he squirmed.

'Luckily,' I whispered, holding him tight, 'we both know someone very close who actually works on a newspaper – but asking my boy Adam about those other articles can wait until tomorrow, after—'

'After?' Josh said, pushing me away and holding me at arm's length as he gazed at me with grey eyes that smouldered with lascivious intent.

'After a good night's sleep,' I said demurely and, as best I could at my age, I slipped out of his grasp and scampered from the room.

chapter six

Tuesday

Josh left early the next morning for his usual twenty lengths – he says – in the local leisure centre's swimming pool. As soon as he'd gone, and still snug in dressing-gown and slippers, I went into my office and checked my *Penny Lane Panorama's* website and e-mails. Most corporate orders for landscapes and abstracts come in that way, orders from private buyers via e-mail or snail mail – I have a couple of ads running in magazines most likely to be read by prospective clients. Enquiries for the wedding service I started up when Annabel Lee arrived on the scene, come in all of those ways but also – and very importantly – by phone: I find that couples planning a wedding often have lots of questions and problems they like to talk over, so first it's the phone conversation, then the interview. I leave that to Annabel. Once I'd taken her on and she had her hands on my big Nikon digital SLRs, she arranged to photograph a friend's wedding and now uses those images as her portfolio. She's cleverly mixed monochrome, colour, candids and the more traditional formal poses. If that lot doesn't close the sale, Annabel certainly will.

By the time Josh got back looking pink and damp and smelling vaguely of chlorine I'd spoken on the phone to a couple of corporate art directors, finalized their orders and reached agreement on prices, and was on my way out. We kissed in the space between cars where autumn leaves were falling from the overhanging silver birch, then went our separate ways.

I start most days with a drive which takes me up the A540 past Thurstaston and Caldy to that part of the Wirral peninsula with a coastline on the Irish Sea. At Hoylake, I meet Joanna Lamb at the golf course end of North Parade in a café called the Thirsty Goose. Joanna is a slim blonde who used to work for Gareth Owen, Welsh solicitor turned serial killer. Apprehending him in a blistering climax in a boathouse on the River Dee at Chester brought to Ryan Sharkey the excitement he craved, and with Gareth now banged up inside and Joanna a newly qualified solicitor, the business sort of fell into her lap.

As Josh might say, what better lap is there to fall into? and I was smiling secretively at the thought when I pushed through the door to the merry tinkling of the café's bell.

'Someone's happy,' Joanna said, pushing my cappuccino across the table. 'And of course, me being privy to all sorts of classified info, I just happen to know why.'

'What on earth are you talking about?'

I sat down, hung my bag on the back of the chair, slurped some coffee and managed to look mystified.

'Hah!' Blonde hair whipped back and forth as Joanna shook her head in mock disbelief. 'Two murders is what I'm talking about—'

She broke off as I reached across and touched her sleeve. Cups had stopped clinking, and the murmur of conversation from an elderly couple sitting near the window had stopped as if wires had been cut. They were looking our way. The grey-haired lady in an expensive camel-hair coat smiled tentatively when she saw me looking, then leaned forward to whisper to her husband from behind her hand.

'Murder,' I said quietly to Joanna, 'is a subject best not bellowed from the rooftops.'

'I'll bear that in mind,' she said. 'Nevertheless—' said she, furtively '—murder's what I'm talking about and, looking about your person, it's not difficult to notice that the bag holding your expensive Nikons has been left at home. The evidence is there for me to behold. I'm a member of the legal profession, and I have no trouble in interpreting it correctly: today is not the day to be tramping the beach looking for found items to snap, because you're in PI mode – right, Penny?'

'Mm. Taking snaps is not how I'd describe the way I acquired my reputation – and no funny cracks, thank you – but thanks anyway, because you've reminded me about the cameras. One of the murder victims was getting married this weekend. I'll have to call Annabel, let her know the wedding shoot's off.'

'So you admit it?'

'To a solicitor? You really are joking.'

'Oh, now that is nasty—'

'Us PIs,' I said loftily, 'must watch our backs when walking the mean streets.'

'Shouldn't that be we, not us?' She giggled. 'However, on second thoughts the image that conjures up, like, you know, *wee* PIs—'

'*Now* who's being nasty?' I sniffed. 'All right, if I come clean will you let me pick your brains?'

'Pick away, my dear, but at nine in the morning and me still waiting for my caffeine kick, I wish you the best of British.'

'Right, then, yes I do know about the murders, of *course* I do – but, tell me, what do *you* know about the secret life of Larry Galleywood?'

'Well, I take it you've heard about the rare coin Galleywood bought, because yesterday morning you told me you were planning to interview him.'

'That's right. Only that never happened, because Galleywood, er—'

'Died. In a locked room.'

'Yes, and I was there.'

'If you were there in a locked room,' Joanna said, looking at me from under raised eyebrows, 'then you must be the murderer.'

'Damn it, stop being the precise legal eagle. You know what I mean.'

'I know what you said: he died in a locked room, and you were there.'

'Joanna!' I said warningly.

'Sorry.' She slapped the back of her hand and went on, 'Right, you were there when the police broke in, you charged in with them and you saw the body.'

'Yes, I did. And now the subject's been raised, once again my sluggish brain's been given a nudge: I've just remembered I've got photographs, of room and corpse, on a memory card I slipped into my pocket.'

Joanna pulled a face. 'I seem to remember you slipping something into your pocket when you saw your very first corpse out there on the beach. That little Buddha started you on a crusade that sent my employer to prison and changed your life.'

Her voice had gradually crept back up to its previous level, and there was a sudden clatter and a furious tinkling of the doorbell as the elderly couple left in haste.

'Changed yours, too,' I said, when they'd gone. 'OK, so what have we got, what else is there on Galleywood besides the coin? There must be a lot of serious stuff, because Melanie Wigg let something slip about other newspaper articles.'

'Yes, well, those would have been journalists speculating rather vaguely about the Greek scam.'

'Melanie mentioned scam, too,' I said, my scalp tingling with sudden excitement. 'Go on, tell me more.'

'Well, so far it's all speculation and rumour. It seems that British holidaymakers have been getting ripped off in the Greek Islands. Nothing new there, but this time it was by a couple of British con-merchants. Sort of like those time-share thingies, only involving outright purchases with more money involved.'

'Round figures?'

'Oh ... three million? Pounds, I think, but even Euros is impressive.'

'So how was it worked?'

'I'm not sure. I think someone was selling luxurious villas in the sun that didn't exist.'

'So why Galleywood? Where does he come in?'

'Perhaps nowhere. But his name came up, firstly because he's an estate agent, and secondly because he's been away from the shop for the whole of the Greek holiday season. And when he came back, it was rumoured – again – that he had loads of money.'

'Ah. I told you I was in his kitchen. Well, it looks and smells brand new.'

'There you are then.'

'Melanie went with him, didn't she?'

'Yes, she did. They were both away. Galleywood's son, Andy, was left in charge of the legal side of the estate agent business. That was pretty basic, down-market; they sold terraced houses to first-time buyers without much ready cash, did some rental work. But – rumour yet again – it's possible Andy was also involved in the Greek scam, because someone was needed to get the right images and sales spiel on to laptops. He is – was, sorry – a bit of a computer geek.'

Joanna was stealing glances at her watch and I knew she was anxious to get away to her office in Market Street. Visualizing her in Gareth Owen's old office with desk piled high with briefs, I frantically tried to dig up another question and realized that my image of a stodgy old philatelist living in a crumbling Victorian pile didn't gel with my idea of a criminal mastermind.

'If Andy set up the computer images and Larry and Melanie were the sales team out there in shorts and flip-flops and a mist of Ambre Solaire – who was the brains behind the scam?'

'Funny you should say that,' Joanna said, on her feet and wrapping her trench coat about her tall, slender frame. 'There's been very little speculation, but it does make you wonder when two of the three people rumoured to be involved die within hours of each other. What went wrong, one might ask. Whose toes did they tread on – and what on earth happened to all that lovely lolly?'

The police station in Hoylake is an old building in Queens Road, and has long been known to veteran coppers in the force as the Wendy House. Cute, yes, but I didn't feel that it was an accurate description of such an establishment. I don't consider them to be the best of places to visit, even at the best of *times* and, as I drove my red Ka into the car-park, I was remembering with a frisson of guilt my late-night sleight of hand. Last night, or some time today, DI Dancer would be looking at a memory card handed to him proudly by PC Faraday. It was brand new, and there was absolutely nothing on it.

I also realized with a second slightly stronger frisson that when I left Joanna the memory card containing the crime scene images had been transferred from skirt pocket to the handbag now swinging from my shoulder. Suddenly the bag was ten pounds heavier and glowing as if radioactive.

Despite feeling as embarrassed as a schoolgirl who's just been caught smoking behind the bike sheds, I made it all the way to Dancer's office and was greeted with complete indifference by the untidy DI. The man I looked on as his permanent sidekick, DS Hood, was on his way out. His red hair was gelled into a glistening fright wig. He was holding a digital camera, and looked puzzled. My heart started a wild thumping.

'Yeah,' Dancer said, as I took the chair he indicated, 'you might well shiver and shake. What you did could be construed as perverting the course of justice – whatever that might be.' He grinned, at once softening the hard lines of his thin face. 'Doesn't

matter anyway. All you got was pictures of a dusty study and a
bloke lying dead on a Chinese rug, and the official photographer's got those. And of course, you're not going to sell yours to
the highest bidder.'

'Wouldn't dream of it.'

'No,' Dancer said, holding up crossed fingers, 'and I wouldn't
con my dear old granny out of her lottery winnings.'

'Talking of cons or scams,' I said, but Dancer stopped me with
a raised hand.

'We might get to that later,' he said, and the good humour had
drained from his dark eyes. 'First off, this is a murder investigation, and what I need from you is what you were doing at the
Galleywood house, and what happened before my men got there.'

'He was a philatelist, and I was planning an article for *Gibbons
Stamp Monthly*,' I said. 'Then I heard rumours that Galleywood
had bought a valuable coin from under the nose of a serious
collector, so that raised the possibility of a second article for *Coin
News*, or similar. I was there to interview him.'

'And?'

'I was invited in by a lady called Melanie Wigg who'd been
sitting too close to the brandy. She took me through to the
kitchen and told me Galleywood was in his study, and couldn't be
disturbed. We chatted. Then both of us heard a bang.'

'What d'you mean by bang?'

I thought for a moment, trying to recall the sound.

'It was from upstairs. Muffled. Deadened by all those walls and
floors getting in the way.' I shrugged. 'Sorry. I can't elaborate. It
was a bang.'

'A shot?'

'Melanie thought so.'

'But you didn't?'

'It hadn't occurred to me. I remember I said something silly
about Galleywood dropping a book.'

'And there was a book up there, wasn't there? A big thick one,
and it *was* on the floor. So what was it, shot or book?'

'Well, Galleywood had been shot – hadn't he...?' I hesitated,
trying to follow Dancer's train of thought. 'Ah. You're after the
time of death. The study was locked and there was nobody in

there, but if this was a book I heard falling then Galleywood could have been shot earlier.' I frowned. 'Doesn't make any difference, does it? Because whatever the time of death, we can't get away from the locked room.'

'I hate to say it,' Dancer said, 'but this looks like just the kind of mystery to interest a certain Josh Lane who writes crime books and knows a bit about impossible plots.'

'He'd be flattered,' I said, 'but he's a bit of a plodder. Give him time.'

Dancer's face was impassive. 'Didn't actually say I was asking for his help, did I?'

I grinned. 'Well, you can bet your boots he's working on it. We talked about it last night, and he was … intrigued. We were at the Easter house – but you know that, of course.'

'Yeah.' Dancer nodded. 'OK, so, moving on, what was that about a scam?'

I blinked. 'Erm, I heard rumours.'

'We've all heard rumours, but how close are you to turning rumours into fact? Your son's a journalist. Maybe he's got information that didn't get into the papers, information that would help us in our enquiries.'

My smile was sweet to his sour. 'Maybe he has, but the first I heard of the Greek Island scam was from Sheila Easter.'

As soon as the words left my mouth I knew I'd said the wrong thing. Dancer stopped rocking in his chair. His dark eyes had narrowed, and I could almost see his mind working.

'Yeah, right, and Steve Easter's currently being questioned about a body found in the luggage box on top of his car, said body being that of the son of a man who's *also* died violently and may possibly have been involved in said scam.'

'Whoa, hold on a minute,' I said. 'Actually, thinking back, all Sheila said was that Galleywood and Melanie Wigg had been away for some time and she knew there'd been talk of something fishy going on.'

'Like what?'

'That's it. That's all she said.'

'No it's not. When you walked in here I recall you saying something like, "and talking of cons". That must have come from somewhere. Seconds ago, you said the first you heard of a Greek Island scam was from Sheila Easter. Then all of a sudden you change your tune and all you've got is "something fishy going on"—'

'I got it wrong, that's all. Actually, yes, I do know something about holidaymakers being ripped off, but I heard it from someone else.'

'Ah. As DS Hood was in North Parade and happened to espy you in the Thirsty Goose, your informant wouldn't happen to be Joanna Lamb, would it? Gareth Owen's assistant who couldn't wait to step into a dead man's shoes? Remind me to talk to her about traps, and keeping them shut.'

'Espy?' I rolled my eyes. 'How about descry? Anyway, we were talking over coffee. Remind me to talk to your Robin Hood about noses, and keeping them out.'

But, overtaken by memories that were lurking in the background waiting for the right moment to waylay me, the banter was being pushed to one side as my mind replayed the instant when Steve Easter's luggage box opened and Sheila collapsed in a heap on the wet gravel at the sight of Andy Galleywood's bloody body. Tragedy had come into their family at the turn of a tiny key, and I knew, no, I was absolutely convinced, that they had done nothing wrong.

'Steve Easter,' I blurted, 'had nothing to do with any scams and nothing to do with Andy Galleywood's death. He's not involved.'

'I don't know where that came from,' Dancer said, 'but you're wrong. He drove straight home from a car-park outside his place of work. A witness had seen a man answering Easter's description watch a body being put in the luggage box sitting on top of a black BMW. He photographed the scene, got a picture of the vehicle involved, including its registration number. When the police arrived at Easter's house, a body was found in the locked luggage box on top of his car. The key to the box was with his car keys. Andy Galleywood had been badly beaten; he was either being taught a hard lesson, or he had something, knew something …' He spread his hands and shrugged. 'Whatever, we'll find out soon enough, but the point is he died from those injuries, or from suffocation by being bent double in a confined space with very little air. And as it was Easter's car and he was *seen* – well, the conclusion any investigating officer would come to is that Easter committed murder, thought he was safe, and drove home to wait until such time as he could bury or in some way dispose of the body.'

I came out of my chair in a rush, almost sweeping Dancer's desk clean as I grabbed my bag and swung it over my shoulder.

Dancer was up, too, and as I strode away, speechless, he gave me the expected warning but added a coda that took me completely by surprise.

'Remember, by profession you're a photographer, Penny. First time out as a PI you were trying to save your own reputation and you got lucky, but even then without the arrival of the police you'd have been so much dead meat in a Chester boathouse. Stay away. Let the pros do the investigating, the necessary tangling with very dangerous criminals.

'As for Greek Island scams, yeah, we're looking into it at this end – meaning the UK – and have been for a while now. But there's limits. We can listen to rumours, and follow them up, but we can't make arrests based on rumours. So while the Greek police work on the same case out there in the sun, we watch, wait, enquire. Us. That's me and my men, not you. Also,' he went on, 'in case you're wondering, we did know all about the trouble between Galleywood and Dr Moneydie, and Moneydie's already been questioned. Routine. Knowing he couldn't have done it; knowing, with what we've got so far, that *nobody* could've done it in the way it was done. Apparently,' he added, and grinned in a manner that suggested tracking down Galleywood's killer was something he was going to enjoy.

Then, as I stood half-turned in the doorway, he stuck that little bit on the end that tamed my furious gaze and almost brought hot tears to my eyes.

'However, knowing you,' he said, 'all of that'll go over your head. So if you want to help Steve Easter, ask yourself this question: if, as you believe, he's not involved in any way with Andy Galleywood's murder, why did someone get a spare key to the luggage box on top of *his* car so they could stuff a corpse inside it? Why his, and not one of the hundreds of boxes that must be all over Liverpool bolted to the top of other, more expensive cars? What has Steve Easter done to make him the focus of some very nasty attention?'

chapter eight

'Annabel?'

'Hi Penny. How's tricks?'

'Sadly, I'm the bearer of rotten news. You can put your cameras away for the weekend. The wedding's off.'

'Damn. What happened, has Andy got cold feet?'

I stared out of my office window and felt an inappropriate smile twitch my lips as I wondered how to answer that.

'You could say so, I suppose. He's dead.'

'OhmyGod! What happened?'

'He was murdered.'

There was a silence. I knew what was coming next, and closed my eyes.

'Knowing you, this is really weird. His death isn't by any chance connected to your visit to his dad? 'Cos you were going there last night, weren't you?'

'I was, and I did.' I paused. 'He's dead too.'

'Bloody hell,' Annabel said, her voice shaky. 'Weird turns bizarre. You're not the *bearer* of bad news—'

'I *am* bad news. Yes, I know.'

'And, like last time with the body on the beach, you're going to put it right.'

'I think. I suppose. Which is why I must rush. How'd you like to pop over – say, Thursday evening – for dinner? We can talk business over drinks, see what's in the pipeline. I'm also about to phone Adam, and I'll invite him too so you won't feel—'

'Spare?' She giggled. 'I thought Adam was involved with that

Church Army tambourine shaker. With the made-up French name.'

'Desirée. No, that's over. And it was the triangle she played, in the Salvation Army band.'

'Wow. And ting-a-ling.' Another giggle, this one sounding strangled. 'OK, Pen, I'll be there. But don't for one minute think I'm not up to why you're doing this.'

'Oh, *really*, Annabel—'

'Yes, really. Drop the injured tone, because I've already agreed. I spoke to Andy and his fiancée lots of times about the wedding shoot. Between now and Thursday I'll try to recall anything he told me that might lead you to his killer. Happy?'

'Of course, but also shocked that you would think—'

She made a rude noise, and put down the phone. The smile that had been twitching my lips became a full-blown grin. Annabel Lee was a blonde-haired delight who never failed to brighten my day.

I'd got back home from Dancer's office soon after half past ten. Josh was laptopping away at his latest crime novel, and in the hour or so before I called him for lunch I had several telephone calls to make. The first had been to Annabel Lee, and that pleasant chore was now out of the way. Those still to come had a direct bearing on the second of the murders to be plonked in my lap, and I was determined to make the most of DI Dancer's advice. I knew he'd given me a valid question to start my investigation on its way: Steve Easter might in my eyes be innocent of murder, but if he was then for some reason he had been targeted.

My first task was to find out why.

On the drive home I'd worked out that the person most likely to know something was the eyewitness who'd reported the crime and taken photographs. What I hadn't worked out was how to get in touch with him – even Dancer in his generous mood wouldn't give me that – so I'd naturally thought of my clever journalist son, Adam Wise.

That's right, Wise, not Lane.

The conflicting surname's part of a long story that really did begin at the bottom of Liverpool's Penny Lane. I was born there. My father's name was Mark Black – try filling that in on forms where the surname comes first. He was a philatelist with a tiny shop on Smithdown Road, and being blessed – if that's the right word – with the infamous scouse wit, he naturally called me Penelope. For more than twenty years, I was a living breathing specimen of that most famous of British postage stamps. In 1974 I met Peter Wise, when we were both newly qualified teachers. We got married, I changed my name, and the most charitable thing I can say about the union is that for a time I became the complimentary half of a well-known proverb. We had two children, Adam and Jacqueline, but in 1985 that proverb came back to haunt me. Penny Wise I might have been, but I'd known for a long time that, over Peter, I'd been foolish in the extreme. One rainy evening he went out for cigarettes and, on that short walk, decided he fancied a pack of Winfield. A couple of months later I found out he'd bought them from a shop in Sydney, Australia. In 1994, when she was seventeen, Jacqueline went Down Under to live with him (she later moved north, and now works for the *Brisbane Courier Mail*). A year later I married Josh and sort of went full circle: born in Penny Lane, I'd *become* Penny Lane.

As I picked up the phone for the second time I knew what I was in for. Talk to my son face to face or on the telephone and I might as well be talking to his father. Peter may be 12,000 miles away, but his fair hair, fresh skin and dry, slightly mocking voice have all been passed on to his son and remain there to haunt me. In addition, Adam, used to reporting the seamier side of life, is dead against my PI activities.

With that in mind, I began with the good news as a softener. I should have known it wouldn't work.

'Adam, how does Thursday evening sound for a slap-up feed?'

'Brilliant, if I didn't twig it for a clever ruse to get me into the house and pick my brains.'

'Oh, *really*, Adam, you're as bad as Annabel—'

'Yes, and I know that tone of voice, too. Frequently used. Deeply hurt on the surface, but mental fingers crossed and the gaze steely—'

'Have you heard about Andy Galleywood?'

'Yes. With considerable shock. I have more than once spent a happy and productive evening with the Seasoned Scribblers. He

was a good bloke. Frequently helped me with computer problems.'

'I was going to ask you about newspaper articles relating to his
misdeeds, but Joanna's given me some answers. I need more, of
course, because I'm hoping to discover the truth behind those
tragic events—'

'Which is Penny Lane speak for poking your nose into the
activities of dangerous criminals as you hunt for a killer. Come
on, Mum, you're not setting off on that bloody high-stepping
hobby horse again, are you?'

'It's difficult not to. There were two murders, Adam.'

'Yes, I know, father and son.'

'I was there for both.'

'You are *joking*!'

'Well ... not joking, but not entirely accurate, either. There, but
not in at the death, so to speak. I heard the shot – or think I did
– when Larry Galleywood was murdered. I was downstairs in the
kitchen with a woman who calls herself a domestic without portfolio. Melanie Wigg. I think she's much more than that, which is
one of the lines I'll be pursuing. Then I was at Steve's house –
Steve Easter? – when he drove in from work minutes ahead of the
police with Andy's body stuffed in his luggage box.'

'Jesus!' Adam said softly. 'Is that what happened? And are you
saying Steve was arrested?'

'Mm. He's still helping with enquiries. I just wish I could do
something for him.' I paused to let that sink in. Then, twisting the
knife, I said, 'I could be wasting my time here. You don't know a
lot about either murder, do you, which is a pity because that's bad
news for Steve.' I put a hefty measure of disappointment into my
voice, then held my breath.

'I have read the brief reports. I know one death's a complete
mystery, there was an eyewitness to the other.'

'Not to the death. This person saw Andy's body being put into
the luggage box, even took some photographs. I haven't seen
them, but the description he gave to the police of one of the men
helping with the putting sounded a lot like Steve. The thing is, I'd
talk to this bloke, but I don't know his name.'

I heard papers rustling, then the faint rapping that I knew was

Adam turning a pencil in his fingers to tap each end in turn on
the desk. Concerned. Trying to make his mind up, wanting to
help me but uncertain. Then I heard him sigh with what sounded
like resignation.

'I'll see what I can do. Hang on, Mum, I'll put you on hold.'

I jumped as a hand touched my waist. Josh had left his office
and crept up behind me. His finger slid up my spine, and with his
nail he gently traced the skin at the nape of my neck. I scrunched
my shoulders and twisted to look at him.

'It's not lunchtime, not bedtime, and I'm talking to Adam. Go
away.'

'I'm fascinated. I caught most of your side of the conversation.
It sounded like a cold-blooded mixture of bribery, blackmail and
bullying. You've used the same tactics before now; if they don't
get you what you want, you play on a person's good nature. Very
cruel. All Adam wants is for you to be safe.'

'Finished?'

He grinned. 'I'm thinking of using you in the book, giving you
a Boston accent and a .357 Magnum and changing your appearance with nips and tucks to tighten the loose bits and create a
hard face, top it all with a blonde wig and—'

I held up my hand as the phone chirped in my ear.

'Yes, Adam.'

'I've been talking to my pals on the crime desk. They've come
up with a name. You can have it, on one condition.'

'Which is?'

'When you go to see this guy, take Ryan Sharkey with you.'

'I intend to. He's my next phone call.'

'All right. This eyewitness, his name's Joey Lox. Early twenties,
unemployed. Shaven head, tall and skinny – that's the best I can do,
and there's a lot of his kind about. I haven't got an address for him,
either, but I do know he lives somewhere in south Liverpool,
possibly the Dingle. You'll be coming in through the tunnel, so your
best bet is to make your way to Belvidere Road and try to wangle
your way into the club that's on the left a little way before the posh
school. The club's called SCENE SOUTH, and that's where Joey hangs
out. Get there early evening if you can, and nurse your drinks. Ask
the barman to give you the nod when this Joey walks in.'

'I will. And thanks, Adam—'

'Mum.'

'Yes?'

'Remember ... Take Ryan Sharkey.'

The phone clicked. I put mine down and swivelled to face Josh. He was leaning against my filing cabinet as he looked out of the window at the willow tree trailing naked branches over his unfinished pond. He liked to call it his dust bowl. Or Death Valley. Not funny.

'He told me to take Sharkey. This Joey Lox character sounds rough. That's stereotyping, I know, but images spring to mind unbidden, don't they?'

'Yes, well, right or wrong, taking Sharkey along as bodyguard is a clever step in the right direction. Full marks to Adam.'

He came away from the window and I saw he had his Olympus micro recorder in his hand. He always carries it with him to capture those clever ideas that come out of nowhere and can so easily slip away into the ether.

'Sharkey really is next on my list of calls, you know. Always was, from the moment I knew I was back on the crime beat.' I smiled. 'That's the wrong term, isn't it? More in Adam's line of work. Or am I miles out? And sounding a bit wobbly and ... melancholy? Always do, don't I, when I've been talking to my son who's the spitting image of that ... that—'

'He looks like his father,' Josh said quietly.

I took a deep breath, let it out slowly.

'Yes. Anyway, I know Sharkey will be chuffed. I spoke to him about a week after the Gareth Owen case, but since then there's been no contact.' I chuckled. 'Remember all those nasty stories? About him being a cross dresser, and dossing in a shed where he survived on Pedigree Chum?'

'Yes, and you half-believed them because he was an unshaven tramp in a wrinkled suit when you first saw him – where was it, that Liverpool club, JOKERS WILD?'

'That's right. The place run by the late Terry Lynch, who kidnapped Annabel then died at our very own OK Corral shoot-out. But instead of a tramp looking as if he'd just downed fifteen pints, Sharkey's a professional gambler who makes a bundle, most of it through his mobile phone or laptop while he looks out over the Welsh hills from his classy Albert Dock penthouse.'

'And d'you know what?' Josh said. 'That professional gambler bit is something I only half-believe. If Sharkey spent most of his time in Las Vegas, fine, but—'

'Times change, Josh. It can be done, it *is* done.'

'I know, I know. I mean, that's what I'm writing about at the moment, a novel set in Arizona.'

'No, what you're doing at the moment is what most writers do for most of the time, and that's stall.'

He grinned. 'I've been sussed. OK, phone Sharkey. I'll carry on stalling to good effect in the kitchen by preparing lunch.'

He slipped away. I found Starkey's land-line number in my Filofax, punched the telephone keys and got his answering machine and was about to hang up when he came on.

'Sharkey.'

'It's game on, Sharkey. Isn't that what they say?'

'That must be Penny Lane,' he said with a smile in his voice. 'Still trying hard to be cool when the term went out of fashion—'

'Ten years before you were born?'

'Ouch. You're probably right but, as you're well aware, if it was still in I'd be its shining epitome.'

'Well, I hope being cool doesn't apply to our relationship and make you unreachable, because I need you this evening. I'm going to a Dingle club to talk to a man who witnessed a crime. I need someone with me who's got menace, muscle, and is also cool.' I giggled. 'What I mean is cool as in able instantly to assess dangerous situations and come up with the right response. Unflusterable, if there is such a word. If there isn't, try unflappable. Does that sound like you?'

'Absolutely.'

'And you're free tonight?'

'What time?'

I had my mouth open to speak when Josh again touched my waist. He'd sneaked back into my office. Serial eavesdropper sprang to mind, and I covered the mouthpiece to bite his head off when he shushed me with a finger.

'I'm going to the writers' group this evening,' he said in a low voice. 'It's because of Andy, and Steve's involvement, a sort of extraordinary meeting. Just a few of us, but I'd like you there. Can you put this Joey feller off until after nine?'

'He's not expecting us, got no idea we're on to him. So, yes, of course.'

He kissed the top of my head and drifted back to his lunch-making, and I became aware of Sharkey burbling in my ear.

'Sorry. That was Josh. I thought I'd need you early this evening, but he's got me booked.' I hesitated, thinking, then said, 'On the other hand, you could go ahead of me, and I could meet you there.'

'I could indeed, if you tell where and what this is about.'

I spent the next few minutes bringing him up to date with two murders, gave him the name and description of the scally who had witnessed the start of Andy Galleywood's last journey, told him where he liked to hang out, said I'd see him there some time after nine.

'One important point, for future reference,' he said. 'I'm having trouble with the phones here, so you'd better take my mobile number and use that if you need to get in touch.'

He gave it to me, I jotted it down. Then, farewells said and my mouth watering as the aroma of grilled Lincolnshire sausages and gently percolating coffee came wafting into my office, I went through to the kitchen to eat lunch with the chef.

Yesterday's rain had given way to November sunshine which was still strong enough to warm the conservatory. An after-lunch nap has been a habit of Josh's since his army days, mine since we got married. With a small glass of red wine beside us to complement the after-taste of the delicious midday snack, we stretched out in the conservatory's cushioned wicker chairs with the patio door half open to let in the cooler air that carried with it the fresh scent of wet grass.

Thinking in the hours after midnight is rarely productive and often depressing enough to cause despair – one of my unbreakable rules is never to go over heavy issues or make important decisions while lying awake during those dark night hours.

However, I think it was Confucius who said that *meditating*

with warm sun beating on closed eyelids is pathway to enlightenment.
If he didn't, well I've just made it up because I know it's true. So
with Josh sprawled opposite me and his bare toes a comforting
couple of inches from mine, I embarked on some serious
thinking on what I'd let myself in for, and why. Eyes closed, of
course.

I've got enough common sense to admit that success on my
first venture into criminal investigation was probably down to
beginner's luck, but not quite enough, it seems, to understand
that this second time out I might not be so fortunate. Well, OK,
putting it like that does suggest that I recognize the dangers, but
if that's true, why do I go on?

Buzz is probably the first word that springs to mind. I felt it
throughout the Gareth Owen case. That buzz arrived to set my
brain sizzling with excitement on top of a gradual realization that
I'd reached a plateau and gone as far as I could in my chosen
profession of photographer. It was pretty hard to resist. Still is.
For me, the spurt of adrenaline that sets the senses singing during
so many phases of a murder investigation puts the necessary
magic back into my working life – and probably gives DI Dancer
nightmares. It's irresistible.

So, without probing too deeply, I was happy privately to accept
that unique buzz as my reason for setting out to investigate two
puzzling murders, and publicly to use helping Steve Easter as a
more acceptable excuse, if anyone was interested.

Which was great, for me. But if my conscience was clear, the
way ahead was anything but. I was hoping to solve two baffling
murders – but where did I start?

Talking to Joey Lox was a beginning, but I didn't really expect
to get anything new. An eyewitness can only describe what he's
seen. Peering through the rain at Steve Easter's house, I'd
already heard the stocky detective go over that grim scene in the
car-park in some detail. The police would by now have inter-
viewed the eyewitness and looked at the photographs from his
phone – which left me with what? A forlorn hope that Joey Lox
could put names to one or more of the men he had seen?
Unlikely, and in any case the police questioning would have been
exhaustive: if Joey had recognized anyone, after a couple of hours

in the interview-room he'd have been spitting out the names like bits of broken teeth.

Well, we'd see. Later that evening, with Sharkey the menacing presence at my side, I'd smile pleasantly but work my butt off (I read that in the Arizona novel Josh is working on) to get Joey Lox to spill anything missed or overlooked by the police. And with that being my one forlorn hope of progress in the second murder I was back with the intriguing first: the murder of Larry Galleywood.

That was easier, because it was impossible and I had absolutely nothing to go on. Melanie Wigg had travelled abroad with Galleywood and I might get her talking about that, but locked room murders? They were the stuff of fiction. Outside crime novels they just didn't happen, and even there the possibilities had long been wrung dry.

My relaxed, reclining body shook as I chuckled softly, and I felt Josh's foot nudge mine as he stirred and changed position.

If he knew what I was thinking he would probably have scolded me for using wrong terminology. I think possibilities should be exhausted, not wrung dry – is that right? – but it didn't matter anyway. Labelling Larry Galleywood's murder an impossible crime meant I needed help; calling it the stuff of fiction told me exactly where to get it. Before meeting Sharkey I was going with Josh to a meeting of the Seasoned Scribblers. Most of the members were crime writers. Between them they had written countless intricate plots. I would arrange a brainstorming session, then sit back in the shadows outside the circle of light shining on those clever novelists while they slowly and methodically solved the Larry Galleywood murder.

Easy. See what I mean about thinking with the hot sun on closed eyelids? It's enough to send you to sleep.

chapter nine

My first meeting with DI Dancer had been in the lounge of Heswall's Golden Fleece public house, when Josh and I had gone there hoping to return a small statuette of the Great Buddha to Dr Sebastian Tombs. This was a couple of months ago, at the start of the Gareth Owen case, and by that time Tombs was missing, probably dead. But the visit to the Golden Fleece left a favourable impression on Josh, and when he and Steve Easter formed the Seasoned Scribblers writers' group, that's where they went seeking a suitable venue to hold their monthly meetings. They got the room at the back that had been a big vestry in the pub's former existence as a church. The front half of the building had been rebuilt to present a suitably attractive pub façade to the Wirral's winers and diners. At the back, the old vestry remained intact, and its mullioned windows – still leaded – looked out over grassland rolling down to the wide Dee estuary.

At eight o'clock that evening we drove on to the circular drive and around the floodlit pool with its central fountain. Cars were bright splashes of wet colour. There were two I recognized in the marked parking bays. One was an old Jaguar XJS. The other was an even older Nissan Cherry. Josh had also spotted them.

'Someone's got here early.'

'Yes, I see two different pods for two very different peas: Vince Keevil and Deakin Chatto.'

'That's a new twist on an old saying, but spot on.' Chuckling, he backed the Range Rover under overhanging shrubs and switched off. 'What is it the Americans say: Ike and Mike they're both alike? I think I've got it wrong and it's *think* alike, but it makes the same point: I doubt if I've ever met two people who are as near as dammit direct *opposites*.'

It was drizzling and cold. I'd donned a warm skirt and slipped on a pale yellow cashmere sweater – courtesy of Oxfam – under the inevitable blue waterproof. Jacket rustling, I got out and waited with hunched shoulders for Josh.

Once inside the Golden Fleece we walked past the small bar with its tall stools and a carpeted space where an old loose-covered settee and a couple of comfortable chairs were placed for the convenience of unsteady drinkers, then made our way along the edge of the dining area to the back room. The door was ajar. Josh glanced in, counted heads, then gave my shoulder a squeeze as he turned and went back to the bar.

I carried on, and not for the first time got the strange feeling of going from pub to church in one stride. Warmth turned to cool verging on chill, walls that in the public areas of the pub were papered in fiery reds and rich gold became blocks of naked stone, and the rain-splashed mullioned windows and huge refectory table with its wheel-back chairs suggested we were attending a mediaeval banquet.

That impression was immediately dispelled by the appearance of the three people already in the room.

Vince Keevil was in his mid-fifties, had the raw, shaven-headed look of an iron man tri-athlete and was wearing white trainers and a navy tracksuit in some expensive fabric with a sheen. The tracksuit top's zip was open far enough to reveal gold glinting in crinkly chest hairs I liked to believe were the result of a trans-plant. Joanna and I had often speculated, with considerable merriment, on their original location.

I'd met him several times and on each occasion he had been in deep conversation with Gay Tirril. The name evokes an image which that not-so-young lady tries hard to match by fighting tooth and nail against reality. Reality was winning hands down. I'd said something along those lines to Josh, and he'd repri-manded me for everything from the overuse of clichés to mixing metaphors. But needs must (sorry), and if the language fits the situation then rules must be broken. Gay was pushing fifty, but was dressed like someone wobbling out on high heels to present the bouquet that comes after the medals at national swimming championships. Her dress was lime-green and cut for a figure less full than hers. I knew from experience that the hemline swooped dizzily on the opposite side to the split and, as she leant across the table with head tilted and her cobalt contact lenses fixed on Vince, her long blonde hair fell attractively across skin that was less than flawless.

So far everything as it should be. Yet, perhaps because of heightened awareness now that I was once again involved in crime, I couldn't help noticing that their manner seemed strained. There was something in Keevil's steel-grey eyes, noticeable even from a distance, that looked very much like a warning. Gay had an elbow on the table. Her chin was resting in her cupped hand, and in the fingers lightly touching her cheek there was a faint tremor. It was difficult to tell at first, but I did get the impression that her eyes were swollen, possibly from weeping. No surprise there, of course. Andy Galleywood had been one of the group's more popular members. He would be missed.

Nevertheless, it appeared to me that as far as Vince and Gay were concerned, they were alone in the room, lost in their own timeless world of ... of what? Gay might have been weeping for Andy Galleywood, but what else was troubling them?

Deakin Chatto was watching me watching the two uncharacteristically uncomfortable poseurs, and as I tore my fascinated gaze away and looked his way he winked, rolled his eyes and shrugged. Harder to do than you'd think. Try it. But Chatto's an original. I can't stand the man, but according to Josh he writes like Hemingway, the beard has been there since the day he should have started shaving (about twenty years ago), and he dresses like a scarecrow because – rumour has it – that's where he gets his clothes.

I was hanging my jacket over one of the wheel-backs and settling on to the hard wooden seat when Josh reappeared with a rattling tray. He plonked it down, passed a bottle of Old Peculiar to Chatto, gin and tonic with a slice of lime to Gay, something pale green in a liqueur glass topped with a red parasol to Keevil. I got an excellent Merlot.

The brolly in Keevil's drink was Josh's little joke. Keevil was not impressed.

'Bad business, Josh. Not the time for frivolity.'

'Rubbish,' Josh said, getting rid of his jacket and settling into a chair. He tasted his Glenfiddich, smacked his lips and said, 'Might as well say it's not the time for drinking, Vince, but you'll do that, won't you?'

'Different thing altogether. A man's dead, I'll drink to his memory.'

Gay was glaring at me. 'How about givin' us the details, tellin' us what really happened?' she said, in a strong Liverpool accent enriched by smoke and drink. 'The papers're useless. All we know is we've lost a good friend who was also a fine writer.' She shivered. 'Apparently the poor lad was stuffed in Steve Easter's luggage box.'

'That's about all anyone knows up to now,' I said. 'A young scally witnessed that gruesome business and took photographs before calling the police. But that was the termination, for want of a better word. As we've no idea what happened prior to that, we were hoping that a crime writers' brainstorming session might at the very least come up with possible reasons for the murder.'

'There were two murders,' Chatto said.

Keevil shook his head. 'Only one concerns us.'

'Father and son,' Chatto said. 'If they're connected—'

'They're not.' Keevil was adamant.

'Why?'

Keevil swung on Josh. 'You should know. In your novels, doesn't a different *modus operandi* almost always mean different killers? Besides, one murder was in Liverpool, the other very close to here no more than an hour later. Given the distance, I'd say it was impossible for the same killer to be in both places.'

'You know a lot,' Chatto said, suddenly wise in demeanour as he stroked his beard. 'Where did you get all the info?'

'It was in the morning paper.'

'Not about different MOs. There was nothing in there about how they were murdered.'

Keevil put pained weariness into a thin smile. 'One was in a locked room, one in a locked box—'

'That's remarkably similar, not different,' Chatto said.

I flicked a finger to ping my wine glass and grab their attention.

'That's similar place of death, Deakin, not similar method,' I said. 'As for the MO, then you should have asked me before arguing to a standstill. I was there at both crime scenes: in Larry Galleywood's house when his body was found in the study, and in Steve Easter's house when the police discovered Andy Galleywood's body. Larry Galleywood had been shot through the eye. The bullet apparently ricocheted from a book he was holding. He'd been to the library, and may have been engrossed enough to, well, not see what was about to happen. That's just my reading of the scene, by the way, but I was very close to the body and I think I'm right about the book and the ricochet. I couldn't tell what had happened to Andy. I was further away, and everyone was shocked rigid when he tumbled out of that box. However, I spoke to DI Dancer this morning. He told me Andy Galleywood had been badly beaten, and died from his injuries.'

Nobody said anything. Josh finished his single malt, downed the glass with a flourish and looked around the table with his eyebrows raised questioningly.

'Everyone happy so far? Right, then for argument's sake and to give us something to get our teeth into, let's say that different MO does mean two killers,' he said. 'Has to be, anyway, as Vince pointed out: time and distance between crime scenes rules out a single killer.'

'No it doesn't,' Chatto said, 'because we don't know what time Andy died. All we know is he was seen being put into that luggage box at, what…?'

'Seven-thirty,' I said, 'according to the police.'

'Yeah,' Chatto said, 'and he could've been alive, couldn't he? Could've been driven there in that big Jeep SUV.'

'Now who's privy to information not readily available?' Vince Keevil said. 'Come on, Deakin, where did you get that Jeep from? That *certainly* wasn't in the paper.'

'We're brainstorming, dickhead. If you want it put another way, we're hypothesizing, creating could've-been situations out of nothing. And what I'm saying is Andy could have been kicked, beaten, tortured almost anywhere and any time within the last couple of days, then taken to that car-park so he could be put in Steve's box.'

'Taken in a phantom SUV.'

'No, not phantom, Vince,' I said. 'It *was* a Jeep SUV, with tinted windows. I heard the police describe it to Steve.'

'So how does Deakin know so much about it?' Gay said, as if taking her cue from Keevil. It was the first time she'd turned her face fully towards the rest of us. Yes, her eyes were swollen, and I was convinced she'd been crying.

Josh was getting impatient.

'Cut it out, all of you,' he said firmly. 'If information pops up in this session, we'll use it and worry about it later. The point is that the different MOs don't rule out the Galleywoods' murders being connected. Again, for argument's sake, let's agree they are: father and son were murdered for the same reason, the same motive. Going a step further, I reckon the killer or killers were probably hired.'

'Contract killers?' Keevil frowned. 'So who was paying them, and what was the motive?'

Josh looked around the group.

'Any ideas?'

'All Andy did was work hard in his dad's office, and play with computers,' Gay said. 'He wasn't treading on toes, wasn't doing anything serious enough to get himself killed.'

She'd almost finished her gin and tonic – definitely not the first – and alcohol was turning her cheeks a glorious shocking pink. Keevil and Chatto just looked baffled. Josh seemed to be waiting for me. I thought for a moment, then came at them from a different direction.

'What about Steve Easter? Andy's body was put in his luggage box. What can we make of that? Hardly coincidence, because whoever did it had the keys to the box. That points to premeditation. So what was the idea? Was Steve being warned off: back off, or you're next? If so, why? What was he on to?'

'He mentioned something to me about a property scam,' Deakin Chatto said, and smiled when Keevil snorted derisively. 'Nice work if you can get it, apparently: fleecing British suckers dazed by sun and sangria. Or in this case, ouzo.'

Keevil was scornful. 'Galleywood didn't have the brains.'

'Which one?'

'We're talking about Andy.'

'Yeah, well, I'm talking about Larry, and he had the brains *and* the tan.'

I nodded confirmation. 'He certainly had the tan, and that's because he was out of the country for six months with Melanie Wigg. And I've heard that same story of fishy goings on in the Greek Islands, but always as rumour. Once with a fair amount of detail, though, and from someone I can trust. Let's say it's true, and there *was* a big fiddle going on involving lots of money. Andy was here minding the shop, so why was he murdered?'

Josh was steepling his fingers thoughtfully. 'You're back to motive again, Pen. Work out who murdered one, and why, and you've solved both crimes.'

'Yeah, well,' Deakin Chatto said, 'that puts the ball in Penny's court and, as I should have been elsewhere half an hour ago, I'm off. Before I go …' He hesitated, glancing around as he stood up and shrugged into his black leather jacket. 'You know, it might be prudent to consider what Penny said about a warning. Steve's a member of this group. If Andy's body was stuffed into that box as a warning to Steve to back off, I reckon it could be taken as a warning to all of us. If anyone here does know anything about scams or iffy deals in the sun, it might be wise to think twice before broadcasting the info.'

He shaped a wristy curlicue in the air with his hand, bowed with the camp grace of a departing actor, and was gone.

A glance at my watch told that I was also cutting it fine if I was hoping to make it across to Liverpool in time to talk to Joey Lox. Thankfully, as if Chatto's words had effectively brought to an end a cold room discussion that seemed to be going nowhere, chairs were pushed back and everyone grabbed their coats and charged towards the door leading to warmth and fresh drinks.

I hung back with the idea of casually watching each of them in turn, and that immediately bore fruit when I saw Vince Keevil wait for Chatto to leave the room and at once take Josh to one side. Keevil had his arm draped across Josh's shoulders, the kind of buddy-boy contact I know Josh hates, and was whispering to him with his lips uncomfortably close to my tall hunk's ear.

After a few moments of that Josh nodded, wriggled free, then clapped Keevil on the shoulder and sent him on his way. The door closed behind Keevil with a bang. Josh returned to where I was standing by the big refectory table, his eyes blazing.

'Prick,' he said. 'I should have used the edge of my hand on the back of his neck.'

'And ended up in A & E with broken metacarpals.'

'Might have been worth it, though,' he said, visibly relaxing with a rueful grin.

'What did he have to say?'

'He asked me if I'd noticed the menace in Chatto's dark eyes when he – in Keevil's opinion – issued that warning.'

'Issued?'

'Mm. Keevil's of the opinion that Chatto's in some way involved in the murders. He again mentioned the Jeep – and I have to say he seems to have a point. We know about it, because we were at Easter's house when it was described by the police. But how *did* Chatto come by that information? And what about torture? Chatto also brought that up. Do we *know* Andy was tortured?'

'I could phone Adam again. He should know what details have been released, and what haven't. Or you could, of course. My main concern at the moment is getting to Liverpool.'

He glanced at his watch.

'You'd better get moving. It's after eight now. Getting there after nine is one thing, but after ten could mean a wasted trip.'

'Best I can hope for if I am late is that Sharkey uses his initiative. I gave him everything I know over the phone. If he can't conjure up some searching questions from that ...'

I was crossing the room with Josh behind me as I spoke. I reached for the door's old iron handle, only to find it dropping away from my fingers as I touched it. I snatched my hand back as if hit by an electric shock. Suddenly the heavy oak panels were rushing towards me. I hastily stepped backwards, cannoned into Josh, trod on his instep and would have fallen if he hadn't caught me under the arms. I sagged in his grasp. His hands thrust all the way through and somehow ended up gently cupping my breasts.

The door swung all the way open.

'Oops,' a grinning Steve Easter said. 'And here's me thinking the party was over.'

chapter ten

'Barnaby backed my alibi.'

'Who's he?'

'My editor.'

'That's not the name I remember.'

'You're thinking of Sinclair. He got done for libel, defamation of character or something, left in a hurry.' Steve Easter shrugged. 'But that's his problem, mine was squirming my way out of a murder charge. You were watching from the house when you heard me tell the police it couldn't have happened because I was in a meeting. That was confirmed. By Barnaby. And I was in his office much later than I thought. I couldn't possibly have been in the car-park at seven-thirty.'

I looked across at Josh. He pulled a face, and came up with the obvious objection.

'What about the photographs on that kid's phone, Steve?' he said. 'How were they explained?'

'Easy. Upon examination the police realized that although the bloke looked like me from a distance, he was too tall, too skinny.' He spread his arms wide and grinned. 'Anyway, look at me. Can you see me running from the office down to the car-park and back again? Because that's what this guy did.'

As soon as we'd recovered from the shock of Steve's unexpected arrival and enfolded him in warm, congratulatory hugs, we'd hurried from the chill of the old vestry. Deakin Chatto had gone. Gay and Vince Keevil were studying menus at one of the tables. In the bar area the sagging settee and chairs looked as comfortable and inviting as worn slippers, and were vacant. Josh had ordered drinks – an orange and tonic with ice for me because the Liverpool trip was still on – and we had settled ourselves on those worn and faded loose covers to listen to Steve's story.

'What about Sheila?' I said now, absently running the tip of a finger down the condensation on my glass as I looked at him with concern. 'Have you spoken to her? Does she know you've been released?'

'Of course. I rang her at once, but she's still at Mark's flat in Chester. She'll stay there tonight, get a good night's sleep, and I'll pick her up in the morning.'

There was silence for a few moments. The place was almost empty, which was just about right for a Tuesday evening, and all three of us were busy with our thoughts. The arrival of the unexpected always brings with it a dizzying array of questions clamouring for answers, and Steve's sudden appearance was especially exciting because the meeting of the Seasoned Scribblers had confirmed – if I ignored Keevil's suspicions of Chatto – that I had very little to go on. Steve was at the very centre of a crime, whereas at that moment I was an amateur investigator with nowhere to go: two murders, no suspects, no motive, no clues. All right, perhaps that's me being a bit hard on myself because I was the only person at the scene of both crimes, and I did have a few ideas. Nevertheless, I waited impatiently as Steve closed his eyes and savoured his drink, then leaped in like someone starved of affection when he cast his eyes in my direction.

'Did you see any of what went on in the car-park, Steve?'

He shook his head. 'No reason to look. I think I did when the meeting began, glanced out of the window automatically to check my car, but nobody's going to steal a clapped-out BMW, are they?' He smiled. 'So there it was, rusting away in the rain, I turned away and after that we were too busy.'

'What about the man who was deliberately done up to resemble you? Did you know him?'

'No. The police had downloaded the pics from the mobile phone, but the larger images were still no help. The lighting was poor, he kept his head down, there was no way I could recognize him.' Steve shrugged. 'It was professionally done, and that's what I'd expect.'

Josh lifted an eyebrow. 'Why?'

'You mean why professional? Because ...' Steve hesitated, either carefully considering Josh's question or how best to reply. When the answer came, it was totally unexpected.

'I'm not sure if I mean professional or ... uncanny – and that sounds daft, doesn't it? OK, yes, that bit was professional, the person looking like me, emerging from the building where I work, keeping his face hidden even though he had no idea anyone was watching. But the other ... You see, I'm writing a book, fiction, crime – which is what most of the people in Seasoned Scribes are doing. The difference is I've told nobody about mine, until now; nobody except Sheila, and I know she wouldn't breathe a word to anybody. And yet ...'

'Come on, Steve,' I said, 'spit it out, you're giving me goose bumps.'

He frowned, absently brushed back his errant forelock.

'Imagine what it's doing to me. I went out with Sheila one day to buy that luggage box, not because we needed one, but because we wanted to test it; we, I, wanted to see if it was possible to squash a man's body inside one of those things.'

'Christ,' Josh said. 'You mean you were thinking of writing a scene like that in your novel?'

Steve nodded. 'Already done. I wanted to see if it was plausible.'

'And this reality matched your fiction.'

'There was a body; it was squashed in a luggage box.' He shrugged. 'How close a match can you get?'

Josh hesitated, thinking. I jumped in ahead of him, asking the obvious question.

'They were seen opening the box, Steve. How did they get keys?'

'There's a serial number on the locks. Duplicates can be obtained from the manufacturer.' He was watching Josh. 'I've got a strong feeling that disposing of Andy's body in this way was done as a warning to me. Had you considered that?'

Josh nodded. 'Penny raised it as one possibility when we were brainstorming.'

'From knowledge, or guesswork?'

I did some side-to-side, maybe-yes maybe-no kind of head wagging.

'Bit of both, I suppose. Sheila said Galleywood might have been involved in something fishy in the Greek Islands. I thought when she was telling me that she must have got the story from you' – he nodded – 'and that meant that as well as a novel you were also researching an exposé type of article. Then Joanna Lamb added some details: Galleywood was suspected because he'd been away all summer, the scam had something to do with expensive properties that didn't exist outside a computer. That brought Andy under suspicion, because he is – was – a computer geek.'

'Of course he was,' Steve said softly. 'I should have thought of that. I was doing some probing, concentrating on Galleywood senior and not really getting anywhere because, if you disregard Melanie, he was your typical loner. Bringing Andy into the frame gives me several potential leads.'

Josh nodded approvingly. 'So you're pressing on with the article, despite that gruesome warning – if that's what it was?'

'Definitely.'

'You know, putting those two together, article and warning, brings us to another interesting question: who, of the people who knew what you were up to, either betrayed you to the baddie, or actually is the baddie?'

'I've thought about that, of course,' Steve said, 'but it's incredibly difficult to answer. I've never gone into great detail about a possible scam that raked in millions for the perpetrators; couldn't, because I haven't yet got all the details. I've at least raised the possibility of an exciting exposé to people I work with, and I suppose almost everyone at Seasoned Scribblers knows about it.'

'We didn't,' I said, pouting.

Steve's eyebrows went up. 'Really?' And then he grinned. 'I think I probably did drop a hint in your presence, so it must be an age thing creeping in, you and Josh two wrinklies getting a bit past it.'

'Watch it, sonny,' Josh growled. 'Either take back that remark, or give us some inside information as compensation. For instance, if there really was a scam, how was it worked?'

'You shouldn't be asking Steve,' I said. 'DI Dancer thinks you can help unravel this complicated plot.'

'Me?' Josh said, eyebrows raised in amazement.

'It was a hint more than a request – and a shamefaced hint at that. The poor man couldn't believe what he was doing, the voice of authority asking for help from a crime writer.'

'Well, a crime writer still asks what-if questions. So how about it, Steve, *do* you know how a scam like this Greek thing might be worked?'

Steve pulled a face. 'Not a clue. All I've worked out so far is that it's likely the property existed inside a laptop, but nowhere else. Yet I can't see that being enough to get canny people to part with their cash.'

He broke off as my phone tweeted like a strangled canary. I struggled to my feet, excused myself and fumbled in my tote bag as I made for the end of the bar.

It was Sharkey.

'The informant's here, the lights are low, the music's seductive and the drinks are on ice – so where the bloody hell are you?'

'If that's supposed to be one of those fabulous Aussie holiday ads, your accent's all wrong. The best I can say is I'm about to shoot through, Blue.'

'Yeah, but how long?'

I closed my eyes and chose the first number that came into my head.

'Thirty minutes.'

He chuckled. 'I'll hold you to that.' And the phone clicked in my ear.

I actually made it in forty-five minutes, spent five looking for a place to park – which happened to be behind a Lexus I recognized as Sharkey's – and four more walking up the slope to SCENE SOUTH. The rain had stopped, I had my tote bag but had left my blue waterproof in the car and put on the dark red gilet I always keep on the back seat. Good decision: it took another three minutes to gain entry to the club, and there was a cold, cutting breeze.

SCENE SOUTH was a very large and very old private house with its decadent innards hiding behind a sober Victorian exterior. When he finally answered my impatient ringing the huge black doorman, obviously confused by my Chartered Institute of Journalist's press pass, bundled me inside with a swift, searching glance over his shoulder as if I were a spy being ushered into a safe house. And guess what? Sharkey's description had been spot on. As I crossed a tiny vestibule where a row of coat hooks nailed to the wall acted as cloakroom and stepped through a scruffy panelled door into a long inner room that was packed with drinkers and as stiflingly hot as a midsummer wardrobe I was bathed in soft red light and enveloped in relaxing music that was mostly moody jazz guitar accompanied by the whisper of drums and the tinkle of ice in glasses. Josh would have been in his element, transported high enough to float through the open window and over the moon.

The bar stretched the full length of the room, with a few tables in the centre and red plastic booths down the other long side as if the owners were trying to create the atmosphere of a New York gin joint. I rested my hand on someone's beefy shoulder and stood on tiptoe to peer over the extended line of T-shirts and smooth naked shoulders and heavy gold glittering at throats slender and muscular, and quickly spotted Sharkey. Dark and elegant, he'd chosen a stool almost as far away from the door as he could get. He was talking to a young man with a severe haircut I knew must be Joey Lox. The bartender, skinny, tattooed, with red hair like thin scratches raked across his pale scalp, was leaning on his elbows as he listened to the animated conversation. As I pushed my way nearer, treading on more toes than I missed as my eyes watered in the warm waves of perfume, after-shave and beery breath, I remembered that this was Liverpool and – surprise surprise – the talk was about football.

'If they'd got to the European final they'd have lost,' I said, unbuttoning the gilet as I slid on to the stool Sharkey's bum had been keeping warm, 'so they saw losing to Chelsea in the semi as a crafty way of avoiding humiliation.'

Around me, the room went silent.

'Oops, sorry,' I said, hand to mouth, 'I thought I was among Evertonians.'

'If there was a ref in here,' Sharkey said, 'he'd be brandishing a red card. Look around you. The room's full of *good-looking* men, the conversation's *intelligent*—'

'Yes, I know,' I cut in, 'and even the lights are red so there's no mistaking the allegiance. Right, with all that football nonsense out of the way I'm here, I'm waiting for one of those ice-cold drinks you mentioned, and I'd very much like to be introduced to your friend before all my clothes turn to rags.'

'Joey Lox, meet Penny Lane,' Sharkey said, with a grin and a sweep of the hand. And to the bartender he added, 'The lady with the death wish is driving home, so you'd better make that ice-cold drink orange juice on the rocks.'

'After the things she's been sayin', the barman said, 'I was thinkin' on the lines of the finest champagne – which means there's no mistakin' *my* allegiance,' and, tugging with his fingers at the shoulders of his blue T-shirt, he winked at me then turned away to reveal the logo across his back and fix my drink.

'So, Joey,' I said, as the hum of conversation all around us picked up again, 'what can you tell me about the night you saw sinister goings on in a Liverpool car-park?'

'No more than I told the police and him,' he said with a nod at Sharkey.

'Which was?'

'Bloody hell, this'll be something like the tenth time.'

'All right, skip the main details, what about the three men you saw?'

'That's all. That's it. Three men. Four if you count the guy gettin' stuffed in the box.'

'Recognize any of them?'

'No.'

I looked at Sharkey, caught his slight nod as he sipped what looked like coke, then back at Lox.

'That was too quick.'

He grinned ferociously. 'How about noooooooo?'

'You'd still be lying.'

'Yeah, an' if I am, it's for good reason, isn' it?'

'I'm sure it is. Two men murdered already, you don't want to be the third bloody victim – and that's not me swearing, I'm describing how you'll look when they've finished with you.'

'You're tellin' *me*?' He shook his head in disbelief. 'Listen, those guys don't take nothing from *nobody*. I know that for a fact. Once, the big guy did a job, and he didn't get paid. So he went after the guy who hired him and put him in hospital. That happened once, right? Word like that gets around. It didn't happen again.'

I swivelled on the stool, flipped a hand one way then the other to take in the whole room. 'All right, we both understand that, but look around you, and listen hard, Joey. There's so much noise even Sharkey's wondering what I'm talking about, and nobody's looking at you, nobody's interested in you. If you're going to get this off your chest, now's as good a time as any.'

Lox shook his head. He shot a glance at Sharkey, then frowned and stared moodily down at his drink. Under the short hair his scalp was glistening. His shoulders were stiff with tension.

If I'd been telling him the truth I would have said that *hardly* anybody was interested in him. Fact was that a bull of a man in a tight dark suit sitting at one of the nearby tables was sweating into his white shirt as he tried to look at us without making it obvious. His being on his own was what had singled him out to me – which sounds like a very bad unintentional pun but happened to be true. Almost everyone I could see in SCENE SOUTH was in a tight knot of three or four people and, as I waited for Joey Lox to reach a decision I mentally retraced my steps and tried to recall if anyone had followed me when I walked up the road from my car. Or was it Sharkey this man had followed? Or, much more likely, Joey Lox himself, the eyewitness who had put himself on the spot by going to the police?

I snapped myself back to the present, aware that Sharkey had taken over the talking.

'What about the phone?' he was saying to Lox. 'Did the police confiscate it, or the SIM card, or simply download the photographs?'

'Downloaded,' Lox said warily.

'And then deleted them?'

'No. They didn't bother.'

'So the photographs are still on your card, and if I had another SIM card you'd be happy to swap?'

'No way. There's stuff on mine I need.'

'But you'd be rid of those pictures. They're red hot. If those blokes come after you, if the *killer* comes after you ...'

Sharkey was looking past Lox and at me as he said that, and I saw in his eyes that he too was aware of the man at the table. Lox, however, was unaware of possible danger, and continued to bluster.

'I'll handle it. Anyway, nobody saw me.'

'But you saw them,' I said, 'and recognized them. You as good as admitted that when you said you had good reason for lying.'

'So? One way of handlin' it is to keep quiet, isn' it? So you can ask all you like....'

But he was only half listening to what he was saying and his voice trailed off because Sharkey had taken a mobile phone out of his pocket and was waggling it so that it glinted richly in the red lights.

'Latest model Sony Ericsson,' Sharkey said. 'Powerful camera, Bluetooth, Vodaphone Live, 3G. Never used. New SIM card. All you have to do is register. So here's the deal: a straight swap, yours for this one.'

'I told you, there's stuff—'

'Everything you've got inside your old phone tells a story. You made one mistake by going to the police. Don't make a second by clinging to evidence that could get you killed.'

Lox was licking his lips, either from nervousness or greed. He hesitated for a moment longer, then took a phone out of his shirt pocket, looked at it, then handed it to Sharkey. Sharkey took it, fiddled with some buttons, looked at the display. Nodded. Slipped the phone into his pocket.

'I always check. Once bitten and all that crap. But it's OK, you were telling the truth, the pictures are there.'

'So ...' Lox said, and held out his hand.

Sharkey was still grinning, but at me.

'Handing over your phone was just part of an excellent deal

that's made you much safer,' I said, taking his cue. 'To complete, we need names.'

Lox was shaking his head violently. 'No, that's not what he said.'

'It's what I said,' I said sweetly, 'and Sharkey does what I tell him – just like you're going to.'

'No—'

'If you want the phone.'

'He took mine so now I *need* that fuckin' phone, but givin' names is too risky.'

'It was more risky giving us the phone, but that's done. Think about it. A SIM card with photographs of a crime being committed, visible faces that today's technology can enlarge, enhance. Names can be put to those faces, but it would take time. You can do it now, you *will* do it now.'

Lox took a deep breath. He dragged the back of his hand across his mouth as his gaze wandered, looking everywhere, nowhere. I flicked my glance sideways. The table where the big man had been sitting was empty. I hadn't seen him leave.

'Jimmy Rake, Ellis Barnes,' Lox said, almost under his breath.

'Those names don't ring any bells,' Sharkey said.

'That's your problem.'

Sharkey held out the phone, but gripped it firmly and moved it back as Lox reached for it, tantalizing him, keeping it just out of his reach.

'That it, nothing more to tell us? For a bonus?'

'Like what?'

'Twenty quid. Put some credit on the phone.'

'Forty.'

Sharkey took blue notes out of his shirt pocket with the first two fingers of his free hand, folded them alongside the phone.

'There's a connection,' Lox said, licking his lips. 'To another guy. He wasn't there in the car-park with Rake and Barnes, but he's someone I've seen Rake with more than once. Feller called Reef—'

Still talking, he snatched at the phone and cash as a big man sitting at the bar behind Sharkey stepped down, stumbled, and lurched sideways. One beefy shoulder with all his weight behind it rammed into Sharkey's back, and I heard Sharkey grunt. The heavy blow knocked him forward. He flung out an arm to regain his balance. My drink with its melting ice-cubes flew from my hand. The glass shattered. Cold orange liquid soaked the front of my lovely second-hand cashmere sweater.

His face dark, Sharkey spun around. In the same movement his two hands came up. He grabbed the big man's lapels and slammed him back against the bar. I saw a shaven head, scarred eyebrows, a nose that had been broken more than once and each time badly set; colourless eyes, and a face that was placid and untroubled, lips twisted in a sardonic smile.

'An accident, pal,' he said in a soft whisper of a voice that carried to every corner of that hushed room. 'Don't make it into something it never was.'

For a moment, Sharkey held him hard against the bar. He held him without effort and I knew he was demonstrating his strength, emphasizing that if he chose to take it further the big man would come off second best. Then the tension left him as he relaxed. He eased the big man down, let his fists unclench and removed his hands from his lapels. Straight-faced, he smoothed the crumpled cloth by stroking it with the backs of his fingers – only for his hands to be roughly brushed away.

'Forget me and my suit, pal, and see to your young friend. I think he's walked out on you.'

Using the disturbance as a diversion, Joey Lox had slipped silently away into the night taking with him Sharkey's phone and leaving us with two-and-a-half names. The problem was, which half of the third name was missing?

'I hope that wasn't your phone you gave away, because I've already put the number you gave me into *my* phone.'

He shook his head. 'No, I thought I might need a bribe, and mobile phones to scallies are are like beads to natives.'

'Not very PC,' I said.

But Sharkey wasn't listening.

'That guy who banged into me. He said it was an accident, but it was much too convenient for that.'

'I didn't even see him. I was paying too much attention to Lox, and that man at the table.'

'Who melted away without us noticing.' Sharkey smiled. 'I saw him watching us, but now I think about it I'm sure it was you he was interested in.'

I gaped. 'Me? I'm pushing sixty, going grey—'

'And very attractively, too, even in a sopping wet sweater.' He shrugged. 'All right, so he was gay and it's me he was lusting after. The point is all our attention was on the wrong man, and unbeknown to us the bloke who slammed into me from behind had probably been listening to every word we said.'

'You said that violent contact was convenient, no accident. D'you think he acted deliberately, knee-jerk spur-of-the-moment stuff to stop Lox when he started feeding us names?'

'I'm sure of it.'

'And that's why Lox scarpered?'

'Oh yes. And I tell you what: I reckon when we download those photographs on to your computer—'

'*My* computer?'

Sharkey grinned. 'Of course. I'm coming home with you. You lead in your little Ka, I follow.'

We were sitting in Sharkey's silver Lexus. The interior smelled richly of leather and woodwork and subtle aftershave that could have been Paco Raban but was probably something much more expensive. The street-lighting shone on the rich burgundy of his leather jacket, on black hair as glossy as a raven's wing. That's yet another cliché, I know, but in some ways Sharkey is a walking bundle of clichés that pile on the compliments. Even relaxing in the driver's seat his strength was palpable, and I remembered when I'd first entered his Albert Dock penthouse and seen him dressed in baggy lounging pants and a dark green singlet and how, on being confronted by his tanned, muscular frame, I'd thought beefcake and tried not to drool. Well, if I hadn't already been too old to remember what drooling over a man was like, of course. If one ever can be.

The point was he was right about coming home with me because I knew he'd like to see Josh again and three heads are always better than two, especially when one of them is sitting on a crime-writer's shoulders. We'd already made considerable progress that night and at 10.30 it was by no means over. Indeed, Sharkey had already left something unfinished.

'You were saying,' I said, 'when rudely interrupted?'

'I was talking about downloading photographs. I think we'll find that when we do, the man who barged into me and caused me to bathe you in ice-cold orange will be one of those three in that Liverpool car-park who sent Andy Galleywood on his final journey.'

'Well, if he's a regular at SCENE he won't be hard to find. Which suggests, to me anyway, that it wasn't his own identity he was trying to keep secret. Thinking back, he didn't act, didn't do anything to announce his presence until Lox gave us the name Reef. So who is he, and who's this Reef? Does the name mean anything to you?'

'Nope.

'Be nice if he turned out to be the big boss.'

'Be nice if we knew what he was big boss of.'

'Mm. Good point. I'm assuming Greek scam, aren't I?'

Sharkey grinned. 'If you're right, I'll travel with you to the scene of the crime, hold your hand—'

'—smooth on the tanning lotion, soak up the sun. You're on – but we might never get the chance.'

He nodded. 'We've been sussed, haven't we? Exposed. Cover broken.'

'That's right. Our involvement in whatever it is we're involved is no longer a secret. I was seen asking questions by what could be a very nasty piece of work – and you were right there with me.'

chapter eleven

Wednesday

'There,' I said softly. 'You were right, Sharkey. The taller of the two men tossing Andy Galleywood around like a rag doll, that's the big bastard who tried to ruin your kidneys.'

Sharkey grunted. He was behind me, bending close so that I could feel the heat of his body as he concentrated on my computer monitor. He was intent, studying the surprisingly clear photographs of a Liverpool car-park taken by Joey Lox on a wet November evening.

Josh, pressed close on my other side, had his warm hand on my shoulder as he peered at the screen.

'What about the others?' he said. 'The other man doing the lifting. And the bloke in the fleece – he's the one supposed to be Steve Easter, isn't he?'

'Hah! That man in the fleece is nothing *like* Steve,' I said. 'As for the other ...' I hesitated, frowning, clicked the mouse and brought up the next photograph. 'Clear – but not clear enough. I'm sure I've never met the man ... and yet ...'

'And yet?' Sharkey said.

'And yet I've got the feeling I *have* seen him somewhere. But why would that be? Where do I go to mix with people like that?'

'Ouch,' Josh said. 'People like that might be respectable lawyers who happen to be built like big brick thingamajigs and enjoy frequenting sleazy night-clubs.'

'And now you're at it,' I said. 'Sleazy it was not.'

'Titillatingly raffish?' Sharkey suggested.

'Don't be rude,' I said, flashing a quick grin. 'It was refreshingly unsophisticated, but the point is that bloke could be the Pope's right-hand man, but we've got him on camera committing a dastardly crime.'

'Dastardly I like,' Josh said. 'The question is, what have we got in total, and where do we go from here?'

'*We* go out of my office and into our cosy conservatory armed with refreshment suitable for discussing tense situations at a late hour. Where I go with *my* investigation is part of what we'll be discussing over those strong drinks.'

It was after midnight. I'd stopped off with Sharkey at his Albert Dock penthouse on the way home to pick up a USB cable that would link Lox's phone to my computer, driven through the night to Heswall with the lights of Sharkey's Lexus in my mirror, brought Josh up to date with events when he came yawning out of the kitchen then gone straight to my office. Well, not straight. First I slipped into the bedroom, removed my stiffening orange sweater and thick skirt and donned a silky dressing-gown that was light-weight, comfortable and classically patterned.

Then, Josh looking tousled and comfortable in slippers, sloppy pants and sweater and Sharkey down to tight taupe T-shirt, jeans and socks, we downloaded the photographs. Is that right? I'm never sure of the terminology. Could be uploaded – couldn't it? Anyway, our tale of events and the shock of seeing what two thugs were doing to Andy Galleywood had brought my big hunk fully awake in a hurry. Now, each of us clutching a crystal glass charged with several fingers of the Macallan, we wandered like sleepwalkers into the conservatory where Josh had thoughtfully switched on the electric heater long before we arrived home. He'd also lit perfumed candles, which added spice to the occasion but their light, in the circumstances, gave our cosy little conservatory an air of the sinister.

'You shivered,' Josh said, as we sat down on plump cushions and leant back against more of the same and wicker that creaked.

'*No fue nada, no te preocupes*,' I said, and winked at Sharkey. 'He's writing a crime book set in Arizona, so he's proud of putting a bit of Spanish in there. I got that off Google's translation doodah. I think it means "It was nothing, don't worry".'

'It does,' Josh said, 'but the shiver I saw remains unexplained.'

'Put it down to me experiencing a delicious tingle at being in the same room as not one but two impressive, mature males – then let's get down to business. Who'd like to start?'

'Me, with a message,' Josh said. 'It comes from Eifion Owen.'

'Ahah.' I glanced at Sharkey. 'In case you don't remember, he's the brother of the lawyer turned serial killer, Gareth Owen. Eifion's a senior police officer, nearing retirement.'

'And in case you don't remember,' Sharkey said, 'Eifion's my brother-in-law.'

'Damn, that's right, Ffion Lynch was your sister.'

'So Sharkey'll know he's *past* retirement,' Josh said, 'but still with his finger on the pulse and a host of contacts. He wanted to talk to you about the Larry Galleywood murder, but was happy to give me the information to pass on. First, the bullet that killed Galleywood has been examined by ballistics, and it seems he was shot with a .38 revolver. It looks as if Galleywood was either reading or had in his hand a thick stamp catalogue. Stanley Gibbons, British Empire, Colonial Commemoratives or something like that – which probably isn't important, a book's a book. Anyway, when he was threatened, he must have raised it to protect himself. The bullet hit the book, it was deflected, and finished up in his eye.'

'I'd worked that out, more or less. I think I mentioned it at the meeting tonight.'

Josh nodded. 'The second part of the message from Eifion is that the police have discovered that the sash window in Galleywood's office *has* got broken cords, but *can* be opened. However, they can't determine if it's been opened recently, and in any case the broken cords mean it won't stay open.'

'So nobody could get in that way?'

'Definitely not. Anyway, you were there when the police examined the grounds. No sign of an intruder, no means of getting *up* to that first-floor window never mind entering the house that way.' He paused. 'He also had something to say about Andy Galleywood. He *was* tortured. He was also alive when he was stuffed into that luggage box – that information comes from the police surgeon, and also from the eyewitness who went down to the car and heard him moaning.'

'Jesus,' I said softly. 'We didn't ask Lox about that. Should have done.'

'Wouldn't have helped.'

'Mm. Well, anyway, I've got an idea Eifion's info about Larry Galleywood could be helpful. Don't ask me how. All I know is Steve's out on police bail – is that right? – so the priority is clearing his name. To do that, we've got to find Andy's killers.'

Sharkey was sprawled in his chair, legs crossed, nursing his whisky and half-listening to the rain that had started up again and was pattering on the conservatory's glass. Windows were ajar to freshen air warmed by the heater. The lush smells of wet soil and grass were battling with the scent of the candles and, in my opinion, coming out on top. There was a half smile on Sharkey's face that, if asked to describe, I'd have called rueful. I couldn't blame him. He'd been listening to us with interest, and his next words told me – bless him – that he was very concerned about the immensity of the task I'd set myself.

'I remember that first case,' he said quietly. 'Up against Terry Lynch and serial killer Gareth Owen, all three of us ending up facing a gun in that dank Chester boathouse. We were lucky – yes, I know, you've already admitted that several times, Penny. Trouble is, here we are, amateur sleuths setting out to solve another crime or two, and I'm wondering if luck's enough – or even if it'll hold.'

'You make your own luck,' Josh said bluntly.

'Saying that to a pro gambler is like teaching your granny how to patronize,' Sharkey said with a warning look. 'And despite what sounds like me whinging, the omens are looking good. We've struck lucky already: a SIM card with photographs of a crime being committed has practically fallen into our hands, and tonight we literally bumped into one of those men.'

'Both of them.' I grinned in triumph. 'Not actually bumped, but I've just remembered where I've seen the other man in the car-park photographs. And I'm kicking myself. He was the perspiring bull of a bloke in the tight suit, sitting watching us from the table in *scene south.*'

'Well spotted,' Sharkey said, 'but not too helpful. From their looks, they'll have form, which means by now they'll have been picked up. That takes care of the thugs, but not the man who ordered the killing.'

'Which brings us to suspects,' Josh said.

I frowned. 'Be helpful if we knew where to start.'

'Think back to what Steve told us after the Seasoned Scribblers meeting. We were sitting in the bar, and talk got around to his exposé article and who knew about it. Remember that?'

'Damn. Yes, I do. He told us the only people he'd shared details with were members of the group.'

'Which means,' Sharkey said, 'that each member of Seasoned Scribblers has to be a suspect.'

'Mm.' I frowned. 'At the meeting Josh and I arranged a brainstorming session. It wasn't very successful, but I noticed two of the members were looking unusually uptight.'

'Vince Keevil and Gay Tirril,' Josh said.

'Yes. They were as close as budgies when we walked in, twittering away in undertones. Vince's face was as black as thunder. Gay's hand was shaking, and I think she'd been crying.'

'Possibly not,' Josh said. 'I know she's got something wrong with her eyes. Conjunctivitis? Or ingrowing eyelashes? Something like that anyway and, interestingly, she's been seeing your favourite doctor.'

'What, Moneydie?'

'That's the one. Which, if you stretch your imagination a bit, gives her a connection to Larry Galleywood.'

I pulled a face. 'Not exactly killer material, though, is she?'

'That depends,' Sharkey said. 'You did say she and Keevil were unusually uptight.'

I hesitated. 'Good point. And if we're looking for suspects, we could attribute the increased tension to their having prior knowledge of one or more of the murders. As in being involved.'

Sharkey grinned. 'So, despite her not being killer material, our first suspects are Vince Keevil and Gay Tirril.' He waggled his empty glass at Josh. 'I think that calls for another drink.'

'If Keevil's a suspect,' Josh said to us half-an-hour and a shared plate of ham and mustard sandwiches later, 'it gives new meaning to what he said to me on his way out of the meeting. Remember that, Penny?'

'I do. He was of the opinion that Deakin Chatto was involved in those murders.'

'And if Keevil's guilty of murder, he could have been saying that to divert suspicion.'

'He had a point though, didn't he?'

'Why?' Sharkey said.

'Two points actually,' I said, and Josh nodded agreement. 'One, Chatto had an important detail not yet in the public domain: he knew that the men in the car-park had been travelling in a Jeep SUV. Secondly, I suggested that Andy Galleywood's death could be a warning to Steve to back off and abandon his investigation into the scam. On his way out, Chatto pointed out that it could be a warning to every one of us.'

'And why would he do that,' Sharkey said, quickly catching on, 'when the only person interested in the scam was Steve Easter? Why would others be in danger?'

'Exactly. The only reason I can think of is that we were being warned *not* to get interested in the scam story. And, in my opinion, that makes Deakin Chatto our third suspect.'

'Is that it?'

'No. We've got one more possible suspect,' I said, 'as you well know. A man with a name like a knot.'

'Reef,' Sharkey said, and at Josh's questioning glance went on, 'Joey Lox reckons the heavy at the club who jostled me – whose name, incidentally, is Jimmy Rake – was seen with this bloke Reef.'

'Interesting,' Josh said. He looked at me with a faint smile. 'Make a mental note: tomorrow must talk to Adam about man called Reef.'

Sharkey was half asleep, his eyelids drooping, his glass once more empty but now slack in his lean hand and resting on his thigh. Josh had stopped at his first whisky and drunk fresh orange juice with his sandwiches. I had drunk coffee with my sandwiches and later slipped through to the kitchen for fresh orange juice from the fridge. Another empty glass. The dull throb of a headache brought on by weariness.

'If there really is a scam,' Josh said, 'and for the sake of argument—'

'Hypothesis,' Sharkey said, eyes closed.

'—we assume that's what this is all about, then what can we
deduce from two murders—?'

'If they're connected,' I interrupted.

'Christ,' Josh said fiercely, 'will you two let me finish?'

'Sorry.' I put fingers to lips, sank lower in my chair.

'OK,' Josh went on, 'for the sake of another argument, another
hypothesis' – this with a glare at Sharkey – 'we'll assume those
murders are connected. So, let's look at some possibilities.'

'Some *hypothetical* situations,' Sharkey said, eyes still closed,
and there was a sudden, awkward silence. I looked at Josh, bit my
lip, tried not to giggle.

He sighed. 'OK, Sharkey, why don't you give us the first?'

The dark eyes slowly opened. Half asleep had been an illusion,
a pose. He was wide awake, alert.

'That's the easy one, Josh. The scam worked, the scam boss has
got the cash, and the Galleywoods were murdered to stop them
talking and also so the boss could pocket their cut.'

Josh nodded. 'Right, so that's theory number one. However, it
doesn't ring true. Andy Galleywood was tortured. You don't
torture someone to shut them up, you torture them to make them
talk. So what does that suggest?'

'The Galleywoods had worked a double-cross,' I said. 'They'd
kept the money, stashed it away. Andy was interrogated on the
orders of an irate scam boss looking for his cash.'

'And we have theory number two,' Josh said, nodding approval.
'But if that's what happened, how do we account for Larry
Galleywood's death which came within hours of his son's
murder? Was he murdered because they got the information from
Andy, knew where the cash was stashed and no longer needed
Larry? Or was Larry's death an accident – a questioning that
went wrong?'

'Or was he,' I said, 'murdered by someone else, for a reason we
have yet to fathom?'

'Bringing us back to an unconnected death,' Sharkey said.

'And giving us theory number three,' Josh said. 'If that is what happened, we've now got a very angry scam boss whose last chance of finding his cash seems to have snatched from his grasp.'

He paused, looked at Sharkey, then at me.

'Or does it?'

'Probably not,' I said. 'Because if theory number two explains Andy Galleywood's death – it really does seem the most likely – and if theory number three explains *Larry*'s death – an unrelated killing – then what we're left with is Melanie Wigg. Why is she there, in Larry Galleywood's house, knocking back the wine and enjoying all the fruits of recent prosperity? Melanie was out there in the Greek Islands with Larry Galleywood. For the whole of a long hot summer she was, as far as we know or assume, running the scam with Larry; she was closer to him than his own son Andy, who was back in the UK minding the shop. OK, so Andy was a computer geek. But if there was a double-cross – and the Galleywood residence really does have the look of a place suddenly flush with money – then surely the person most likely to know where the loot's stashed is Melanie Wigg?'

Josh has pretty well given up marathon running, which makes each weekday morning when he swims, and each Wednesday when he works out on the leisure centre's nautilus machines, two very important parts of his weekly routine. However, after the late-night lengthy discussion about murders and methods and theories and suspects, I wasn't too confident he'd get out of bed in time for the nautilus – and you'll realize how unusually decadent that would have been when I tell you his sessions always take place in the afternoon. That we did rise well before mid-morning coffee time was down to two reasons: Josh is a man who abhors unpunctuality, or appointments missed for no reason other than sheer laziness, and I didn't want Sharkey to see us as oldies who have to spend half the day in bed if they have a couple of strong drinks and retire one minute after midnight.

But how would he know, I hear you ask? Very easily: Ryan Sharkey spent the night in our conservatory, because when Josh and I did finally go to bed he was already fast asleep and snoring. Which, of course, put the boot well and truly on the other foot, and gave me the fuel for all kinds of snide remarks. Would I stoop to that? Well, let's just say should the need arise....

So, I showered first, all three of us had breakfast in a kitchen brightly lit by cold sunlight, then Josh wandered off for what my ex-army man calls his ablutions. Sharkey leaned against the breakfast bar and talked to me of this and that but nothing in particular for a few minutes. Then, looking strangely thoughtful, he pecked me on the cheek, climbed into his Lexus and went off to back horses, roll dice, flip the pasteboards or whatever it is a professional gambler does on a cold Wednesday morning in November.

I must admit that his behaviour was making me a little uneasy. He'd looked and acted drunk the first time I caught sight of him in JOKERS WILD during the Gareth Owen case – as knobbly as a beggar's cane was the way I'd thought of him, with bloodshot eyes, and thin lips a mean gash in dark designer stubble – but when I later met him face to face in his penthouse he was bright, clean, stone-cold-sober and the picture of physical health and fitness. Nevertheless, that first sighting had been in a nightclub, we'd been in a nightclub of sorts last night, and now I tried to recall what Sharkey had been drinking when I strolled into SCENE SOUTH. It had looked like straight coke, but that could have been laced with one of several strong spirits and I wondered how many he'd downed before I got there.

Had I discovered a major flaw in the dark, handsome gambler's character? I smiled at that. As an investigator, I could always investigate sneakily – but I could also come straight out and ask him.

With a glance at my watch I realized, shock horror, that it was already ten o'clock. Using the phone in the kitchen I quickly rang Joanna and apologized for not making it to the Thirsty Goose for our morning coffee, brought her up to date with Eifion Owen's information about the first Galleywood murder (damn, she already knew), then phoned Annabel Lee and suggested it might be a good idea to get together in about an hour's time and talk photography. She was delighted.

Josh was out of the bathroom, and he poked his head into the kitchen. I told him where I was going and he nodded and smiled, but his grey hair was wet and he was scratching it vaguely and I knew he'd got into his Arizona novel in the shower and was on the way to his office trying to hold a new and exciting plot twist in his head.

I blew a kiss, and waved him away.

Then, in the time left to me, I got on with my main business.

The only new twist in that was an e-mail from a man wanting

111

a framed print for his wife's birthday. He'd left a mobile telephone number. I decided to call him when I had more time.

Then, dressed in a different skirt and jumper but last night's gilet, I jumped in the Ka, and off I sped.

With, it has to be said, ulterior motives aplenty.

Annabel Lee's delightful rented cottage in the town of Parkgate is just a short way upriver from Heswall – the river being the Dee. I love the snug living-room which has an arched opening leading through to a rear eat-in kitchen overlooking a tiny walled garden, and when I got there Annabel had the usual cafetière of coffee sitting snug under its colourful knitted cosy alongside two china mugs.

The young and talented photographer is blonde, slim and as bubbly as a mountain stream. Like the stream, she's also ice-cool in the toughest of situations, which comes in very handy for a wedding photographer, or for someone who might be called on to help an amateur PI track down a killer. Oddly enough, her background could also come in handy in such a situation.

Annabel is the niece of the late Terry Lynch, who had murdered over and over again in his relentless search for the man who planted evidence that had sent Lynch's brother to jail, then arranged his murder. Lynch's brother's murder, that is, in case you got lost. Again during the Gareth Owen case. I know for a fact that Annabel's not averse to placing herself in perilous situations. When I first saw her she'd been sitting on a stool in the bar of the Golden Fleece, dressed like what the Americans used to quaintly call a working girl and on her way – or coming back from, I forget which – to watch a local GP sink into a drunken stupor, then signal to his killer.

Sounds unforgivable, and it would have been if she'd known exactly what was going to happen to the poor doctor. She didn't, of course, and was horrified when she found out, but you see what I mean about her being, well, a kindred spirit.

Doesn't stop her also being highly critical, as her first words after a warm welcoming hug confirmed.

'I can't believe you're at it again,' she said, pouring coffee and sliding the biscuit tin towards me.

'How d'you know I am?'

Her snort was unladylike, but expressive.

'You know my roots. With the family I've got I hear everything, most of it underworld stuff. And what I hear is you were seen in a south-Liverpool club talking to a young guy who's in deep trouble.'

My heart fluttered.

'His name's Joey Lox. I went to talk to him because he'd witnessed a crime. He'd also photographed the criminals. And it turned out that those men were there, in that same club, close enough to listen to every word I was saying and—'

'Take it up with him later?'

'Exactly. And not a pleasant thought, after seeing first hand what they did to Andy.'

'Andy Galleywood?'

'Mm. They tortured him, then stuffed him in the luggage box on Steve Easter's car, which is where he died.' I saw her narrowed eyes, and flapped both hands to forestall any questions. 'Oh damn, damn. I was already worried and now you've convinced me I've set Joey Lox up. I'll have to do something, talk to Sharkey, tell him to warn the lad.'

'It's too late,' Annabel said bluntly.

'You don't know that.'

This time a roll of the eyes. 'Of course I don't. I'm guessing. But in an educated way, as I'm sure you'll agree when you've calmed down. Incidentally, I knew about Andy, because you told me, remember? Because I was about to do the photography at his wedding, and you phoned me?'

I closed my eyes, opened them again and shook my head.

'I'm going daft. Of course I did. Though not the grisly details.'

'Well, no. But you also told me that, just like the last one, you're going to look into it; put it right – you suppose.' She raised her eyebrows. 'You are involved, aren't you? That nasty stuff about Andy *is* what that young guy witnessed, and part of the reason you were in that club?' She caught my nod, and reached across to touch my hand. 'Look, it's not your fault. Think about it, Pen. Were those villains there in the club when you arrived, or did they come in later?'

'They were ... yes, I'm sure they were there already.'

'There you are then. They'd followed him. You talking to the young guy didn't set him up, he was already a dead duck as soon he took those pics and dialled 999.'

I shuddered. 'Oh God, don't say that.'

Annabel sipped her coffee, her intelligent blue eyes watching me intently.

'So, back to the beginning: why *are* you doing it?'

I hesitated, comforting myself by warming my hands on my china mug. To be truthful, I, too, was wondering what the hell I was playing at. And it's only when such questions arise, when the process of something close to self-analysis seasoned with self-doubt begins that true feelings emerge.

'It's funny isn't it,' I said quietly. 'I'm not a licensed private eye – I don't even know if UK private investigators *need* a licence – and yet I'm not a true amateur.'

'How d'you work that out?'

'Well, as I said yesterday in a moment of foolishness, I dabble – don't I? That's really all I do. You know, poke about on the fringes of a police investigation, not expecting anything from them, not even expecting much from myself.'

'So why. Why do you do it?'

'Getting involved in the first crime was easy, as you know: I'd made a mistake, it had to be put right. This time? Well, to paraphrase mountaineers, because I was there. And despite not really knowing what I am, I believe I'm good at it – whatever it is.'

Annabel's chuckle was a gurgle of delight.

'That's what I love about you, you're so ... loopy. You don't know what you are, but whatever it is, you're good at it? Right. Sounds a bit like doing a crossword without knowing the clues.'

'Which neatly sums up the way I've been fumbling my way through crime investigation,' I said, grinning. 'Anyway, I've just worked out that the perception acquired through years of work as a photographer gives me a special aptitude for seeing things others often overlook. And that's invaluable.'

'Especially when you do have some clues. And suspects. You do have suspects, don't you?'

'Oh yes. And that's partly why I'm here.'

Annabel groaned. 'Subterfuge, am I right? Talk of photography was the bait on the hook I swallowed in one gulp. Now you want – whoa, hang on a minute, that young guy photographing villains didn't give you the bright idea of sending me out with the Nikon?'

'Lord no,' I said firmly. 'And I did say suspects are just part of the reason I'm here. The other really is photography—'

I broke off, because Annabel was shaking her head.

'Only in a roundabout way. Or photography as in dead and buried – if you'll pardon a truly dreadful pun. This is to do with Andy's fiancée, Kirsty Tremayne, isn't it? I know you're not in a remembering frame of mind, but on the phone you wanted me to think back to my talks with them and see if anything they'd said had a bearing on Andy's murder. I haven't got back to you. So now you're about to take the bull by the horns.'

'I like to call it taking the initiative.'

'Yeah, whatever, but you want me to be the sucker standing in front of you flapping the crimson cape.'

'Diversionary tactics.' I nodded. 'Sort of. I thought it would be less stressful for Kirsty if a familiar face was there.'

Kirsty Tremayne lives in a flat over a newsagent's shop in the ancient rows that are the historic heart of Chester. When it comes to parking a car my standard practice is to avoid the frustration of driving round and round looking for a non-existent vacant slot on the streets and instead go for the most convenient option and hang the cost. So I drove straight off Pepper Street into the high-rise parking above the Grosvenor Precinct, and from there it was a quick skip down windswept concrete steps and through the warm shopping malls and a short walk to the wooden boards of the rows above Eastgate Street.

The flat and its occupant were a surprise. Andy had been a big, powerful young man of twenty-five, wide-shouldered and with a swaggering walk that was the opposite of the stereotypical computer geek image. No John Lennon glasses. No bowed back from hours slumped in front of a flickering monitor.

With that clear picture in my mind I'd been expecting a matching, tanned young woman, who could hold her own in a clinch and perhaps use a crippling arm-lock to nip in the bud unwelcome advances made before that 'special' day. Wow, listen to me. Air quotes definitely necessary, because talk about old-fashioned. Wildly out of touch would be closer to the mark, but, anyway, what confronted us when we walked up the narrow stairs was a tiny woman I guessed was looking forward to her fiftieth birthday, dark hair streaked with grey, elastic-banded into a pony-tail reaching a waist that was less than three feet from the floor, and sharp blue eyes gazing at us from a smooth, serene face.

Annabel, true to her nature, immediately enveloped Kirsty in a warm embrace, and for a few moments I listened to muffled whisperings as I gazed around the flat.

Overlooking Eastgate a window propped open at the bottom with a book was letting in the myriad sounds and smells of a bustling city, and at either side pretty curtains made – I'd have sworn – from Kirsty's grandmother's wedding train were wafting gently in the cool breeze. Once upon a time I'd have described the look as Habitat. Nowadays functional furnishings of that nature can be bought almost anywhere, and Kirsty had added to the feeling of – what, a penny-pinching ascetic? – with truly bizarre decorations. Like, apples and oranges that had been left to wither and grow mouldy on top of the TV; objects nailed to the wall that seemed to be dentist's tools from the Victorian age and scraps of muslin that could have been used to strain sour milk when making cottage cheese; and, visible through the open kitchen door, a bread bin – with an organic loaf poking out of the door – I'll swear was originally a stainless steel sterilizer for surgeon's scalpels.

Behind me, in a voice that was huskily Scottish, Kirsty said, 'That's exactly what it is, if you're wondering. Cost me nothing because they were throwing it out, so what the hell.'

Grinning, Annabel broke the awkward silence by doing the introductions. Kirsty went into the kitchen and was back in a trice with three mugs of instant coffee (I refused to speculate in what she'd used to boil the water), and as we settled with our drinks on settee and chairs that were more comfortable than they looked, she fixed me with an enquiring gaze.

'I've heard impressive tales about you,' she said. 'You're very successful, if a wee bit short on experience. However, that's as maybe. If you can find the bastards who beat Andy to a bloody pulp I'll be truly grateful. So, tell me, what do you want to know?'

'You've heard the rumours?'

'About the property scam?' She pulled a face. 'Well, rumours abound, facts are scarce, but Andy's dad and that Melanie Wigg were certainly up to something out there in the Greek Islands. I can only go by what I've been told, but if you're thinking Andy spilled the beans under that duress, forget it, because I don't think he ever knew all the details.' She shuddered. 'That's what makes the beating such a terrible thing: there was no way he could tell them what they wanted to know.'

'They?'

'Him, then. Yes, OK, thugs without brains waded in with the baseball bats, or steel-capped boots, or whatever it was they used. But we all know they were under orders.'

'And you haven't got a name?'

Kirsty shook her head. 'All anyone knows is a clever villain came up with a bright idea for making a lot of money.'

'Involving properties in the sun that didn't exist outside a laptop?'

'Oh, so you've heard? Well, they existed, right enough, but they weren't for sale. They happened to be vacant because the owner was away on business, or a long holiday.' She grinned. 'My guess is some of them were holiday homes, owned by Brits, being sold to Brits.'

I nodded, thinking back. 'Steve Easter guessed a laptop would be involved, with stunning images to pull in the suckers.'

'Well, I don't know where he gets his info, but he's certainly on the right track.' She looked pensive. 'I suppose if anybody could find the missing money – outside the polis, of course – it'd be a clever, persistent journalist with his scruples well hidden.'

'Mm. I was thinking, though, this business of actual properties: wouldn't it be difficult to come up with necessary and convincing paperwork if someone made an offer?'

'A *cash* offer.'

'Goodness. *Always* cash?'

'Definitely. On the nail. And you can forget the paperwork, because that'd be a doddle. Today's computers can churn out a perfect Magna-bloody-Carta, and if you've got a pet local solicitor willing to make everything legal and above board, where's the problem? Which brings us to Larry Galleywood: he was an estate agent; he was short of money, but he knew houses and was good enough to sell ouzo to the Greeks. This was property; the sales were all going to be to Brits, so the villain decided Larry was the right man to do his dirty work.'

'Straightforward.'

Kirsty grimaced. 'Is anything ever?'

'So what went wrong?'

'Over six months or so, Larry Galleywood deposited a lot of money in a Greek bank. But when the big man trotted along to withdraw his ill-gotten gains, the coffers were empty. According to the Greek bank officials, the whole bloody lot had been moved to an unknown destination. A perfectly legal transfer in their eyes. Larry Galleywood swore ignorance, said it had to be internet fraud. The big man was having none of it. As far as he was concerned, Larry was telling fibs and had put three million quid where it couldn't be touched.'

'Yes, that's the figure I've heard mooted – though possibly in Euros,' I said. 'Either way, it's no wonder Mr Big went berserk.'

'Which brings us to Andy,' Annabel Lee said softly. 'But why Andy, why didn't this villain go straight to Larry?'

'Because of computers. Andy was very clued up in that department. Although he didn't come right out and tell me, I'm sure he produced all the scam's impressive paperwork. The big man would have known that, of course. If there was jiggery-pokery going on then, in the villain's eyes, Andy would be deeply involved.'

I frowned. 'Didn't they go to Andy and ask him nicely before beating him to a pulp?'

'Aye, he was asked.'

'And?'

'I told you, Andy knew very little, certainly none of the details and nothing about any missing money.'

'So what did he tell them when they asked?'

'Her. It was Gay Tirril doing the asking.'

I was aware of my mouth dropping open. 'You're kidding. Gay Tirril as of Seasoned Scribblers?'

'The same. I mean, she didn't go about it as if she was the villain's emissary, you know? No, it was done more jokingly, like, "Come on, Andy, you can tell me, where's your dad put all that lovely money?"' Kirsty shook her head. 'But she was fooling no one, was she? Andy knew at once what was going on, and he told his dad, and, well ...'

For a few moments there was a contemplative silence in the

room. I could hear the chatter and laughter of shoppers on Eastgate, the roar of double-decker buses making the tight turn from St Werburgh Street, the thud of feet tramping the boards of Eastgate Row directly beneath the window. Half listening to that background hum and throb, I was acknowledging that what Kirsty had told us bore the ring of truth because it had been one of the theories I'd cooked up with Josh and Sharkey in our conservatory discussion – though that theory had included Andy in the rip-off. However, I was also trying to accept Gay Tirril's involvement, and I just couldn't do it. I was much more inclined to believe that the questions really had been asked in a light-hearted, wheedling, go-on-share-your-secret sort of way which Andy, tormented by guilt, had taken seriously. OK, so I had got Vince Keevil on my list of suspects, and he and Gay were as thick as thieves....

I chuckled at the unintentional pun, and shook my head. When I looked up, Annabel and Kirsty were watching me expectantly.

'Sorry. A bout of serious thinking terminated in a silly play on words. Or thoughts. However, mention of Gay Tirril brings us to the other female connection and to the obvious question: what about Melanie Wigg? You said at the beginning, Kirsty, that Andy's dad and Melanie were certainly up to something. If she and Galleywood were in it together, surely she'd know what happened to the money?'

'Not according to Andy. He discussed it with Melanie, because with the money gone he was also a loser. She's in the dark and, I must say, very angry.'

'Why? Because they were all going to get a big slice of the loot, then Larry decided he wanted it all for himself?'

'Partly. A big part, too, right enough, but she's also angry because by taking that cash Larry put her and Andy in danger. I haven't spoken to her since Andy ... died ... but I can imagine what she's feeling right now.'

Annabel stood up and stretched. 'Absolutely. Big shock to the villain, Andy won't talk, and Larry goes and dies before they can get to him. Ho hum, nothing left for it, we'll just have to go and talk to Melanie.'

'A sickening thought,' I said, 'but I'm sure it's one that will have occurred to the police. DI Billy Dancer said they were looking into the Greek scam, but couldn't make arrests based on rumours. That was yesterday, and I'm sure they're beavering away. But what about us?' I looked at Kirsty. 'You've been very helpful, but I'm still struggling. Got any more suggestions, based on what you know?'

'Well, the scam boss must have gone to Andy first because he thought computers held the answer. If you want to take that approach, Andy spent a lot of time with a guy called Rieff.'

'Reef?' I said, startled. 'Reef as in knot?'

'No, Rieff as in R-I-E-F-F.' She looked puzzled. 'Surely you've heard of him? You're friendly with Steve Easter, and Rieff is Easter's editor.'

'No,' I said, 'he's not. Steve's boss used to be Sinclair, now it's a bloke called Barnaby.'

'Aye, that's right,' Kirsty said. 'Steve Easter's editor is this guy I just told you about. His name's Barnaby Rieff.'

I was itching to talk to him. I couldn't believe the identity of the man known to have been seen with broken-nosed thug Jimmy Rake had come to me out of the blue to a skirl of distant bagpipes, couldn't believe that when the name Barnaby came up in support of Steve's alibi neither Josh nor I had asked for the editor's full name. If we had, the information Joey Lox had so reluctantly leaked in exchange for Sharkey's mobile phone would have given me something to act on. Instead, I'd been guilty of assumption – I'd believed Barnaby to be the editor's surname – and it's through such stupidity that wars are lost.

I chuckled. A bit over the top? Well, probably, but Josh's military background has soaked into my psyche, osmosis has made me army barmy and I was all fired up, chasing my real first clue, metaphorically champing at the bit on my way to Liverpool and, I suddenly realized, doing so at ten miles an hour over the speed limit.

Steady, Penny, I thought, lifting my foot. Think of ice-cool Annabel Lee, and do it her way, not yours.

We'd left Chester at midday and I'd dropped my pretty blonde photographer at her cottage in Parkgate half an hour later. However, before letting her go, we sat in the Ka. I phoned Steve Easter, got his editor's phone number, at once phoned his office and looked wide-eyed at Annabel as Rieff agreed to give me fifteen minutes of his time, starting at 2.30.

Then Annabel and I spent ten minutes talking business.

With Andy Galleywood's weekend wedding off the books and

the next wedding two weeks away, she had nothing to prepare for. At least, nothing to do with my work. But before being employed by Penny Lane Panoramas she'd had considerable success selling her own informal portraits taken in settings ranging from lush meadows to moody interiors, and she'd done well with brooding Scottish castles set against wooded backdrops printed in infra-red I knew had been created on the computer. Also, the coloured prints of flowers I'd seen on my first visit to her cottage, done in periods when she'd been winding down from what she called her serious work, would win prizes anywhere.

So Annabel had plenty to keep her occupied without the work I might provide but, sitting chatting to her, I'd been finding it difficult to forget her earlier shocked reaction when she'd thought I was about to send her out with her Nikon looking for villains to snap. Suddenly, it sounded like a good idea, and the mission I was envisaging wasn't quite so risky.

Risky enough, though. As I drove down the ramp into the car-park from where, on Monday evening, Andy Galleywood had started on his final journey, I was wondering at the wisdom in sending Annabel Lee out to take photographs of the Galleywood residence. And just what I was hoping to gain.

Barnaby Rieff was definitely not my idea of a newspaper editor. No green eye-shade, no glittering arm bands encircling shirt sleeves rolled back from hairy wrists, no stubby fingers stained with printer's ink, no stogie jutting from the corner of a mouth that was either snarling or snapping orders.

What I saw instead, after walking through a large open-plan office where jeans-clad journalists of both sexes stabbed with two fingers at computer keyboards while holding a telephone against one ear with a shoulder and a lot of luck, was a dark-haired man in a crumpled light-grey suit with his dark tie hanging down from an unbuttoned collar. The unusual, layered brown eyes behind rimless glasses must have watched my approach through the half-glazed door. When I entered the office they were blank, unreadable.

'This is not what I expected,' I said, as I sat in front of his desk on the hard chair he indicated and let my tote bag slip to the floor. 'Not out there, not in here. For years I've been carrying this vivid picture in my mind—'

'Hollywood, 1974,' Rieff said, lazily swivelling his chair. 'Walter Matthau as newspaper editor Walter Burns in *The Front Page*. Fourth or fifth film reincarnation came out as *Switching Channels* in 1988. Burt Reynolds.'

'Impressive. Your start in journalism must have been as a film critic.'

'Maybe it was, but that's not why you're here.' He looked at his watch. 'You've got a little over ten minutes to tell me what you want.'

'Hang on, you said fifteen—'

'From the time you entered the building. What do they say adds tension to your husband's crime books?' He held up his hand and rocked the index finger back and forth, left, right, left, right.

'Yes, I know: the clock is ticking. OK, first question: did you deliberately prolong an editorial meeting so that a body could be planted in the luggage box mounted on Steve Easter's BMW?'

'No.'

'Do you deny being seen in the company of Jimmy Rake?'

He stared at me hard, rocking now, not swivelling, the brown eyes as hard as onyx. Then he reached forward and used an expensive Schaeffer pen to scribble something on a yellow pad.

'Oops,' I said. 'That's me for the chop.'

'Not at all. I've got to pick up some tripe and some eyewash at the supermarket on the way home. You reminded me.'

And then he grinned, and there was a sparkle in the onyx and the office lit up as if the sun had burst through the clouds and banished all gloom. I grinned with him. He shook his head.

'I've heard about you, but nobody told me you were feisty.'

'I'm not. I'm petrified. I once discussed crime with a man holding a gun, and that was as nothing compared to this.'

'I'm flattered – I think.' He fiddled with the pen, his eyes still amused. 'I know Jimmy Rake because it pays me to do so. And others like him. This is a newspaper. That means bad news is good news.'

'D'you know why I mentioned Rake?'

'Because he was one of the men doing the lifting in the car-park.'

'How do you know? That's not been in any newspaper.'

'Maybe I've seen him since. Maybe he told me.'

'An admission of guilt to a newspaper editor, even a friend, is hardly likely. What about the second man? Do you know his name?'

'Frank Stock.'

My stomach lurched. I looked into those unusual stratified eyes, strove to hide my excitement; saw the return of coldness that had never been far away and knew the laughter that had lit up the room had been this man marvelling at his own brilliant wit at my expense.

'I suppose it all depends on who you consider to be the second man,' I said, keeping my voice steady. 'The one I meant was the person helping Rake with Andy Galleywood's body.' I paused, waiting for a reaction, got none. 'I suppose Stock is the man who had the key and opened the box?'

'*Take Your Pick*,' Rieff said softly.

I nodded. 'I know. Michael Miles, 1955, and now you're a TV critic. OK, I will take my pick. Stock *was* the man who used keys to open the luggage box. You've slipped up, Rieff, because even the police haven't identified the third man—'

'Neither have I.'

'But you said—'

'Who heard me? You?' Then his face hardened, and his hands slapped the desk as he leaned forward. 'Are you recording this?'

'No.'

'Prove it. Open that sack you're carrying; show me—'

I stood up so fast my chair fell backwards. Swiftly I scooped up my bag and turned towards the door.

'My time's up, and anyway I've got another appointment—'

I heard a low growl behind me. There was a faint whirring sound. I knew it was his swivel chair spinning, knew that Barnaby Rieff was on his feet and charging round his desk to get to me.

My hair prickled. I felt my legs go weak. I opened my mouth to cry out – and then, in front of me, the door was flung open. A man in shirt sleeves with damp patches at the armpits burst in, his eyes blazing with excitement.

'Barns, there's trouble out at Speke factory; I've sent Appleby to cover, Chadwick to take the pics …'

I squeezed past him, and ran. My tote bag was flying, my eyes staring – I'll swear the skin was pressed back against the bones of my face so fast did I run as I pelted through that big newspaper office on my way to the open air and freedom.

chapter fifteen

Josh was in the bathroom when I got home, probably fresh out of the shower and with a towel knotted around his waist as he used tissue to wipe steam off the mirror so he could check to see if the nautilus machine he'd been working out on was keeping his muscles hard as rocks. No, that's not right. A mirror can't measure hardness – can it? Bulk, yes, so I imagined him standing flexing, full-frontal first, then more flatteringly side-on and leaning slightly backwards to flatten his stomach, face turned towards the mirror and tilted slightly upwards to reduce the unsightly slackness under the chin ...

You'll have gathered by now that my experience in Barnaby Rieff's office had left me so traumatized that forty-five minutes later I was still babbling – and of course you'd be wrong. Assumption gets you nowhere, as demonstrated by me when I heard the name Barnaby and grasped the wrong nettle. Oops, and that's a non-sequitur – isn't it? Or utter nonsense?

OK, yes, all right, you win, so I *was* incoherent, if only in my thinking; but as I told Josh when he eventually emerged from the bathroom dressed in something more modest than a posing towel – jeans and T-shirt, actually – I'd just had an awkward conversation with a killer.

'Really,' he said, loosely sprawled opposite me in one of the conservatory's wicker chairs. 'What's Annabel been up to now?'

'I'm not *talking* about Annabel,' I said. 'That was hours ago, and since then I've seen someone else.'

'Kirsty Tremayne. In Chester.'

I blinked. 'How'd you know that? And do you know who she is?'

'Andy's fiancée. She's been on the phone. Said she remembered something after you left. Andy, it seems, was looking into offshore banking. She said he started soon after his dad got back from the Greek Islands.'

'Did he now?' I said. 'That's very interesting, because it ties in with what we were discussing with Sharkey last night, but in what could be an unhelpful way.'

Josh was grinning. 'Go on.'

'Well, we'd more or less decided the Galleywoods had worked a double-cross and nicked all the scam money, right? However, Andy studying the intricacies of offshore accounts could have been the father and son looking for somewhere safe to hide all that loot – or it could have been Andy trying to find out where his dad had put it.'

'Mm, I can see where this is leading. You mean Larry had already taken it, without Andy knowing? Or at least without telling him where it had gone.'

'Or anybody else. Yes, Kirsty thinks that's a possibility. It'd been some time since his wife died, so maybe he had a lady friend.' I hesitated, letting my mind roll in all kinds of weird directions. 'Remember at the Scribblers' meeting I thought Gay Tirril was crying, and you told me she had an eye infection? Well, what if I was both right and wrong: she *was* crying, but over Larry Galleywood, not Andy. Makes more sense. Larry was her age....'

Josh was nodding, seeing the sense in what I said, seeing another avenue opening up.

'Lady friend sounds good, though I don't know about Gay.' He stretched out, crossed his legs the other way. 'Bit flashy, isn't she – but, then, who knows Galleywood's preferences?' He narrowed his eyes speculatively. 'So, what d'you think happened? The scam was in the Greek Islands, week by week, month by month, the money was deposited in a Greek bank, and before he returned to the UK, Galleywood managed to shift it?'

'Something like that – if we're agreeing that it was Larry Galleywood going it alone—'

'Or with a lady friend?'

'Yes, with a lady friend, but cutting out his son.'

'Sounds good,' Josh said, 'though I'd amend it slightly: I can see Galleywood keeping it a secret from absolutely everybody, *including* this mythical lady friend. But either way it doesn't bring us any closer to finding the cash, or the killer. And, talking of killers ...'

'Wait there, I'll get the drinks.'

I went through to the kitchen, put the jug on, then on impulse picked up the cordless phone and called Steve Easter. I told him what had happened, told him his editor had come up with the name of the third man in the car-park. He couldn't believe it. Said he'd talk to him, ask him what the hell was going on. Without saying why, I told him to be careful, then put down the phone.

The jug was still purring away. I sat on a stool, leaned on the breakfast bar.

It was heading towards four o'clock on what had turned out to be a grey November afternoon. Getting dark, actually. The drizzle was like pale mist drifting across the garden and the unfinished pool that would, I thought, be dry for the foreseeable future if fine rain was all we were going to get. If I knew Josh, he'd be praying for a heavy downpour. Looking for the easy way out.

I chuckled as I waited for the jug to boil. Almost, but not quite true. Josh never looks for the easy way out, he just avoids altogether those tasks he doesn't like, doesn't want to do. But isn't that the same thing, rephrased, put another way? Isn't stopping before you've started the easiest of easy ways out?

There was a wry smile on my face as I carried coffee through to the conservatory. Then, through the glass a movement caught my eye. Josh saw me pause with coffee mugs poised, and raised an eyebrow.

'There's a scruffy moggie out there by our dust bowl,' I said, staring through glass misted with fine droplets.

'The rain will drive him away.'

'He's prowling. I think he's got a vivid cat imagination and can see those fat koi carp lazily swimming just out of reach.'

'Yes, well, moving on, common sense is telling me that my wonderful wife only imagined a conversation with a killer and she's now desperately stalling—'

'He tried to stop me leaving.'

'Who did, and leaving where?'

'Barnaby Rieff. I pointed out his slip, and he became very angry. I ran from his office.'

'Perhaps,' Josh said, 'you'd better explain.'

I handed him his coffee and sat down on the edge of my wicker chair.

'I found out from Kirsty Tremayne that Barnaby Rieff is Steve Easter's editor. I won't explain *that*, because you can work out where we went wrong over the name. The point is, I went to see him. We knew he was acquainted with Jimmy Rake, I wanted to know if he knew the second man. So I asked him the second man's name.'

'Ellis Barnes.' Josh nodded.

I shook my head. 'You know that and I know that. According to Barnaby Rieff – incidentally, one of his colleagues came barging in and it seems they call him Barns—'

'Bloody hell,' Josh said, grinning, 'do get on with it, Pen.'

'OK, according to Rieff,' I said, leaning forward, 'the second man's name is Frank Stock.'

Josh closed one eye, twisted his mouth, rocked his head.

'Right,' he said slowly, 'and you believe the name he gave you was that of the third man; the man done up to look like Steve who ran from the office block, turned the key to—'

'Open the box. Yes. Though that's not what I said to Rieff. I just told him he'd slipped up, meaning he'd named the wrong man, given me a name that wasn't known to *anyone* except the guilty. He went mad, wanted to know if I was recording the conversation, slammed his hands on the desk. I got up and ran.'

Josh stood up and wandered towards the window, mug in hand. He stood looking out at the damp garden.

'Very fishy,' he said softly, 'and Rieff's slip certainly gives us another suspect. Bad enough being friendly with the others, Rake and Barnes, but knowing *that* name ...' He swung around. 'Phone Dancer, Pen. See if the police have caught up with – who was it, Stock? If they have, then this Rieff will put his knowledge down to good contacts within the force, and he's off the hook.'

I slipped through to the kitchen, dialled Dancer's number, got through first time and asked the question. He objected at first. I said all I wanted from him was a simple yes or no: had the name Frank Stock come up in the Andy Galleywood investigation. He grunted, said it hadn't. That set me tingling with excitement. I told him Stock was probably the third man in the car-park, then quickly put down the phone before he could start asking questions.

When I returned to the conservatory, the door was open and Josh was standing in the middle of the lawn in the fine rain, looking down at the hole that should have been a pond but had never quite made it. I wondered if it ever would. The cat thought not. He'd given up on the koi carp and was nowhere to be seen.

I poked my head out. A wind had sprung up. Cold rain stung my cheeks. I shivered, gathered my hair at the back of my neck.

'Josh? What's up?'

'I came to chase the cat but got distracted. Could you come here, Pen, please.'

His voice was as bleak as the November weather. I glanced around for a jacket, couldn't see one, quickly folded my arms and walked with reluctance across the wet grass. Slowed. Stopped when he raised his hand.

'Far enough, Pen – for the moment. I want you to brace yourself. There's … there's a body in this … our …'

'Death Valley,' I said, and my voice was a weak croak.

'Christ, yes, we did call it that, didn't we? Many a true word. Oh, hell. Look, if you feel up to it, come and have a look. He's … on his back, and I'm pretty sure from what you've told me that I know who it is.'

I took a deep breath. The skin tightened across my cheekbones. When I stepped forward I felt as if I were floating. I edged closer, looked down into the shallow hole, and swayed. Josh reached out quickly to hold me steady.

'Easy, easy,' he said softly.

'Yes,' I said, 'it's him.' And then I swallowed hard. 'It's the scally, Joey Lox.'

'You're sure of that?'

'Absolutely. Sure of that, sure that Lox wouldn't be lying there, dead, if he hadn't been seen talking to me and handing his phone with those damn pictures on it to Ryan Sharkey.'

And with a soft whimper of utter despair I turned and buried my rain-wet face into the hollow of Josh's hard shoulder.

'There's two things that strike me as very odd,' Josh said. 'They point in a direction I really don't want to take – and yet, for the killer to go in that direction seems close to an impossibility.'

It was three hours after the discovery of the Body in the Dustbowl (that's me masking the horrific with the banal) and we were sitting in the living-room with DI Billy Dancer. At the rear of the bungalow our garden looked like a wet paddock enclosed by sagging crime-scene tape, Joey Lox's sad remains had been removed, the Scenes of Crime Officers had done their work and departed.

For most of those three hours I had wandered about in a daze, pottering in my office without having a clue what I was doing, going occasionally into the kitchen to drink ice-cold water and watch without interest the police activity, sometimes staring moodily out of the front windows where police cars parked in the driveway were attracting the interest of respectable (as in curtain-twitching) neighbours.

When everything that could be done by the police had been done, Dancer had knocked on the conservatory door and been invited in. Dressed in his usual baggy alpaca suit which was stained dark at the shoulders by the persistent rain he had asked me, with politeness that masked steely intent, to tell me everything I'd done or discovered since our talk in his office. I complied. It turned out to be not very much. From the photographs on Lox's SIM card the police knew all about Rake and Barnes. Joey Lox had served his purpose, and in any case was now history. I'd already given Dancer the name of the car-park's third man. That was being looked into, he told me, then listened without reaction when I told him that the name, Frank Stock, had been given to me by newspaper editor Barnaby Rieff.

After that I'd left him talking to Josh while I fled to the bathroom to soak under a hot shower. I felt dirty, yet after five minutes under scalding hot water and a liberal lathering with Royal Jelly shower gel I knew it was the kind of dirt that no amount of scrubbing would remove. What I was feeling was guilt, and it was with a heavy heart that I dried myself, got dressed and prepared to face the evening.

Now, with the living-room curtains closed, the heating pleasant enough for Dancer to loosen his tie and the soft light from table-lamps glinting on crystal glasses of red wine, I was putting on a brave face and the gaunt detective was looking intrigued.

'What two things are those?' he asked Josh. 'Which direction, and why impossible?'

'Well, the police – meaning you – know Andy Galleywood's battered body was put in the luggage box on top of Steve Easter's car. What you possibly don't know is that the luggage box was bought for one reason: Easter's writing a crime novel with just such a scene in it, and he wanted to know if it was possible to get a body into one of those boxes.'

Dancer was already seeing where that led, already nodding. 'Then Easter told somebody,' he said bluntly, 'and I suppose that's the direction you don't want to take. He'd only tell his friends, so the logical conclusion is that one of his friends is a killer.'

'Exactly.'

'And the impossibility?'

'I'm also writing a crime book, this one set in Arizona. In it, there's a scene in which a body is discovered in a hole in a woman's back garden – back yard, as they call them over there.'

'And?'

'I've told no one, not even Penny.'

'No,' I said, 'you haven't – told me, I mean. But that doesn't mean I couldn't have found out.'

'Yes,' Josh said patiently, 'but that's because you live with me and you can walk in and out of my office, rummage through my notes.'

'I don't have to, Josh, and neither do other people who are up to dirty tricks. You don't take your laptop everywhere you go, but you *do* take a USB memory stick. Always. And that's got all your books on it.'

Dancer was listening intently, his eyes alight with intelligence. Josh's face was grim.

'Damn it, you're right. It's one of those that clip in an inside pocket, and I hang my jacket in lots of places.'

'Harriers, leisure centre … library …' I nodded. 'All it needs is someone with a laptop, your USB thingy and about sixty seconds.'

Josh shook his head. 'Well, one good thing is it means access isn't restricted to my friends,' he said, clearly relieved.

That didn't wash with Dancer.

'Look, as it stands we've got three suspects, all caught on camera at the scene of a crime,' he said. 'Two were out on bail and are now back inside answering questions, Frank Stock's also telling his story. Looking at the way things are going, I believe the CPS would accept what evidence we've got on those three villains as being enough to charge them with one murder. Two, if I can get them for Lox. However' – he held his hand up as I made as if to protest – 'an investigation is never static and if things do change, if evidence pops up to prove me wrong *and* if I was a betting man – I'd put money on the killer being someone you know well.'

'Maybe you're right,' Josh said. 'Someone murdered Joey Lox and dumped him here, in the garden, in a scene taken straight from my crime book. If it wasn't Rake, Barnes or Stock, then it was someone else who was able to get at my data.' He shook his head in exasperation. 'Damn it, even if those three are the killers there *has* to be someone else involved, someone who could get close to me without being noticed then feed them the information. None of those three could do that, so there's someone out there, someone we know, there *must* be – right, Penny?'

I nodded absently, sipping my wine and still feeling down in the dumps. I'd gazed in horror at yet another dead body, and I couldn't get rid of the feeling that I was responsible for Joey Lox's death; that I was a clever, successful photographer but a bungling would-be PI who repeatedly made mistakes that put other people's lives at risk.

Josh's optimism wasn't helping either, because I knew he was wrong: despite what Dancer had said about his three villains, our three-way discussion with Sharkey in the conservatory had given us our own suspects, and each one of them was a friend, or reasonably close acquaintance. The odd one out was Barnaby Rieff. I'd been excited at the thought that my good work had produced another suspect, but the name hadn't impressed Dancer.

I sighed deeply.

Josh cocked his head, smiling sympathetically.

'The doldrums?'

'Mm. I'm not sure where to go next – or whether to give up.' I looked at Dancer, who looked comfortable and set for the night. 'I suppose you've spoken to Stock?'

'Not personally. But, like I said, he's telling his story.'

'So I have got *something* right, although—'

I broke off. I could see Dancer watching me with a peculiar look in his eye.

'What? What's up?'

'Nothing,' he said. 'Keep going.'

'Well, I was just going to say you've got the man who opened the box and the men who manhandled the body, but there's a sort of criminal stick-together thingy, isn't there? You know, the Code of The West, all for one and one for all, nobody grasses. So, is it likely that Stock or the others will spill the beans, point the finger at Barnaby Rieff?'

'No reason to.' Dancer shrugged. 'Sorry, I wasn't honest with you when you phoned earlier. Frank Stock's name *had* come up; Barns Rieff had phoned and given it to me just ten minutes before you did.'

Josh snorted. 'So what. Doesn't make him an innocent goody-goody. All he was doing was covering for the slip he'd made by giving Stock's name to Penny.'

'Yeah, except that Barns Rieff has long been a great help to the police with his journalistic abilities and complete willingness to share any dirt he or his team dig up. Unlike,' he said, 'a certain crime writer who was asked for help' – he looked at me, and I nodded – 'and from whom, up to now, I've received bugger all.'

'You will, Oscar, you will,' Josh said.

Dancer glared. 'What the hell's that supposed to mean?'

'It's from Monty Python,' Josh said, straight-faced. 'They did an Oscar Wilde sketch. Wilde said that to Whistler – but my meaning's pretty clear, isn't it? You're reasonably certain you've got your killers; Penny and I don't share that conviction so we'll keep looking.'

'I *know* I've got Andy Galleywood's killers,' Dancer said, 'and so do you. What I don't know is if they were hired to do the job. Contract killers.'

'They were.'

'Yeah, well, we'll see. If your take on Barns Rieff is anything to go by I'm not going to get much of value.' Then he looked hard at me. 'But what about you, Penny Lane? Were you serious before about giving up? I can see why you might be: the bodies are piling up again like they did last time, but now in your own back yard. So, what's happening, is it all getting a bit too much for your lady-like sensibilities?'

'I'll treat that remark as an uncharacteristic, ill-tempered snipe, Billy Dancer, and simply say that I really don't know how I feel. I think I'm coming around to the belief that poking my nose into the affairs of grubby little criminals isn't doing me much good, or them much harm.' I shrugged helplessly, feeling the hot prickle of unshed tears. 'To be truthful,' I said, with a quiver in my voice, 'I've got the horrible feeling that if I do keep going the whole world's going to come crashing around my ears. And, yes, if you really want to know, that's me being very scared.'

chapter sixteen

Thursday

If my world was going to come to an end it certainly didn't do so during the night, and I awoke to a cool, sunny day with a determination to follow the course of action Josh and I had agreed on when Dancer had left for home soon after midnight: that was, no action, do nothing. At least, nothing to do with crime.

Easier said than done. That morning a phone call was all it took to rekindle the embers of my PI ambitions, albeit on a different track.

Although Josh had given up marathons, he still enjoys 10k races and training runs with his mates at Liverpool Harriers. Wednesday afternoons are always set aside for his nautilus sessions, Thursday mornings he occasionally goes for a long run from the university sports ground in Mather Avenue. So after breakfast I saw him off to Liverpool in the Land Rover then went back inside, snug in housecoat and slippers, to do absolutely nothing.

The phone rang in the hall. It was Annabel Lee.

'Got the pics,' she said.

'Ah, right,' I said, 'but I'm not supposed to be talking crime. Joey Lox's body was dumped in the pond in my back garden. Josh found him last night.'

'Jesus. You mean he drowned?'

'Er, no. Josh has never finished the pond. It's a dust bowl. No,

Joey was dead when he was dumped – could have been when I was with you in Chester. I really don't want to know. I've not asked questions, don't even know how he died.'

'But you know why. He took those pics, talked to the police and that was it, goodbye Joey.'

'Yes, well, I've had just about all I can stomach.'

'Yeah,' Annabel said smugly, 'but my pics are really, really interesting, this is a different killing – and I've got a theory.'

'Hang on.'

I carried the phone through to the kitchen, hitched myself on to a stool at the breakfast bar, poured lukewarm coffee into a mug and wrapped my housecoat around my knees.

'OK, carry on.'

She giggled. 'My mum always used to say, "with who?". Anyway, we're talking about the photographs you wanted me to take of Galleywood's house, right? The interesting bit was round the back, that overgrown track leading to the private health club. It was raining, water comin' off the trees like a bloomin' waterfall, but I could see the house and the upstairs window – his study, yeah?'

'That's the one.'

'OK. Well, I think I was exaggerating when I said the pics were really interesting, because they're not very. Just a boring old house. No, it's my theory that's good. Taking those pics, I did the normal, you know, lined up, focused, pressed the button. It dawned on me when I was doing it that if Galleywood had been standing in his study, I would have seen him. Clear as day. And then I thought, if this was a gun not a camera – I could have shot him.'

'If the window was open.'

'Well, yeah … but maybe it was, the night you were there.'

'No.' I shook my head, frowning and suppressing a shudder as my gaze was caught by the flapping crime-scene tape catching the sun. 'No, it wasn't open. And anyway, the sash-cords are broken.'

'Big deal. There's always a way – isn't there?'

'Maybe, but it didn't happen. We – well, PC Faraday – broke into the study moments after the shot was fired. Believe me, Annabel, that window was closed.'

'I suppose ...'

She sounded deflated. I'd squashed her brilliant idea. Quickly I reminded her that she was coming over for dinner that night and Adam would be there, asked her to bring prints of the Galleywood pictures, then said a bright cheerio and replaced the handset.

For the rest of the morning I got on with business relating to Penny Lane Panoramas, but always with Annabel's theory niggling away in the background and threatening to destroy concentration. I logged on and checked the website, added a few images, remembered the man who'd telephoned and called his mobile to find out a little bit more about what he wanted to give his wife. Sorry, that sounds a bit coarse, doesn't it? Anyway, he told me, and I made notes and said I'd put some samples in a folder and call him to arrange a meeting. And that was it. I gave up. A quick, solitary lunch was followed by a trip to the bedroom to decide what to wear. Then, looking snazzy in Reeboks, tailored chinos, taupe sweater under a snow-white fleece brightened by a multi-coloured chiffon scarf I'd bought in a shop on Main Street, Gibraltar, I waltzed out into the early winter sunshine, slipped into the car and headed off to Liverpool for a change of scenery and pace.

My eighty-year-old father lives in sheltered accommodation, quite near to the old Strawberry Fields but in a home of a very different kind from that famous establishment and situated on the other side of Liverpool's Calderstones Park. Strawberry Fields closed in 2007, I think – I do know it was saved from much earlier closure in 1984 by a cash donation from Yoko Ono. Dad's place will, I hope, keep going for as long as he needs it.

When I see him we always laugh about the time I'd used his power shower. The force of the hot water had almost beaten me to my knees, left me lobster-pink and as limp as the warm plastic curtain. My father had gone up in my estimation – how he keeps his feet under that steady man-made downpour I'll never know – but I had vowed there and then never again to bathe at his place.

Strangely enough, my odd frame of mind almost had me breaking my promise. The guilt in my soul was still making me feel unclean – tainted, I suppose you'd call it – and the mere thought of standing for fifteen minutes under a cascade of water as hot as I could bear it made me tingle with anticipation. I didn't rush into the bathroom throwing off my clothes, of course. Dad knew something was wrong as soon as he saw my face, and during the course of a wonderful afternoon graced with lots of tea and shortbread biscuits we talked through my problems and he came to agree wholeheartedly with Annabel's opinion: I was not to blame; not for anything; and, going one step further, he told me bluntly that giving up would make me feel worse, not better. I needed success, he said, and packing it in was an admission of defeat.

It was a wintry dusk when I left, and although I hadn't come to a firm decision about the PI work, I had done something positive. Different frame of mind, you see. Thanks, Dad. What I'd done was phone Mr Smith, the man wanting an artistic gift for his wife. I had the print samples with me in a mini-portfolio and, after a brief mobile-to-mobile chat, we arranged to meet at six o'clock at his house in Kensington.

When I drove away from Dad's place it was after 5.30. Through the mirror I could see him standing at his front door waving and, for a reason I couldn't fathom and certainly didn't dwell on for too long, I was swept by a brief feeling of utter desolation.

One of these days I'll learn to take heed of warnings signs.

The address I'd been given was in one of the small side-streets off Low Hill, and I turned off the main road at a little before six o'clock and squeezed the Ka into a space between a huge, rusty Rolls Royce and a Triumph Stag with no wheels. It was full dark, the fine drizzle had returned with added chill and the dimly lit street was so reminiscent of the early days of gas lighting that I half-expected to see the ghosts of pipe-smoking men carrying long poles and short ladders.

The number Mr Smith had given me – six – was easy to find because the front door was one of the few in that murky, littered street to boast a number. In retrospect, hindsight, call it what you will, I suppose that's why it was chosen; that, and the man's name: he was one of about half a million Smiths in the UK, and that should have rung warning bells.

Suffice it to say that I sashayed up to that black, peeling front door with tote bag and flat portfolio slung over one shoulder and didn't even notice that all the ground-floor windows were boarded up. Maybe I thought plywood was the new chic. At that stage, anything was possible.

So, Little Miss Innocent, I blithely lifted my hand to rap with my knuckles on the door. As I did so, something that felt like a band of steel whipped around my neck from behind. A hand came around the other way and clamped over my mouth and nose. Instantly I was choking, struggling to breathe, wild with panic. A knee bored into the small of my back. My moan of pain was smothered by the palm pressed to my face. The front door clicked open, unbidden. I heard a grunt of effort, felt hot breath on my neck. Then the arm around my neck moved to my waist, my captor's groin thrust hard against my backside and I was lifted off my feet, carried bodily into the house and along a black and foetid hall. Another door was kicked open. Like a side of unwanted beef, I was dumped on the dusty wooden floor of an unlighted front room. Out of nowhere, a foot came swinging. It crashed against my head, red flared behind my eyes then everything went black.

I was sitting in an antique wheel-back chair with wooden arms. I knew that because a couple more were scattered about that otherwise empty front room. As my eyes adjusted I could just see them in the light seeping through cracks in the plywood, but I couldn't make admiring remarks on their quality because my mouth was taped shut. What do they call it, duct tape? And I certainly couldn't walk over to give them a closer examination – with a view to buying – because my ankles, like my arms, were taped to the chair I was sitting in.

Couldn't walk away, couldn't speak, couldn't scream – didn't want to cry because I had a blinding headache, and in any case my nose would run and of course I couldn't reach my handker-chief.

If I was going to die, I thought, trying not to giggle hysterically because then I'd probably suffocate or choke on my own spit, I wanted to do it with dignity. Or not at all, of course, which seemed the least likely possibility when the door slammed back and a man walked in from the hall.

If the black clothes he'd adopted were supposed to be slimming, he'd made the wrong choice. He looked enormous: wide at the shoulders, thick around the middle; big fists covered by black leather gloves. His head and face were also covered: he wore a black balaclava, sunglasses to hide his eyes, and when he spoke I knew he was sucking marbles to disguise his voice.

He was alone, but that was no consolation. It takes but one man to commit murder, and I was in no position to protest.

'Stupid, stupid, stupid,' he said, his tongue battling with the sibilants as glass balls rattled against his teeth.

I shook my head vigorously. Big mistake. He stepped closer, swung his right arm and slapped me across the face with his open hand. I rocked sideways, felt the chair teeter on two legs as my ears rang and bright lights flashed. Tears welled. My nose began to run. I shook my head, this time to clear it. Looked at the black shape now blurred by tears; tasted copper and realized with relief that the liquid running from my nose was warm blood.

'Stupid,' he said again, this time having trouble with saliva. He swallowed, went on, 'You interfering, stupid bitch. What's done is nothing to do with you. What's lost is not your loss, not yours to find, not yours to *even think about.*'

The last three words emerged as a muffled shriek. I narrowed my eyes and turned my face away, expecting something hard to shoot out of his mouth. Overcome with anger, he lifted a hand to his forehead to adjust the balaclava, fixed the sunglasses – Raybans clamped to his head near his covered ears – took a deep breath and again brushed at the black woollen cloth I guessed was sticking to his sweating forehead.

Then he took a step towards me. There was a new tenseness in the man's hard body: it was as if he had come to a decision. He was staring at me – but I couldn't see his eyes. I was watching his fists – but if they swung at me I was tightly bound and couldn't ride the punch – slip the slap? Please, Penny, I thought, please don't laugh or this bloody ignorant villain will kill you.

With a hiss of breath, he bent forward. Wood vibrated as his leather-covered palms slammed on the chair's arms. This time when he spoke I could smell his minty breath, could feel the hot wetness of his spittle on my cheeks.

'You understand? You understand you're a stupid, interfering bitch?

I nodded.

'You understand that if you continue to poke your nose in – you'll die?

I nodded.

'You understand that if you walk away from here and the relief of being free urges you to change your mind and you continue investigating killings, looking for cash – you'll die?'

I nodded.

For a long moment there was silence.

Then he straightened, stepped back, flexed his fingers. I knew what was coming. I closed my eyes, thought about dying with dignity; thought, to hell with that. With dignity forgotten, I made my move. A good one: I made about three inches. Then his left hand came out of nowhere and clamped on my head. His fingers locked in my hair and held my head steady. I squeezed my eyes shut, moaned with pain. This time when he swung his arm, he'd clenched his fist. This was no slap to slip, no punch I was in any shape to ride. Bone thinly coated in flesh and leather crashed against the side of my jaw. There was an explosion of pain, gone in an instant, a sensation of falling, then floating.

Then there was no pain, no light, no sound ... nothing.

chapter seventeen

'Dinner with company might be too much for you. I can always stop them coming,' Josh said.

'Over my dead body.' And then I saw the suddenly grave look on his face, and said, 'I'll rephrase that – the hell you will.'

I said the last bit in a John Wayne drawl and saw his lips twitch and then a wry smile cracked his sober face. He dabbed once again at my jaw with lint soaked with hot water and TCP. I winced, twitched. Liquid dribbled on to my dressing gown. He paused, waiting as I gritted my teeth.

'So you came to your senses in the Ka?'

'Recovered consciousness,' I corrected. 'That's where he'd put me.'

'Just the one man?'

'I think so. The others are all in jail. He put me in the front room and knocked me out so he could don his disguise – I mean he couldn't walk around like that, and he'd grabbed me in the street.'

'So he'd put you in the car ...'

'Yep, me and my tote bag and portfolio. Which is now redundant, damn it. The portfolio. Because he didn't really want my pictures, did he?' I touched the damp patch absently. 'I think I truly came to my senses on the way home when I thought, hey, you know what, you really are in the right job?'

'Photography?'

'No. My bow's second string, criminal investigation. Could be the first, actually.'

Josh snorted. 'How did you come to that conclusion?'

'Because of the way I acted under interrogation.' I grinned, then winced again and straightened my face as pain stabbed through my jaw. 'You see? I was a helpless captive, yet I'm even making a joke of that vicious questioning. Well, not questioning, more like dire warnings, actually. Anyway, that's what I'm getting at: the whole time I was in that awful room strapped to a chair by duct tape and with my sweet lips forever silenced – I was seeing the funny side of things. Going along with more or less everything the bastard said – in the interests of self-preservation, of course – yet still, in that horrible predicament, keeping my sense of humour, keeping my wits about me. Doesn't that tell you something? Doesn't that prove I'm a natural, born to be a PI?'

'Depends,' Josh said, taking my mixing bowl with its pink liquid and soggy lint over to the sink and returning to sit with me at the breakfast bar.

I pulled a face. 'I know what you mean. You mean if I'm that good I'd have come away with something positive; with a big fat clue. And you think I didn't. Well, the first thing that struck me right at the start of that ordeal was that there had to be a reason for the heavy disguise. For the mouth full of marbles.' I grinned. 'Or whatever. But you know what I mean. If he went to all that trouble before he could safely terrorize little me – then he must have been scared I'd recognize him.'

Josh reached across, touched my tender jaw with the tips of his fingers, stroked gently. I tingled. He leaned forward, kissed the tip of my nose.

'And did you?' he said softly.

'Did I what?'

'Recognize him.'

'No.' I hesitated, again losing the thread as Josh's hand moved lower and he tenderly massaged and kneaded tense muscles at the base of my neck. 'But you know what?' I said, swallowing. 'There was *something* about him I recognized.'

'And that was?'

'I don't know.'

'Bugger.'

Josh dropped his hand, settled back on his stool.

'I will do, though,' I said. 'Keep your hands to yourself, give me a little time, let me work out what it was I recognized and pin that ... whatever it was ... to a face, a name.'

'In the meantime, time's pushing on so I'd better work out what we're going to do about our guests. You're certainly in no shape for cooking.'

'And it's probably too late anyway.'

'Right, so I'll sort out a takeaway and get the table ready, you get dressed and prepare to be the slightly marked but ever beautiful hostess.'

'Mm, and if you hear a shriek from the bedroom,' I said, getting down stiffly from the stool, 'you'll know I've sussed my assailant.'

With a bubbly blonde on one side of the table, son Adam on the other and Josh and I at head and foot – if you can say that of a table: head, yes, but foot sounds more like bed, doesn't it? – anyway, with four special people gathered together around an elegant dining table, even a dinner delivered by a sullen young man in a van and disgorged from polystyrene containers is bound to be a success. And so it was. After I'd got all the explanations out of the way regarding cuts and bruises and near death experiences, Adam chatted merrily to all while unashamedly eyeing-up Annabel Lee, Annabel fluttered her eyelashes and egged him on cruelly only to shoot him down in flames in the nicest possible way (if that's possible), and Josh and I exchanged lots of amused glances while working our way through – amongst other delicacies – crab stick and sweetcorn soup, aromatic Peking duck, sweet and sour chicken, beef Cantonese style, satay roast pork and yeung chow special fried rice. Washed down, of course, with a wonderful, fruity merlot.

After that it was into the kitchen to put the dishes in the dishwasher, make a big pot of coffee, take the rattling tray through to the others in the living-room where they had retired to the more comfortable chairs and, under soft lighting and to a background of music for relaxation (how's that for optimism), get down to business – and I'm sure you, like Josh, know which one I mean.

★

'You had the right idea when you told me to take Sharkey along to SCENE SOUTH,' I said to Adam, 'except that Sharkey got clobbered and I came away unscathed.'

'Unlike the second time when you went on your own.'

'OK, first time unscathed, next time just a little bit scathed' – I grinned at Josh – 'but at least what I saw in that room has given me a smidgen of hope. It was something about that man who attacked me. I don't know if it was something he did, something he said, the way he moved, the way he talked – no, not that, because it sounded as if he had a mouthful of ollies – but when whatever it was does come to me, then I'll have Andy Galleywood's killer and the man behind the Greek property scam.'

'Before you get too carried away with that thought,' Adam said, 'as you asked me here as a working journalist so you could pick my brains I'd better bring you up to date.'

'Oh, right, so you've twigged what's behind this get together, have you?' Annabel said, giving him a seriously conspiratorial look.

'Absolutely. Big nosh up, then pay back time, Annie,' Adam said, shaking his head gravely.

'Annabel,' I corrected absently.

'No, Annie's fine, I like it,' Annabel said, her blue eyes sparkling. 'And *Adman's* got it right. What I was supposed to bring was vital clues picked up during my pre-wedding conversations with Andy and his fiancée – only we visited Kirsty yesterday afternoon, Pen, and came away empty-handed, didn't we?'

'Er, not quite,' I said. 'There was something there, too, something that set little bells jingling like mad, but for the life of me—'

I broke off as Josh groaned and flopped back on the settee with his eyes crossed.

Adam was grinning. Then, quickly sobering, he said, 'Doesn't matter anyway because as far as the police are concerned the Andy Galleywood case is almost closed.'

'Oh come on,' I protested.

'No, you come on, Mum. Think about it. Jimmy Rake and Ellis Barnes were already prime suspects. Then Barns Rieff gives Dancer the name of the third man, Frank Stock—'

'After he'd let it slip to me.'

'Doesn't matter. He's a respected newspaper editor and the police now have all three men who were seen putting Andy's body into that luggage box. As a newspaper man with contacts I know those three are in custody, I know they're answering all questions with blank looks and that's fine with the police because they know they've got the guilty men.'

'Yes, and Josh and I know all that too because Dancer went through it when we talked after Joey Lox's body was found. Dancer also said the CPS would probably be satisfied with the evidence. However, he also as good as admitted other evidence might turn up that pointed elsewhere – which suggests a degree of uncertainty, or him not being entirely convinced he's got the man behind the killing.'

'But that evidence hasn't turned up, not yet,' Adam said.

'What about the property scam? The Galleywoods were deeply involved and they're both dead because of the man who set up the scam.'

'If there was a scam,' Adam said, 'it's a separate matter and it's being investigated by the Greek authorities. Andy Galleywood was murdered by Rake, Barnes and Stock – a witness has come forward who heard Andy being threatened by Rake. Larry Galleywood was murdered by person or persons unknown, for *reasons* unknown—'

'Tell that to Steve Easter. Ask him why his BMW was chosen as a hearse.'

'It's always possible,' Adam said quietly, 'that Steve is making up that story of a scam.'

'He is *not*. He worked on a similar exposé a couple of years ago. That first case got him deeply interested in that kind of fraud.'

Adam still didn't look convinced. Josh was frowning at him.

'What about the attack on Penny? The threats. If the three men Dancer believes murdered Andy and Joey Lox were behind bars at the time, surely that attack is proof that there's someone else involved?'

'Maybe, but it's not even evidence,' Adam said, 'if it's not reported to the police.'

'My God,' Annabel said, 'that's a must, isn't it? Why haven't you reported it—?'

She broke off as the telephone rang. Josh climbed off the settee, wandered across and picked it up. He turned his back, walked across to one of the table lights and murmured softly. From what I could hear I gathered that he was answering questions. He nodded once, signed off and put the phone down.

When he returned to the settee and threw himself down, I was watching him.

'Steve Easter,' he said. 'Worried sick, wanting to know if you're OK. I told him you're fine, bruised and battered but still able to put glass to lips.'

I frowned. 'Hang on a minute, Josh, weren't we just talking about me not reporting the attack? How on earth has Steve found out?'

'Ah, well, Sheila phoned earlier. She was just making sure you knew she and Steve were back home, that she wasn't still in Chester with her son.'

'And you told her?'

'Of course.'

'That's not the point,' Annabel said, still looking at me as if I'd lost the plot. 'The fact that you haven't reported it, well, isn't that withholding evidence, perverting the course of justice or something?'

'All of that, I suppose.'

Adam was watching me closely. 'So why, Mum?'

'Haven't got around to it.' I found a tremulous smile and fitted it to my lips. 'I think I'm still in shock—'

Josh groaned, and again flopped back theatrically.

'—and endless questions would—'

'Give you the vapours,' Josh said.

'I think she's scheming,' Adam said.

'Doesn't make withholding evidence any less risky,' Annabel said. 'If she's nicked, I'm a photographer out of a job.'

'Or running the whole shebang in my absence.'

Josh, still sprawled inelegantly, said, 'Oh dear, I think I can see where this is leading.'

'Oh God,' I said, yawning, 'the bloody crime writer's been looking at the evidence—'

'We believe,' Josh cut in, 'that one or both of the Galleywoods – with Melanie Wigg – worked a property scam then moved three million quid to where it couldn't be found. Yesterday, Kirsty Tremayne telephoned with the news that Andy Galleywood had been investigating offshore banking. Dancer has made the point that, if there is a scam, it's being looked into by the local authorities.'

He grinned at me. 'How'm I doing so far?'

'Triffic,' I said. 'But you're not going with me.'

'Going where?' Annabel said, blue eyes wide.

'If you can't stand the heat, get out of the kitchen, isn't that what they say? Well, I'm going to nurse my bruises, make myself invisible to both goodies and baddies and weigh up my options while basking in some welcome winter warmth,' I said, and reached for my mobile.

I got through to Sharkey's land line first go. Unfortunately, the tone I got in my ear told me it was disconnected. I frowned at Josh, dialled Sharkey's mobile number.

'Where are you?' I said when he picked up.

'The club. JOKERS WILD.'

'Mm. Remarkably quiet. Funny what they say about mobiles, you can say you're just about anywhere when you're not really and nobody'll be any the wiser.'

'And that's remarkably devious. What d'you want, Pen?'

'I want you to book two return tickets, on any suitable budget airline, for tomorrow morning. At the same time, book accommodation for two. I may not know where you are now, but I know exactly where you'll be this time tomorrow.'

'Which is?'

'With me, on a Greek Island called Rhodes.'

chapter eighteen

Friday

The holiday season was over, so most of the more reasonably priced hotels in the Greek Islands were closed for the winter. Sharkey was aware of this, and had booked us into the brand new Nikos Takis Fashion Hotel. Hang the expense, I suppose, but don't ask me how much he paid. I remember seeing somewhere that the price for fourteen days in the hotel's Vosporous suite is over 3,000 Euros. Sharkey had booked us in for one day, so without the long stay reduction I reckon he'd paid close to five hundred quid.

We flew into Rhodes Diagoras Airport at 10 a.m. carrying only cabin baggage and Sharkey's laptop. Once through customs we strolled out into dazzling sunshine and took an air-conditioned Mercedes taxi to the hotel, which was opposite the clock at 26 Panetiou Street, Medieval Town.

Very impressive, too. If you've ever visited Rhodes old town you'll know all about the walls, the cobbled streets, bridges, gates and archways, and the hotel created by fashion designers Nikos and Takis looked completely at home in those ancient surroundings. At home, however, was not the description I would have given to the suite when we were shown up to the second floor. The atmosphere was oriental, and in my Heswall bungalow the bright blues, greens and crimsons of walls and fabrics would have looked like an out-of-control forest fire. But in Rhodes? Breathtakingly beautiful, and tucked in there with the bedroom and king-size bed and luxury bathroom with bath and jacuzzi I was relieved to see a living room with a sofa bed.

Sleeping arrangements sorted!

I was aware of Sharkey watching me.

'Toss you for the bed,' I said.

'And me a professional gambler? You'd lose. Besides, I'm a gentleman. The bed's yours.'

'What do the athletics commentators say "as of right"? Fair enough, and thank you, kind sir – but I have to tell you Josh has his doubts about your profession.' I studied his eyes, saw in them a new, guarded look. 'Why's your phone been cut off?'

'Not cut off. There's a fault on the line. It's being repaired.'

'What, and that forced you to move out?'

'I hate to say it, Penny, but you don't know what you're talking about.'

'OK.' I shrugged. 'We'll leave that until later.'

I moved my cabin luggage and tote bag to a vacant corner, then flung myself with a deep, contented sigh on to Sharkey's sofa bed.

'I know this trip was my idea,' I said, 'but I must confess to being way out of my depth. Here on Rhodes with big ideas, but without a clue where to start. So, over to you, Sharkey. What's our first move?'

'Something to eat, an early lunch. Then I thought we'd go and talk to the police.'

'Ambitious, but optimistic. What if they don't want to talk to us?'

'They will when they see this.'

He'd been wandering around the room, touching woodwork, running his hand with an almost imperceptible whisper of sound down what looked like pure silk curtains, finally moving to open the window with a loud snick and gaze out across the balcony and old town to the sea. Now he slipped his hand inside his leather jacket, brought it out holding a black folding wallet which he tossed to me.

'Christ,' I said softly. 'This is a police warrant card, complete with … Merseyside police badge.' I flicked it open. 'Detective Inspector Ryan Sharkey. Your photograph.' I looked closer. 'This seems genuine, it's signed by the police commissioner.'

Bewildered, I looked across at him. '*Is* this genuine? Are you telling me you're a—?'

'Copper?' He shook his head. 'No, what you're holding is a genuine fake.'

'Really? You know, that may be an oxymoron, but it sounds like a reasonable description of a Ryan Sharkey I'm beginning to realize I don't know all that well.'

And suddenly I knew I'd said the wrong thing. When he spoke, his face was wooden.

'Ah. Not well, but well enough to ... how shall I put it, use and abuse, right?'

I frowned. 'What's that supposed to mean?'

'Last night you were dining with family and friends and you picked up the phone. You didn't believe me when I told you where I was. Then you didn't ask, you *told* me what *you* wanted: I was to go on a trip with you, you wanted two tickets to Rhodes, plus accommodation. I was to book on line – using my money.'

'Christ, Sharkey,' I said, 'I thought we were in this together.'

'You mean you don't mind working with a genuine fake, a man who apparently doesn't fit your husband's image of a professional gambler? Tell me, what *does* Josh think? Is he going by first impressions, as described by you? Does he believe I'm nothing more than the down-and-out you saw that night in JOKERS WILD? How did he react when you told me you didn't believe I was there in that same club last night? Smirk, give you a knowing look—'

'Were you there?'

'Yes.'

'It was very quiet.'

'Thursday evenings are always quiet. The lull before the weekend storm. You should have realized that.'

The room throbbed with tension. In the sudden empty silence I could hear through the open window the sound of footsteps hurrying over cobbles, the sudden loud bray of a donkey, the chirpy toot of a boat's whistle out on the harbour.

After several moments of that I said, 'What brought this on, Sharkey?'

He shrugged, took a deep breath, spread his hands.

'I don't know. Jet lag?'

'What ... after a four-hour flight?'

'Maybe I'm a poor traveller.'

'But good at ... other things.' I waggled the fake warrant card I was still holding, then tossed it to him.

'Look,' he said, 'let's take a couple of steps back, rewind the film. The easiest way of forgetting the last few minutes—'

'Suppose I don't want to forget? Suppose I want to know the real reason behind your ... outburst.'

He smiled, and when he did so his face softened and suddenly I was sitting in the Vosporous Suite with the old familiar Ryan Sharkey.

'What was it you said a little while ago, Pen? We'll leave that until later? You were talking about my disconnected phone line' – he waited, and when I didn't remark on the changed explanation, went on – 'so, yes, let's do that. Talk later. In the meantime I suggest we don't waste the adrenaline but skip the eats and get on with the job. That means the Greek police.'

'Not the Leith police?' I gave him a few seconds to recall the old tongue twister, saw his lips twitch and said, 'D'you know where to find them?'

'Tourist police HQ's on the corner of Papagou and Makariou streets. If you want to phone first it's 22410-27423.'

My smile came from the heart. 'Where would I be without you, Sharkey?'

'We'll talk about that later,' he said enigmatically, and reached out his hand to help a remarkably weary PI to her feet.

Police stations are much the same the world over, and but for the lazily rotating ceiling fans and the preponderance of dark moustaches we could have been in DI Dancer's HQ in Queens Road, Hoylake. We'd decided not to phone ahead in the firm belief that refusals come harder face to face. And so it proved. Sharkey's genuine fake warrant card was flashed and we sailed past the desk like the crew of a racing dinghy rounding a buoy. A stone-faced constable emerged and took our names, then led us along a corridor and showed us into the office of Police Warrant Officer Kostas Kostopoulos – a rank, Sharkey whispered, about equivalent to a UK police inspector.

Kostopoulos was a small man with dark, liquid eyes and an earnest expression. Sitting behind a huge desk, he let his eyes linger for a moment on my jaw where the dark bruise was already turning yellow, then listened intently. It took Sharkey, the English policeman with an attractive assistant, no more than a couple of minutes to state our mission. After just one of those minutes Kostopoulos was already nodding.

'But of course,' he said, 'this illegal activity in the Greek Island property market did exist. We have known of it for some time but, as I am sure you are aware, there are many islands off the Greek mainland or close to the Turkish and Albanian coasts. You will have heard of course of Kefalonia, Santorini, Skiathos, Zante, Corfu' – he shrugged his narrow shoulders – 'and each one of those islands, and each of the others, has many large towns and villages.'

He paused, his dark eyes wide as he looked at us with expectancy.

'You mean,' Sharkey said, 'that the geography is such that it's possible for a crook to skip from island to island, town to village, and always stay one step ahead of the law?'

'Exactly. One step, ten steps, always just far enough to begin again, you see?' Kostopoulos shrugged again, and his white teeth flashed in a broad grin that quickly faded. 'In addition, of course, false names were being used. All we know is that a man and a woman were involved, and that they were English. It is possible to study the passenger ... er ... itineraries, and that is being done.' Again the brilliant smile. 'But it is time consuming; if they used small boats there would be no itineraries, and even if there were there would still be no guarantees. However, we are of course very patient.'

'Names are easy,' I said. 'The man was Larry Galleywood, the woman Melanie Wigg. Galleywood was an estate agent, so he knew houses.'

'That is helpful,' Kostopoulos said. He was sitting back, nodding, not bothering with notes, and I guessed that he had a micro-recorder silently spinning its reels somewhere out of sight.

'So, you now have names,' Sharkey said, 'but can you tell us how they worked it?'

The little warrant officer looked puzzled. 'Worked it?'

'How did they manage to sell houses that were not up for sale?'

'Ah. But, you know, there is always a way.'

'Of course,' I said, 'and one possibility we'd looked at is that they searched for vacant property – the owners away on holiday, or on business – then broke in and, well, sold the property using a crooked lawyer and forged documents.'

'But why break in?' Kostopoulos said. 'Many of those vacant properties would be for rent. We believe that this man you say is called Galleywood actually paid rent for those properties in a perfectly legal way. By so doing, he and the woman would appear to be the genuine owners when potential buyers came to view. But you must understand,' he said, 'that this is only what we believe. We have no proof, and until we have that proof we can do nothing to bring this man to justice.'

'Then you don't know,' Sharkey said, 'that Galleywood is dead?'

Kostopoulos's eyes widened. 'Αλήθεια; Αλλά αυτό είναι τρομερό,' he said under his breath, then quickly switched back to English. 'Really? But that is terrible. And, no, of course we did not know, because until a few minutes ago we did not know his name. We were already facing difficulties because we knew these crimes were committed by foreign nationals who had returned to their home country. It is perhaps true that we were biding our time in the hope that they would come back to continue their illegal operations, confident that they remained undetected.' He shook his head, expressing sadness. 'But if the man is dead then our investigation is at an end.' Then he thought for a moment, and suddenly brightened. 'But of course,' he said, 'there is still the woman. We have her name, and we know that she was as much involved as the man Galleywood.'

'True,' I said, 'and she's alive and well and living in Galleywood's house. Sadly, as far as we know the money is missing. All of it. Something like three million Euros.'

Kostopoulos pursed his lips. 'It was cash, of course. Are you perhaps surprised that this business was conducted in such a way?'

'No,' Sharkey said. 'It couldn't be done any *other* way. The transactions had to be speedy and that ruled out mortgages.' He paused. 'But the cash *was* banked. It seems it simply disappeared.'

Kostopoulos shrugged. 'Of course, and that is a problem for the bank. We knew there were large sums of money involved, but *our* main concern was and is with apprehending the criminals. One thing first, then the other follows – you understand?'

I nodded. 'We believe Galleywood and Wigg were small fish; they weren't the brains behind the property scam. But Galleywood got big ideas—'

'He wanted to be the big fish.'

'Yes. He decided he wanted all the money for himself.'

'And this is why he died? He was murdered for his stupidity?'

'We're not sure. However, his son's a different matter. He was tortured, then left to die, and we know the son was looking into offshore banking. That suggests the money had been moved, or was going to be moved, and the scam boss – the real big fish – was desperately trying to find it.' I paused. 'That's one of the reasons we're here in Rhodes: we are trying to locate the money before he gets to it, or at least find out what happened to it – trace the route it's taken, if you like. If we're going to have any chance of doing that and perhaps eventually locating it, where should we start?'

'Find the bank,' Kostopoulos said.

'Sure,' Josh said, 'but that's easier said than done. If I know banks, they're unlikely to divulge confidential information. Also, we have no account number, and if Galleywood was banking under an assumed name ...'

Kostopoulos was nodding thoughtfully.

'You say three million Euros. And you think the money has been moved. So, you must contact all the banks and ask a question that requires a simple yes or no answer.'

Sharkey was grinning and nodding. 'Has a sum of that size been moved to an offshore account, or simply disappeared, in' – he glanced at me – 'what, the past four or five weeks?'

'I'd say so; the end of the holiday season.'

'And for us to ask even that simple question and expect an answer,' Sharkey said to Kostopoulos, 'you'd put your weight behind us? Give us your written authority – perhaps signed by the commissioner?'

'Most assuredly I will back your efforts,' Kostopoulos said, 'and my own signature will be more than enough.'

I sat back and watched the efficient little police officer's chest swell with pride as he reached across his desk for pen and paper and began to write.

chapter nineteen

'Try Cayman Islands.'

Sharkey grunted. He was bent over the ornate, highly polished occasional table. The hotel had wireless internet facilities. Sharkey's laptop was open and he was logged on to Google. I was standing looking over his shoulder. The Vosporous suite's silken curtains were closed, the room's lights were low, and in the pale gleam of the laptop's screen his face was bleached of colour.

'Lots there,' he said. 'Sixty-nine million hits. Where do we start?'

'Try that one. *Cayman Islands information: business, taxation and offshore.*'

'Um. Looks good, but don't get too excited.'

He was smiling. My hand was gripping his shoulder. He clicked on the blue print and the fast connection moved to the chosen page which had more headings, each with one or more blue hyperlinks beneath them. *Cayman Islands Offshore Business Sector* caught my eye. I craned forward to look at its various links.

'*Cayman Islands banking,* I said, but Sharkey was ahead of me, his finger already moving on the laptop's synaptics pointing device. Again the screen changed, and for a few moments we read in silence.

'The only interesting bit,' Sharkey said presently, 'is the additional due diligence procedures which in 2000 required banks to comply with fresh know-your-customer regulations. Sounds like an erosion of confidentiality.'

'Maybe, but look at all those banks, three hundred and forty of them in such a relatively small area. Try another link. Let's have a look at some of them.'

He clicked a couple of times and got the bank section of the Cayman Islands business directory. I saw the familiar and the unfamiliar, the Bank of New York close to Bank Vontobel Cayman; HSBC Financial Services and Midland Bank Trust Corporation then something called the Multi Banking Corporation; and the Wing Hang Bank which had Cayman after it in brackets but definitely had the ring of the Far East.

'Goodness me,' I said, amazed. 'How on earth can they be regulated?'

'With difficulty, but to keep that licence they'd all have to comply with the new procedures. Look further down: new and long-standing account holders must provide proof of identity and physical address, as well as an explanation of their banking activities.'

'That rule may apply only to businesses setting up banking facilities in the islands. If it also applies to individuals, well, I can't see Galleywood being very happy, or willing to comply.' I straightened, eased my back. 'Go back to the main page, look at the headings again.'

He clicked on the back arrow, the page changed, I ran my eye down the headings – but not very far.

'Down two headings. Then the link to *Cayman Islands Law of Offshore.*'

'Where would I be without you?' he murmured, and I whacked him hard on the shoulder. He chuckled, his fingers busy on the laptop.

'Mm,' I murmured, reading quickly. 'I've always wanted to know stuff like this.'

The link stated that banking confidentiality was well-established in Cayman through the common law, and enshrined both in the Banks and Trust Companies Law 1995 and in the Confidential Relationships (Preservation) Law of the same year. Banking staff and government officials faced civil and criminal sanctions if information was disclosed without authorization. A number of laws permitted the enforcement of foreign judgments or the disclosure of information in response to a court order, but normally in the context of criminal activity and drug use or dealing.

'Galleywood's activity was certainly criminal,' I said, 'but if he has put the money offshore, would the losers here be able to push hard enough to get it back from somewhere like the Caymans?'

'The losers being the ordinary people ripped off when they thought they were buying a house in the sun?'

'Well, yes. I mean, we know it was taken from a bank and they've got the clout that would get them court orders or whatever, but it wasn't the bank's money, was it?'

'No, but they might be able to use that clout to help individuals.'

'I don't know. And if they decide they're not going to do that, look at the next bit,' I said, pointing. 'Despite mutual assistance treaties, the Cayman Islands will not normally co-operate with fiscal investigations, and does not normally respond to requests for assistance on fiscal matters.'

'That's like allowing a criminal to put his big pot of gold at the end of his very own rainbow and know it can't be touched,' Sharkey said, 'which won't please the British couples who've lost a lot of cash. Also, powerful lawyers are already arguing against those new due diligence procedures,' he said, reading on. 'According to Michael Alberga, "Privacy is the key to democracy; why should people be asked to provide more information about themselves?" He's saying that people like Galleywood should be allowed to deposit their money, no questions asked.'

'Well, we've both admitted that it's all very interesting,' I said, 'but we're not criminals, we're not into money laundering, so where does all that information actually get us? How does it help us to find the money Galleywood nicked?'

'It doesn't,' Sharkey said, 'because even the bank here on Rhodes seems to be admitting that cash has gone for good.'

He logged off, switched off and closed the laptop. I settled back on to the cushioned sofa bed and watched him pour red wine into crystal glasses from the beautiful decanter brought to the suite by room service. He handed me my drink, sat down opposite me on a chair that looked like a prop from a movie about the Arabian

Nights, and for the next ten minutes or so we sat in silence while
we sipped and pondered.

After leaving police HQ carrying Kostas Kostopoulos's letter it
had taken us the rest of the morning and almost up to the Greek
banks' closing time of 2 p.m. before we tracked down the missing
cash – sorry, tracked down the bank from where the cash had
gone missing. The search came up with the usual perverse
ending: dusty and bedraggled after hours of trudging the streets,
we found what we were looking for only a few yards from where
we set out.

Rhodes National Bank is in Museum Square which is about as
far away from the Nikos Takis Hotel as I could throw a very heavy
stone. We stumbled into the cool interior at one o'clock, stated
our business, and were greeted with open arms and wide-eyed
optimism by a lean man in a grey suit who quickly began registering disappointment. The poor manager thought we'd found
what he was looking for. Our story resulted in dejection all round,
although we did make some progress.

A large sum of money had indeed disappeared. Yes, he thought
it might be as much as several million Euros; no, he couldn't
possibly give us names or account numbers. But what he did tell
DI Sharkey, practically incandescent with hope when he believed
he was facing a British detective, was that the money had not
been legitimately transferred, it had been surgically removed by a
clever computer hacker. The money did not belong to the bank,
but they were responsible for the loss and their reputation was at
stake. If we could help in any way …

So now we were looking. Not for the money, because without
a depositor's name and an account number it would be like
searching for a needle we wouldn't recognize in a haystack we
couldn't find. The best we could do was look at the possibilities.

Josh had once written a crime book about money laundering,
and when doing his research had discovered that the Cayman
Islands was the place to wash all those dirty notes. Isn't that what
they do? Be a lot easier. Actually it's all done through layers
created by moving monies in and out of offshore bank accounts
of bearer share shell companies using electronic funds' transfer.
Given that there isn't enough information disclosed on any single

wire transfer to know how clean or dirty the money is, the sheer volume of daily transactions and the high degree of anonymity available, the chances of transactions being traced is insignificant. The final stage is integration, which is accomplished by the launderer making it appear all that cash had been legally earned. One way of doing it is to establish anonymous companies in countries where the right to secrecy is guaranteed. By this stage it's very difficult to distinguish legal and illegal wealth.

So where did that put Galleywood's stolen millions? I had to admit that at that point I was getting bogged down in technicalities, floundering in misunderstanding and incomprehension. I mean, did Galleywood need to launder his money? And what were the possibilities now, with Galleywood dead? Was the money stuck in limbo, destined to sit there clocking up interest until some greedy government decided to seize the cash from dormant accounts? Like, well, you know who ...

Sharkey was watching me with some amusement, because my face must have reflected my inner excitement. I'm sure you've had a similar experience: even peripheral involvement in an esoteric activity – especially one that's a teeny bit illegal and awash with cash – can create a buzz that draws you ever deeper and is very hard to resist.

I looked at him over my wine glass. He cocked an eyebrow, waiting for a profound revelation. What he got was a problem brought out into the open that had been puzzling me since we left the bank.

'If that money was taken by a hacker,' I said, 'then the finger's back pointing at Andy Galleywood. But if he *took* it, he must have known where he *put* it.'

'And, under intense duress, would have told the baddies.' Sharkey nodded. 'But what if, without his knowledge, where he put it wasn't its final destination?'

'Mm. So Andy told the baddies what he knew, they went looking, and it wasn't there.'

'Because,' Sharkey said, 'Larry Galleywood had moved it.'

'Right. According to Kirsty, his fiancée, Andy had been spending a lot of time looking into offshore banking. He must have found the details he was looking for, and told his dad. His dad moved the money – much easier than computer hacking, because he would do it by EFT.'

Sharkey nodded. 'Electronic funds' transfer, of which there are more than half a million a day worldwide.'

'Show-off. Josh found all that out a couple of years ago. That's what I've been thinking about – although it's not much help. Anyway,' I went on, 'almost certainly unbeknown to Andy, his dad had decided to ditch all helpers, including his son; he wanted all that money for himself.'

'Which means that details of the money's final destination may have died with him.'

'No.' I shook my head. 'Think about Larry Galleywood. He was an estate agent with a modern office, but his staff would have worked the computers. Larry was a stamp collector, which suggests there'd be a little bit of stuffiness in there, a great deal of the old-fashioned.'

'So he'd write things down?'

'Oh yes. Somewhere,' I said, 'Larry Galleywood has written down the details of where he put that money, and the account number. He had to, because he couldn't afford to lose a cool three million Euros because of absent-mindedness. No, he needed to have a reminder of where he'd put it—'

'And a reminder of where he'd put the reminder?'

I smiled. 'No, that's what I'd need – and I'd probably lose that. Galleywood would want to keep the location of his notes a big secret, so he definitely wouldn't write that down. But now we've got to find those notes, and I know, I just *know* we can if we try really hard.'

Sharkey was nodding his agreement and, as he did so, I felt the first faint stirrings of excitement. We're getting somewhere, I thought: this trip has been a success.

'There's something else,' I said, trying hard to keep my voice steady. 'If Galleywood was a compulsive jotter, then he'll have *everything* down – and that includes the name of the man he was working for. All we've got to do is find his diary or notebook or the scruffy bits of paper he used to write down all this information. When we do that, we'll have the man behind the murder of Andy Galleywood.'

★

'Well, we got what we came for,' Sharkey said. 'We know there was a property scam worked by a man and a woman, we know the money they made got to the bank and was then spirited away. Of course it's always possible it was someone else, not Galleywood and Wigg, and if you think we should stay on to dig deeper—'

'Oh, it's them all right. A strong suspicion has turned into absolute certainty. One day's work has given us all we need, so tomorrow it's the earliest of early flights out.'

'Best way. Early flight means no vacating room at midday and waiting around for hours in the hotel lounge.'

'Right, and I'm pretty sure you're about to wipe the cold sweat of anxiety from your brow and breathe a sigh of relief. You paid for this trip on line, so that means a card of some kind. I don't think you can afford it. You're dealing with a private investigator of above average intelligence, Sharkey, so don't expect to fool me. You're in trouble, and there'll never be a better time or place to bare your soul.'

It was a cool, moonlit evening and we were eating at a table in Plaka, a terraced restaurant set above the gift shops lining Hippocrates Square in the heart of Rhodes old town. Just a short walk from the Nikos Takis. Sharkey had chosen stuffed vine leaves followed by moussaka, and was drinking Amstel from a frosted glass. I'd settled for swordfish in a cheese and mustard sauce, with a side salad that came with garlic bread and dips. And red wine, of course. I'd chosen a local vintage with a rich dark label. Deliciously fruity and strong enough, I fear, for a couple of glasses to send me sidestepping on to the floor to perform a dizzy Zorba's dance with my arms across the shoulders of the grinning waiters.

Nurse it, I thought grimly; one glass, and nurse it.

Sharkey was smiling crookedly and toying with his glass of beer.

'Yes,' he said, 'it was a credit card. The latest bill is somewhere, I haven't seen it but I'm pretty sure the card's maxed out.'

'Why didn't you say something? You know I've got a computer.

So's Josh. We'd have done everything from our end if you'd spoken up.'

'But not as efficiently.' He watched me roll my eyes at his sexist impudence, then shrugged his shoulders. 'Doesn't matter, Pen. Taking credit cards to the limit is what nobody's supposed to do but everybody ends up doing when they're about to go bankrupt.'

I frowned, running the tip of a finger moistened with wine around the rim of my glass as if hoping to summon forth a happy tune.

'When's that going to happen?'

'I could download a debtor's petition form from the Insolvency Service website when we get home. Take it along to the county court. Pay the fee.'

'How much?'

'I think it's a hundred and fifty quid. Plus a deposit of three hundred and forty-five for the official receiver's work.'

'Well, if you haven't got it—' I broke off and shook my head in amazement. 'God, will you listen to me, Sharkey? I'm about to offer my help so you can go bankrupt. Isn't there some other way? I mean, how much do you owe?'

Again the shrug. 'The penthouse has gone. I'm living in an airless box of a room above the bar at JOKERS WILD with alcohol fumes rising through the bare boards and doing a lot of late-night passive drinking – but with my phone disconnected and me making lame excuses, you'd already more or less twigged that, hadn't you?' he said, his smile now rueful.

'Mm, and that's why you haven't seen your latest phone bill. You're not bothering with the mail that's piling up behind the door at the Albert Dock.' They were statements not questions, made from bitter experience because my own son Adam had done exactly the same when he'd had a spell of money trouble. 'So was Josh right to be doubtful about your profession? That story about being a professional gambler was all—?'

'Bull?' He looked seriously offended, and I couldn't help smiling. 'Absolutely not. I've been told by those with experience and money that I'm one of them, a born gambler, and for ten years I made a bloody good living from it – the penthouse didn't come from nowhere. But then' – he shook his head, and his face now registered something like bewilderment – 'for some reason it all began to go pear-shaped. I lost my touch; worse, I lost my enthusiasm.' He looked at me. 'High one day, rock bottom for the next two – you caught me on one of those down days, when you saw me for the first time in JOKERS, me looking like a tramp and, I can assure you, feeling a hell of a sight worse inside.'

'And you don't know why?'

He pushed his almost empty plate away.

'When I think about it, when I allow myself to admit it, yes, Penny, I do. And you do, too, if you think about it. If you remember what was going on at the time you first saw me; the crimes committed by a certain Terry Lynch.'

'Dammit, yes,' I said softly. 'That bastard was your brother-in-law. He murdered your sister, Ffion. Sharkey I'm so sorry, I can't believe I didn't put two and two together.'

'*A private investigator of above average intelligence,*' he said, mockingly echoing my words, yet I knew no criticism was intended. 'You were talking about yourself, and with your tongue firmly in your cheek; but, you know, that was the way I was beginning to see myself in every respect, as a *person*: unbeatable in everything I attempted, untouchable in every way. Then, suddenly, forces beyond my control are trying to drive home the message that I can't possibly live up to that description—'

'Unless you climb off that cold, hard floor and get back on your feet – which might be like something else I've said many times: *easier said than done.*'

'You didn't let me finish,' Sharkey said. He looked at his glass of Amstel, reached for it and tossed back the last of his now luke-warm beer. When he put the empty glass down and met my deliberately neutral gaze the bewilderment I'd seen his eyes had been wiped away to be replaced by smouldering ... anger? Determination?

'What I was going to say when you interrupted was that the message those forces are sending has been misdirected. If they think I'm going to buckle, they've got the wrong man. What my father used to say—'

'Back in Wales,' I said softly, risking a second interruption, watching his appreciative nod.

'—was that a man is most clearly defined by the manner in which he meets trouble. Meekly rolling over is never an option, my dad said, but he also told me that it doesn't always pay to meet trouble head on; head on, he said, can too often see you smacking your head against a brick wall.'

'If I put it to Josh he'd probably say that a strong man would drive his way through that wall.'

'Not my way.' Sharkey grinned. 'More subtle, you see – or should that be cunning? Whatever. All I know is the best thing that's happened to me in a long time was getting to know a certain mature lady called Penny Lane, and what we're going to do together is order a couple of strong liqueur coffees, toddle off to the Vosporous Suite and get a good night's sleep—'

This time he was interrupted by the merry but very short burble of my mobile. It signalled an incoming text.

Darling Penny
You'll be interested to hear that Gay Tirril confronted Melanie Wigg in Galleywood's gloomy Victorian residence, and ended up very dead. It's a long story, with intriguing developments. Hurry home and join in the fun.
Love, Josh.

chapter twenty

Saturday

I was dropped off at home in Heswall just before midday. Sharkey didn't linger but backed his Lexus straight out of the drive and headed for Liverpool to begin putting some order back into his life. My good wishes went with him. I managed to lean through the open window and get him in a headlock so that I could kiss him on the cheek before he left, told him in my softest, most motherly, tones to call us that night, without fail, then released him. I'll swear the old softy's eyes were moist. I know mine were, and I was still swallowing the lump in my throat when Josh swept me into his arms.

'Urrgh,' I groaned, as he lifted me bodily over the threshold and kicked the door shut. 'At this rate I'll be running out of places to bruise. And, come on, feller, what's all this lovey-dovey stuff a prelude to?' I said, as he planted me on my feet and held me at arm's length to gaze lingeringly into my eyes.

'I'm drinking in your warmth and beauty while I've got the chance. You'll have so much to do when you've heard all the news I'll feel like a single man.'

Still holding me, he looked at me even more intently. 'Have you eaten?'

'On the plane, yes. Rubber sausage and something pale yellow that looked like scrambled egg. Washed down with lukewarm … I don't know, muddy waters?'

'Wasn't he a great guitarist and blues singer?' He grinned and glanced at his watch. 'Midday's been and gone. Right, so you go and get changed' – he wrinkled his nose – 'make that *shower* and get changed, I'll fix lunch and we'll talk while we eat.'

'It's that serious? That urgent?'

'Oh, yes,' he said, 'it's both of those all right.'

'I said in my text that Gay Tirril died confronting Melanie Wigg,' Josh said. 'What I left *un*said was that Gay was packing a pistol, and Melanie stabbed her to death. She's pleading self-defence, of course. She used a knife that apparently came from Galleywood's desk.'

'Gosh, I remember seeing that weapon – though at the time I didn't think of it as such. Looked antique, but it was probably bought in what we used to call a junk shop.'

'Well, the study's been a crime scene since Monday night, so she must have sneaked it out when you and the police weren't looking.'

'I wonder why? I suppose she must have been expecting trouble, and it came, didn't it, in the shape of Gay Tirril? Where did the argument take place?'

'In the kitchen. Gay was lying in a pool of blood up against the red Aga. We won't know what was going on or what the confrontation was about until you talk to Wigg, or Dancer. Even Dancer might not know, because I'm sure Wigg will be lying. But things are moving very fast. And if you're wondering how I know as much as I do, it's because Dancer was on the phone asking for you a few minutes before you got home.'

'That was nice of him. Did he talk to you instead?'

'Oh yes.'

He paused to reach for his coffee. Drank slowly, his eyes twinkling at me. He'd fixed sandwiches for lunch – brown bread, butter, thin slices of cucumber with vinegar and pepper – and set it up in the conservatory. Needless to say it was raining again, and we'd sat in silence while we ate and let the patter of rain on the glass work its soothing magic. But now we were finished. And I was waiting.

'Well, go on then,' I said. 'What did Dancer tell you?'

'The gun that Gay was brandishing was the gun that fired the shot that killed Larry Galleywood.'

I couldn't help an unladylike gape. 'Bloody hell. So does Dancer believe Gay murdered Galleywood? Has she been charged?'

'Er, no, because Gay Tirril is currently rather dead.'

'Damn, I forgot that.' I felt the heat in my cheeks, knew I was blushing. 'OK,' I said, quickly moving on, 'the police used ballistics to match the bullets that killed Galleywood and Gay, which is standard procedure and just about foolproof – but I imagine tracing the gun's owner might prove more difficult.'

'Nope, that's been done.'

'Really? So whose is it?'

'Malcolm Moneydie's.'

'Her *doctor's*? How the hell did they find that out?'

'The pistol is a Webley .38 Mk IV, standard British Army issue up to 1956. Dancer knows Moneydie was Tirril's GP, and knows he was an army officer.'

'And so he was questioned by the police. What did he have to say?'

'He rather shamefacedly admitted owning the pistol. Said it was no longer issued when he was an officer, but he acquired it as a trophy and sort of sneaked it out when he left the army. However, he was keen to stress that it went missing some weeks ago.'

'Where did he keep it?'

'In his surgery. One of the drawers in his desk.'

'To subdue violent patients,' I said, smiling at the thought. 'Well, he would say it had gone missing, wouldn't he, because if he still had it – hang on, when did all this happen, Wigg shooting Gay Tirril?'

'Last night. You've only been away a day.'

'Well, what I was going to say was that if Moneydie still had it, he could have murdered Galleywood. Unfortunately, about all we know for sure is that *Gay Tirril* had Moneydie's pistol last night, and she took it with her to confront Melanie Wigg. And died for her trouble.'

'We also know something of Gay's movements yesterday. For instance, we know she had an appointment to see Moneydie at his surgery yesterday morning.'

I frowned. 'Dancer's been unusually forthcoming, for a police officer.'

'Perhaps, for a police officer, he's unusually desperate.'

'Mm. You could be right. All hands to the pump. Anyway, back to Gay: she must have gone to see Moneydie about her infected eyes again.' I narrowed my eyes, now thinking hard. Then I pulled a face. 'What if the eye infection was an excuse, and Gay actually went to the surgery to steal the pistol?' I said doubtfully.

'It was stolen weeks ago, if we believe Moneydie.'

'If. What if he's lying? What if it was still there gathering dust in his drawer?'

'Then, yes, he would be in the frame for the Galleywood murder.' He nodded slowly. 'He certainly had a motive. Remember, Galleywood bought that coin from under his nose?'

'Indeed he did,' I said. 'And I did get the impression Moneydie was a weird sort of fish when I went to see him.'

'Unfortunately, most killers look perfectly normal.'

'Yes, but being an odd bod doesn't rule him out.' I frowned. 'So where are the police up to on this? With Gay dead, surely they'll have to take Moneydie's word for when the gun went missing?'

'Maybe Dancer's waiting for you to come up with something,' Josh said softly.

'I wish.'

'I'm not kidding. Dancer is a man who uses every tool at his disposal. He's hard, but he won't let pride get in the way of a result. All hands to the pump, as you so colourfully put it. He was quite happy for me to help out. Unfortunately, I failed miserably. So now it's over to you. Have you got any ideas?'

'Vince Keevil,' I said. 'He may know something, because no two people at the writers' club were closer than those two, Vince and Gay.'

'So … what are you suggesting? You think she told Keevil her plans?'

'Be nice if she had. She had Moneydie's pistol. To steal it – if that's what she did – she must have known he had one. You say he kept it in his surgery, in a desk drawer. Supposing Gay sneaked a look at some time when he was out of the room – you know, simply nosing around?'

'As women do?'

'Well, ignoring that remark, I'll admit it's hardly likely.'

'On the contrary. If we rule out Moneydie himself *telling* her he'd got a gun, or giving it to her because the two of them were in this together and he's the scam boss and he murdered Galleywood and Gay went after Wigg to find the money—'

'Oh, please, Josh, don't make it even more complicated.'

He grinned. 'There's yet another alternative. The gun did go missing weeks ago, Gay Tirril stole it, and she shot Galleywood.'

'Mm. Gay Tirril and a locked room mystery. Or Moneydie for that matter. It all begins to look very iffy.'

The grin was still lurking. 'Well, one way of finding out if you're anywhere near the right track with any of those options is to do as you suggested: go and see Keevil.'

'Yes, and I will. As soon as possible. But before that I'm going to talk to Dancer, thank him for the news, tell him mine – which isn't much.'

I heard Josh putting the dishes in the sink as I went through to my office. He had a blank afternoon so I guessed that very soon he'd go into his office and pick up his electric guitar – I think it's something called a Telecaster. I know it's heavy. He's drifted from blues to jazz, and is studying different scales – modes I think they're called – with names like Ionian, Dorian, Myxolydian. He discusses them with me, which is a sheer waste of time seeing as I have difficulty remembering what comes after Doh, Re, Me. I suppose you could say that's as f-a-h as I go, but that would be an outrageous pun, wouldn't it? Not that I'm miles out, because Josh did tell me once that those scales really are linked to the old Doh, Re, Me ... for instance, Doh is the Ionian and a major scale, Re's the Dorian, and so on.

Sure enough, I'd barely checked for e-mails and phone messages – none of either – when the soft rippling tinkle of what I recognized as an Am7 arpeggio (see, something must be sinking in) drifted along the hall, and I was still smiling when DI Billy Dancer answered the phone.

'Thanks for keeping us up to date,' I said when the niceties were over. 'You gave Josh a lot.'

'Ulterior motive,' he said, 'most definitely not done for your benefit.' Then he paused. 'Christ, where are you, Penny Lane, halfway to Heaven?'

I chuckled. 'That's Josh playing cool jazz on the guitar.'

'Yeah, well, like I said, I was giving information to the renowned crime writer in the hope of *quid pro quo*. Got something off him, though not as much as I'd've liked.'

'Which I'm about to put right, in a pathetically limited way.'

'Oh yeah, so how *did* it go in the islands?'

'Not much more than confirmation of what I'd already guessed – sort of – and nothing to help you find two murderers. There *was* a property scam ripping off Brits, a man and woman *were* involved, the money *has* gone missing – moved by a ghostly hacker.'

'Hold on a sec,' Dancer said. 'That last bit's interesting.'

'Which bit? Missing, or hacker?'

'If you think about it, the money going missing might create problems for the man behind this scam. If he's already rich, no worries. If he's not, well, he needs cash fast, doesn't he? Because if we've got this right, he's been hiring blokes to do his dirty work – pretty nasty stuff, and that requires characters you wouldn't like to meet on a dark street. Blokes like that, they work strictly for cash, and if they don't get paid they're not going to hang about waiting.'

'Yes, you're right. Joey Lox made that point when we talked to him.'

'So the big boy needs that missing money. How's he going to get to it.'

'With great difficulty. Greek bankers couldn't or wouldn't give us names or account numbers. And as for the perps on the scene out there in the Greek Islands, well, it could have been almost any man and woman, couldn't it? Still, it was a day out in Rhodes, the sun helped the bruises to fade—'

'What bruises?'

'Oops. I didn't tell you, did I? I was attacked on Thursday evening, in Liverpool, held captive, warned off. Told to stop looking for killers and missing cash.'

'Jesus,' Dancer said, 'you call that *quid pro quo*? You've been withholding information – again. If you'd rung in and we'd got there fast we could have—'

'Hang on—'

'No, you listen—'

'I mean it, Billy. I've thought of something.'

He went silent. So did I. I could feel my heart thumping. My mouth was dry. I moved my lips. Nothing came out.

'Penny?'

I breathed in hard, said, 'Yes, I'm here. And I think I know who attacked me.'

'OK. I'm listening.'

'He had a … mannerism. At least, there was something about him that off and on has been driving me crazy. Anyway, I went to see somebody the other day. Before the attack. When I was there, he, this man, got angry. He stood up, and he banged his hands violently on the desk.'

I stopped. I could feel my jaw trembling. I put my clenched fist under my chin, pressed upwards, forced my teeth together.

'Take your time,' Dancer said softly. 'We'll fix it, no problem.'

'When I was … strapped to a chair in a filthy house in Liverpool,' I said, 'the man holding me did something very similar: he came towards me and, in a fit of rage, he slammed his hands very hard on the chair. On the arms.'

'OK, so who do you think it was?' Dancer said. 'Give me his name, Penny.'

I closed my eyes. 'When it was done the first time, I was in a newspaper office. I think the man who held me in that room, threatened and beat me, was Barnaby Rieff.'

'They're going to talk to him now,' I said. 'Dancer wanted to know what time I was held, exactly, so that they can ask Rieff his movements. They can ask all they like. I'm right, I know it, and that part of it's over.'

'That part,' Josh said. 'You mean you've got the murderer. What other part is there?'

'The money. The killer can't find it, can he? That's why he's killing. So after I gave Dancer the name I told him that Sharkey and I worked out in Rhodes that Galleywood will have written the information somewhere. Account number, location. He *must* have done. I think the most likely place to look for it is his office, but that's still a crime scene. Dancer's agreed to meet me there.'

'When?'

'Six o'clock.'

'And Keevil?'

'I haven't got his number, don't know where he lives.'

'But Steve does?'

'You're quick. Yes, I've thought of that. I'm going to phone him.'

'When you've recovered.'

I smiled weakly. When I'd finished talking to Dancer I'd wobbled my way into Josh's office with two glasses of the Macallan. He'd put down the Telecaster and hugged me, rubbing my back, his comforting whispers so warm and close to my ear I almost melted.

Then I'd told him about Rieff and we'd sat down, Josh in his swivel chair, me in the old Ercol easy chair he uses for thinking. Sipped the whisky. Thought of it as part medicinal, part interim celebration. Because I knew it wasn't finished. Knew I could be wrong about Rieff – but really knew I was absolutely right about Rieff.

I shivered.

Josh said, 'There you go again. Last time you shivered you were in the presence of two mature studs.'

'This time it's relief. I think.'

He smiled. 'Ring Steve, Pen. It's Saturday. He'll be at home with Sheila, and you're on a roll.'

'Mm. You realize the way it's developing means the murders were unconnected? Andy and Larry, father and son, murdered for different reasons? And by different killers.'

'But stone dead nonetheless,' he said, as he handed me the phone and picked up the extension.

Like a lot of people, Josh and I don't bother storing familiar numbers in a phone's memory. The Easters' was one I knew well. I dialled, got Sheila, chatted warmly for a minute or two then asked her if I could talk to Steve.

'Two things, Steve,' I said when he picked up. 'Well, three actually. The first is Vince Keevil's phone number or his address. Have you got either?'

'Both. Hang on.'

The phone clonked as he put it down. Seconds later he came back with the information.

'That's great. I'm going to talk to him about Gay, see if he knows what was going on. You heard what happened?'

'I did. You were away, of course, enjoying the sun – or not. How did it go? Productive?'

'Well, if you're still doing research for that exposé article, you've probably got as much as me. Man and woman selling Greek-Island property they didn't own, money deposited, money moved by persons unknown to destination unknown. The authorities were helpful but, because of client confidentiality and bank rules and so on, they could give me very little.'

'Well, in a negative sort of way you've saved me a trip. It hasn't helped us, has it, and that's tough for you and for me?' He paused. 'So what else, Penny? You said there were three things.'

'Well, this next one might be very interesting. Sharkey and I came to the conclusion that if Galleywood moved the money, or had it moved, he must have written the information down. Couldn't risk forgetting it, could he? So tonight DI Dancer's going with me to Galleywood's study. It's still a crime scene, but he's going to let me in and together we'll tear the place apart looking for Galleywood's notes.'

'Think you'll find anything?'

'Convinced. He's written it somewhere, in plain English or in some kind of personal code – but wherever and whatever it is, we'll find it. And,' I went on, as I remembered what I'd discussed with Sharkey, 'it's also likely that somewhere he'll have written down the name of his employer – the man who arranged Andy's murder. If he has, we'll find that too – of which a lot more in a moment.'

Steve was quiet for a while after that, and I knew he was digesting what I'd told him and looking at it in the context of his exposé; perhaps looking at names he'd pencilled in for Andy's killer and wondering if the one I was certain I'd find in Galleywood's study would match any of them.

Perhaps he had none, I thought with a delicious tingle of excitement, in which case he was in for a surprise.

177

'Well,' he said at last, 'I wish you a lot of luck in your search, and the code-breaking, if it's needed. What's number three on your list?'

'You'll love this one, Steve, though I'm not so sure about your editor. While I was talking to Dancer about tonight suddenly, out of the blue, it came to me that I knew the man who attacked me. that means I already *know* who murdered Andy – or had him murdered – so finding a name tonight will be like dotting the tees, crossing the eyes. I think that's what they say.'

I looked across at Josh. He was clinging to the extension and shaking his head in mock despair.

On the telephone line there was a moment of stunned silence. I could hear Steve's breathing quicken, and there was a rustle and a rattle and I knew he was reaching for pen and paper.

'Brilliant, Pen, go ahead.'

'There was something about the man who attacked me, something I half recognized. I won't go into details, but when I was talking to Dancer there was an almighty click—'

'A flash of inspiration.'

'That's right, and in that brilliant flash of light it dawned on me that the man who'd been screaming at me, wetting me with his spittle, *punching* me in the face, was your editor, Barnaby Rieff.'

There was a long, breathless silence. I thought I could hear Steve scribbling with the pen. Then something went down with a clatter.

'Oh shit,' Steve said. 'Methinks I'm going to need some powerful backup.'

'*You* are? Why's that?'

'Remember I said I was going to talk to Rieff about the car-park's third man? Well, I'm seeing him tonight.'

My heart leaped. 'Cancel. Or don't even bother to turn up because you could be wasting your time. The police are on their way to talk to him. I'm sure that by tonight he'll be behind bars.'

'You don't know Rieff. He's the police's blue-eyed boy. And he's as slippery as an eel. I think he'll talk his way out of trouble. If he does, he'll keep the appointment with me, and I'll be there. Talking to a cold-blooded killer.'

I looked across at my blue-eyed hunk, sitting on the corner of the desk with the extension to his ear, saw him nod.

'If you need powerful backup, take Josh, Steve.'

He hesitated. 'I don't know; there could be rough stuff and he's getting on a bit—'

'Yes, you do know, and, no, I most emphatically am not,' Josh said firmly, and I heard Steve draw in a quick, shocked breath. 'Yes, I've been listening, I know what this is about, and I'll be there. Just give me time and place.'

'Aren't you going with Penny and Dancer? Hunting for stolen loot?'

'Haven't been asked' – he winked at me – 'so, come on, what about it?'

'I'm grateful, Josh. There's nobody I'd rather have with me.'

'Where and when?'

'Reiff's office, seven o'clock. Old Hall Street, Liverpool. We could meet in the car-park.' He paused again. Then he said, with what I thought was apprehension and the beginnings of serious doubt, 'You'd better come prepared for trouble.'

Like the murder investigations I'd found myself sucked into at the beginning of the week, Saturday was coming to its dark and dismal conclusion. November's not my favourite month, and this year it had demonstrated why. Most days had brought some rain, the past few had brought enough to soak the garden and begin filling Josh's pond (and dampen Joey Lox's cold, sad body), and when I had a hot shower before heading for Vince Keevil's house I made sure I checked my skin for mildew.

OK, so it was my second shower of the day and maybe I wasn't drying myself properly and mildew in hot crevices comes from damp but, joking aside (and, yes, I know it's called athlete's foot), the truth was I was beginning to feel dirty and it had nothing to do with the muckiness resulting from good honest toil. It began when Barnaby Rieff dragged me into the boarded-up house in Kensington and, although I'd kept it to myself, not the luxury of the Vosporous Suite nor the warm Greek sunshine and good salt air could rid me of that soiled feeling.

While I showered, Josh had been out in the rain setting light to some rubbish in the incinerator he's made from an old bin. He'd gone straight from garden to bathroom to gird his loins or whatever it is macho men do before marching into battle – though for reasons already stated I doubted if he and Steve would find an opponent. I'd donned my usual villain-hunting garb of sweater, skirt, sensible shoes (as Mum would say), and my lovely red gilet. My sack of a tote bag was slung over my shoulder, with the trusty Fuji camera in there for photographing secret documents.

.I set off in my little Ka with real optimism: I was convinced I would soon locate the missing cash, and I was on my way to talk to people who just might lead me to Galleywood's killer. Enough, I thought, as I drove merrily on absently humming one of Josh's jazz ditties, to make a girl's heart leap with the joys of spring. Which sounds a bit odd, but … well, you know what I'm trying to say.

Vince Keevil lives in a cottage on the outskirts of Thornton Hough, a village a mile or so inland from the River Dee – almost in the centre of the Wirral peninsula. I parked under dripping sycamores that had shed most of their leaves, tramped carefully across their ochre rain-slick remains scattered across an uneven pavement and saw Keevil, in the glow of warm wall lights, watching my approach through the cottage's leaded front window.

When he opened the door I was pleasantly surprised. The bone-hard tri-athlete had been replaced by a comfortable man wearing slippers, cords and a thick sweater. Behind him as I was shown straight into the cottage's living-room a well padded lady with white hair was waiting with a wan smile.

'I'm sorry about this, Vince,' I said when he'd made the introductions, I'd shaken hands with his wife, Freda, and we were all sitting down. 'I know you and Gay were good friends, and the only excuse I can make for intruding so soon after her death is that I'm here to help.'

'All you're doing is causing mayhem, ruining lives.'

'What's that supposed to mean?'

'That kid, Joey Lox, he died because of you, and Deakin Chatto's been forced to skip.'

'Why?'

'He knew Lox. They used to go drinking. After what happened to the kid, Chatto wants to stay well clear. He works on the oil rigs. To get at him now the man doing all this killing'll have to cross the North Sea and fight his way past a couple of hundred roustabouts.'

I thought for a moment. 'I suppose that's how Chatto knew about the SUV. From Lox. Remember he mentioned it at the meeting, and you thought it very odd?'

'Yeah, then I told Josh and that made him suspicious and he

had me down for a killer, didn't he?' Keevil shrugged. 'So what's this about coming here to help? How the hell can you do that?'

I saw Freda wince, and guessed the hard man wasn't buried far beneath the soft exterior.

'Gay was carrying an army revolver when she went to see Melanie Wigg. That gun was used to murder Larry Galleywood.' I saw Keevil straighten in his chair, his face registering shock. 'According to Dr Moneydie, the owner, the revolver went missing weeks ago. If that's true, then it's possible Gay murdered Galleywood.'

'No.' Keevil was shaking his head violently. 'And I already know whose it was. Gay stole it yesterday. I know that because she told me what she was going to do.'

'That's what she told you. What if she already had it in her possession?'

'No.' Keevil was emphatic. 'She couldn't have killed Galleywood, because I'm convinced she didn't have that revolver until yesterday.'

'OK, then why steal it? What did she want it for? Was she going to ask Wigg about the missing money?'

His smile was cold. 'If you already know, why ask?'

'I'm guessing. Feeling my way. Anyway, you've answered me. So if she knew about the money, and wanted some of it, was she in it with Galleywood?'

'In what?'

'For goodness' sake, Vince,' Freda said softly. She turned to me. 'No, she wasn't involved in that blooming housing fiddle. But she was involved with Galleywood. When it was over, they were going away together – he said. But what he did was double-cross her. And then someone killed him.'

'Wow, they kept that relationship quiet, didn't they?' I said, unable to hide my amazement.'

'A lot of folks manage that,' Freda said, and when she shot a glance at Vince I sensed that these two knew more than they were letting on. But about what? And was it linked to the Galleywood murder?

'Which folk?'

'Doesn't matter, I've said enough.'

Perhaps she had. She'd told me Galleywood double-crossed Gay. I already knew he'd spent six months in the sun with Melanie Wigg. If there was a reason for his dumping Gay, wasn't the reason staring me in the face? Wasn't it obvious that the Grecian sun had turned Galleywood's head and he'd fallen heavily for his partner in crime? And wouldn't that, now, give meaning to Wigg's extraordinary remark when she saw Galleywood lying on his back in the study? 'Christ almighty,' she'd said, 'he's bloody well gone and died on me.'

'You've said *more* than enough, Freda,' I said. 'Galleywood was involved with Melanie Wigg, wasn't he?'

I was watching her when I put the question, and I saw something flicker in her eyes. She opened her mouth to speak. I saw Vince glare at her. She clamped her mouth shut, her lips a thin line.

'OK,' I said, 'so I'll take that as a yes, Gay was a woman scorned—'

'No,' Freda said. 'Nobody else was involved. Larry was all of a sudden filthy rich, and he was keeping it all for himself.'

'I see.' I met her steady grey eyes. 'So he *hadn't* switched his affections to Melanie Wigg?'

She smiled. 'Guess again, love,' she said, and once more I was stranded, wondering what the hell she meant by that.

'Maybe I will,' I said. I paused, decided I'd pushed too far and they'd battened down the hatches. 'OK, so all that happened was Gay decided that with Galleywood dead she was once again in with a chance of getting her hands on some of that money. She had this madcap idea, stole Moneydie's pistol and trotted off to force Wigg into some sort of agreement?'

'Seems like it,' Keevil said. 'She told me she was going to the surgery, and you've already worked out why she wanted the pistol.'

He shrugged broad shoulders, yawned and looked pointedly at the clock. I took the hint.

'But you're absolutely certain about one thing,' I said, getting up from the chair. 'It was yesterday morning that Gay set out to steal Moneydie's pistol?'

'Absolutely.'

'She didn't already have it? She hadn't stolen it at some other time?'

'She was here,' Freda Keevil said. 'We were in the kitchen. She was dead serious, nervous as a kitten, and I gave her a glass of port. She had a handbag, she opened it, showed me. I'm going to put it in there, she said. I've made sure there's plenty of room. And she was right: you could have got a cannon in that bag, because she'd taken everything out but her car keys and some tissues and what looked like a photograph of her and Larry. There was nothing else in there.'

chapter twenty-two

A change of plan.

Vince Keevil had sounded very sure that Moneydie's pistol had been stolen by Gay Tirril on Friday, but I knew that the only people who could convince the police were Tirril or Moneydie. Tirril was dead, which left me with Moneydie. His house lay close to my route from Thornton Hough to the Galleywood place. I phoned DI Dancer to let him know I might be a few minutes late, then turned right and headed for Moneydie's house.

It took me ten minutes. When I drove past the rugged stone walls and pulled into the driveway the white Toyota was gleaming under the low-slung dormer house's security lights but this time, behind it, there was an old Nissan Cherry with oxidized paint-work speckled with rust.

There was no surgery on a Saturday evening, so who, I wondered, had come a-calling?

On the short drive I had thought up a cunning plan, put together some words that would do for me what Open Sesame did for Ali Baba: allow the doors to swing open and let me in.

Moneydie himself answered my knock. It seemed that the Jessica I had heard but not seen on my first visit was doomed to remain forever in the background, the fumes from sizzling steak or stir-fried veggies clinging in hair I guessed was probably grey and framing a face lined by decades of silent sufferance. Did the ex-army medicine man march her each morning into the kitchen? I wondered – and shuddered as I thanked my lucky stars for having found an army man who'd been a senior NCO and is retired Major Moneydie's polar opposite.

Moneydie was watching and waiting.

I said, 'Doctor Moneydie, the police have arrested a man for Galleywood's murder. I thought you'd be interested.'

He wasn't interested, he was astounded. No sexy plastic apron this time so for something to do he wiped his hands on cavalry twill trousers and looked at me as I was mad. Promising. How could the police have the killer, he was thinking, if that killer is me?

'I'm busy for the moment,' he said, and I sensed he was buying time to pull himself together, 'but if you'd like to wait in the surgery ...'

He ushered me into that part of the house where he conducted his business, let me into a room without bothering to look inside and at once I realized he'd forgotten that it was already occupied.

A woman was in there. She wore a loose white polyester duster coat and yellow rubber gloves and for an instant I thought she was a nurse of some kind, or a vet who'd strayed in her search for a cow. Then I smelt polish, saw the vacuum cleaner standing in front of the desk and realized she was the cleaner and owned the red Nissan.

'Don't mind me,' I said, smiling. 'I'll sit somewhere out of your way.'

'All finished.'

She was in her forties, dark, pretty. She stripped off her gloves with a flourish so that they were still inside out, flexed her fingers like a surgeon limbering up. She was eyeing me with curiosity as she took off the overall and went to unplug the vacuum cleaner. Evening, no surgery, yet there I was waiting for the doctor. What could be going on?

'Awful, about that woman,' she said, an angler casting her line with care. 'The one who was shot.'

'Terrible.'

'And poor Doctor Moneydie, him being questioned like that.'

'Routine, just the police doing their job,' I said. 'After all, it was his—'

'Gun,' she said, nodding quickly, her eyes wide.

'Gosh,' I said, 'I didn't know the press had been informed.'

'Oh, they haven't.' Her cheeks were flaming. 'I was here, doing the hall, you know, the main part of the house, when they were in the living-room. Him and the police. I couldn't help hearing what they were saying.'

'Of course not.' I smiled, two of a kind, women of the world unite.

'The thing is,' she said, edging closer and dropping her voice, 'I know I shouldn't have done it, shouldn't have looked, but I cannot believe that it was the same ... you know, the same, the actual *actual* weapon.'

'What was?'

'The gun. The one I saw.'

'Ah.' Understanding dawned. 'Well, he kept it in his desk drawer, didn't he? So if at some time you happened to be polishing the desk and he'd absent-mindedly left the drawer half open ...'

I presented her with the excuse, waited for her to breathe a sigh of relief. But she was shaking her head.

'Yes, it was like that, sort of accidental the first time – but this time I looked deliberately, because it sort of fascinated me, and ... and I actually *touched* it,' she said, and she twisted her mouth into a grimace, shuddering deliciously. 'I got *hold* of it, put my finger on the trigger' – she raised her hand and waggled a crooked forefinger – 'wearing gloves, of course, but then, my God, to think that very same night—'

'Same night?'

'Yes. Last night. That's when she was shot. With the doctor's gun.'

'And you saw the gun there, in his drawer – when?'

'In the morning.'

'Yesterday morning?'

'Yes. That's what I keep telling you.'

I took a deep, deep breath.

'So when you were listening in the hall, today, you didn't hear *everything* the police said?' Meaning, of course, that she hadn't heard Moneydie lying about the gun's disappearance.

'I heard enough,' she said, moving away from me to grab the vacuum cleaner and make for the door. 'That was the actual gun that killed that woman – and I'd touched it.'

★

I could smell whisky on his breath when he came into the room, strong enough to make what must have been an expensive men's deodorant smell like something you dribble on chips.

He sat down behind the desk, razor-cut white hair, confident in pink shirt, cravat and those cavalry twills. Steadied by the strong spirit. In control.

I looked at him and smiled brightly.

'It's a tough one, isn't it?'

He frowned. 'What is?'

'Well, if someone's being held for the murder of Larry Galleywood, what do you do? Do you let him swing for it? – metaphorically, of course. Or you do the honourable thing and confess?'

'I suppose this is what I deserve,' he said, looking down his nose at me.

'What, for dealing with a dabbling woman?' I shrugged. 'Works like anything else: sometimes things drop into your lap.'

That got to him. I'd started by talking in riddles and continued that way. He was becoming irritated.

'I don't know what the hell you're talking about.' He paused, very gently rocking backwards and forwards in his chair. 'What's this man's name? The man being held by the police?'

'Ah, well, actually that was a fib. They haven't made an arrest, but they're about to.'

I raised my eyebrows, waited.

'What does that mean?'

'I means shortly after I make a phone call, they'll come knocking on your door.'

'Why should they do that? The police have already been here.'

'I know.'

He pursed his lips. 'Galleywood was murdered on Monday. I made it clear to the police that my revolver went missing several weeks ago.'

'Oops,' I said. 'That makes two of us.'

'For God's sake—'

'Telling fibs.'

188

And suddenly he was wary. Watching him was like listening to the whine of some electronic recording device running backwards. His cold blue eyes flickered like the device's mechanical counter. He was reliving the past few minutes, what he'd heard, what he'd seen – what he could work out using his innate intelligence. Then he got to it. I saw his face pale, the thin lips quiver just a little before he clamped them shut.

'Mandy Ellis,' I said. 'Yes, I asked her name. She cleans your – what, surgery, is it? – and she's seen your revolver several times. The big thing is, she saw it yesterday morning. And she's willing to stand up in court and testify.'

He took a deep, shuddering breath, then let it out; again wiped his hands on his cavalry twill trousers. A tic. A mannerism, a habit – and I'd thought a lot about those, hadn't I?

'If I did … do it – and I'm admitting nothing – it must have been an accident,' he said. 'I can't go to prison for an accident.'

'A revolver doesn't fire itself.'

He shook his head impatiently. 'Perhaps I fired at the house. At the window. He had my coin, and perhaps I wanted to frighten him.' He smiled absently, loving that 'perhaps', proud of it. 'Perhaps I'd already made a mild attempt to … harm him. He had angina, maybe something more serious. I told him to take plenty of strenuous exercise.' He shook his head. 'So perhaps I went to see if that had worked, and he was there in his study, standing there—'

'Reading?'

'No. No, just standing there. In fact, I thought he could see me, thought he was probably laughing.' He sighed. 'So it's possible I took a pot shot at the damn fool's house – I really can't remember – but I know that I left quickly, didn't even stop to see the result.'

I almost felt sorry for him. We were watching each other, both waiting to see who'd make the first move. When nothing happened, I fumbled in my tote bag and came out with my mobile. He saw it, slammed a hand on the desk and shook his head.

'Leave it,' he said fiercely. 'You've done enough. At least have the decency to let me finish it my way.'

As he reached for his phone I couldn't help wondering why, at that moment, I had felt an icy chill wash over me that left me feeling physically sick. I know I wasn't worried about suicide: the man didn't have the guts. So was it anticipation, dread, the awful realization that mistakes were about to come back and haunt me?

As always, I was soon to find out.

chapter twenty-three

I was expecting the Galleywood house to be festooned in drooping crime-scene tape like a huge brown-paper parcel that's been left outside to disintegrate in the rain. Instead, as my Ka crunched up the drive, all I saw was the same mouldering Victorian mausoleum with its dusty basement windows peeping at me over their parapets and, parked under yet more dripping trees shedding the last of their leaves from branches flailing and rattling in the rising wind, two cars, two people.

DI Dancer, the shoulders of his baggy alpaca suit once more stained dark by the rain, was talking to Melanie Wigg who was clutching about her slim form what looked like the devil's black cloak. As I stepped out into the gathering storm and slammed the car door I saw her turn and toss a bunch of keys to him as she walked, hair flying in the wind, towards her car. He called something after her. She ignored him, slid into the silver Vauxhall Corsa and sped down the drive towards the road so fast and so close to me I was buffeted by her car's slipstream.

'Where's she going?'

'Who knows? She wouldn't tell me, and it doesn't matter anyway.' He lifted the keys and jingled them. 'We've been given the freedom of the house.'

He grabbed my arm, pulled me towards the steps and we ran up to cower against the front door as the wet wind gusted.

'Just you and me?' I said, as he turned the keys and pushed open the door. 'No uniformed officer to ensure protocol, see there's no funny business?'

He slammed the door, cutting off the roar of the wind. We stood in the gloomy hall. Ahead of us the stairs rose towards faint light seeping through landing windows. Somewhere high up under the roof the wind was moaning.

'Funny business?' Dancer said. 'As a favour to you I'm here in stinking November weather about to poke around a crime scene looking for some clue that'll lead us to a pile of money that's gone missing from a Greek bank. Things don't come much funnier than that, do they? Funny, as in peculiar.'

He was already talking over his shoulder. I followed him up the stairs and, when we turned along the passage towards the study, there across the door was my crime-scene tape. Dancer was shaking his head. He ripped the tape away, pushed the door with the tips of his fingers – the jamb was still splintered – hesitated for a moment as it swung open then stepped inside and clicked on the light.

'Last time I was here,' I said, looking around, 'there was a body on that Chinese rug, an ornate knife on the desk.'

He grunted. 'Yeah, well, there's been another body since then and that fancy knife ended up in Tirril's throat.' He looked at me, must have seen the horror I was fighting to hide, and pushed on, 'OK, Penny Lane, where d'you suggest we start looking for clues?'

I forced a grin. 'You're just as keen as I am. Never mind doing me a favour, finding that loot would be a feather in your cap.'

'Get on with it,' he growled.

We split up. I began with the desk, Dancer with the big wooden filing cabinet. Both of us were dragging out drawers, flipping through files, scrutinizing papers large and small, crumpled, faded, legible, indecipherable; neither of us, I realized belatedly, knew what we were doing. OK, we knew we were looking for something written down. But this was an office, a *study*, for God's sake. Most of the stuff we'd find in a place like this would be writing in some form.

I looked across at Dancer. He had his hands in one of the deep drawers but was returning my glance.

'We need a plan,' he said.

'Or a miracle – like Galleywood's ghost pointing a finger.'

He was casting his eyes heavenwards when his mobile rang. He took it out of his pocket, strolled to the sash window that overlooked the back garden as he listened. Nodded several times. Switched off. When he turned towards me his eyes were gleaming.

'The quack's confessed,' he said. 'Moneydie rang in, said it was him, he killed Galleywood.' He paused. 'Of course, the fact that one minute he's lying about having the revolver at all when the killing happened and the next he's confessing to committing murder with it has got nothing to do with you phoning to tell me you'd be late?'

'Sort of. I haven't got a plan now; I didn't have a plan then. I just called at his house, unannounced. He made me wait, but the cleaner was there and we got talking. She'd seen the revolver in his desk drawer on the same day Gay Tirril was murdered.' I shrugged. 'When I told Moneydie, he knew the game was up.'

'Be nice to have him confirm how he managed to shoot Galleywood, but I suppose that'll come in good time. Right now we're looking for something that might not even exist, and that ghost hasn't answered your call.'

'No, he hasn't. And although I had what I thought was a flash of inspiration just now,' I said, 'I then remembered that on the night he died Galleywood had been to the library so the book he was reading—'

'Wasn't a library book.'

'Really?' Feeling a faint gleam of hope but far from optimistic I made a show of glancing in all directions. 'So where is it? At the police station, I suppose, Exhibit A, sealed in a bag—'

'Nope, it's back on the shelf. We'd finished with it, so it's there – somewhere tucked away in this lot.' He waved a hand vaguely, then cocked his head. 'Why? You think he'd write important stuff in a book?'

'Yes, that's what occurred to me. A lot of reference books, stamp catalogues included, have blank pages at the back for notes. My thought was that if Galleywood does make lots of notes and wanted to write something down but keep it well hidden, there'd be no better place. Crime writers do it all the time: they drop clues into narrative or dialogue but hide them by cluttering the page with distractions.'

But I was talking to myself. Dancer was already over at the bookshelves, looking at titles with his head tipped awkwardly sideways like someone browsing in a public library.

'The catalogue lists British Colonials, going back to when stamps were first issued,' I said, and saw him nod impatiently. He and his colleagues had *studied* the book which would, he was silently suggesting, mean they'd noted the title.

And then *my* phone rang. It was Josh, making a lightning call to let me know he was setting off to meet Steve and go with him to confront Barnaby Rieff. When he got there, he told me, he'd leave his mobile switched off so there'd be no interruptions.

Before I had time to comment, a click announced his departure. I was left with my mouth open and a question for DI Dancer.

'Billy, are your lot still holding Barnaby Rieff?'

'Huh?' He'd moved to the bookshelves near the window and had a thick book in his hand. Wrong one, obviously; he slammed it back into its slot.

'Rieff?' He glanced across, hand reaching for another book. 'No need. I spoke to him on the phone.'

'Christ, is that all? He threatened me, did this' – I indicated the fading bruise on my jaw – 'and on top of all that he's a murder suspect. Why on earth didn't you haul him in to be questioned?'

'Penny, Penny,' Dancer said softly, 'Barns Rieff didn't attack you and he's not a killer, the idea was always ludicrous. I was embarrassed just broaching the subject, and when he'd stopped laughing he presented me with cast-iron alibis then threatened to sue for slander or something.'

'You should have told me.' I shook my head in despair and held up my dead mobile. 'That was Josh calling. Steve Easter's on his way to tackle Mr squeaky-clean Barnaby Rieff. He's going to ask him how he knew the name of the third man and, no doubt, tackle him about the assault on me. Josh has gone along to help with the strong-arm stuff if things get nasty.'

'Then bloody well call them off.'

'I can't. Josh's phone's switched off, and I don't know Steve's mobile number.'

'Call his wife, ask her—'

'It won't do any good. In his present, fired-up mood, Easter's not going to listen to me.'

'Really. OK, then tell me, how did Easter get on to Rieff? Did it come from you, is that how it happened?' Dancer shook his head angrily, almost ripped another book from the shelves. 'Penny, you'd better pray that Easter and that husband of yours don't do anything rash, because Rieff's a powerful man and he's just about had it up to—'

He broke off.

His furious gaze had been flicking absently at the book he'd selected as he raged at me. Now he turned it in his hands to examine the spine and then the front cover across which, even from where I was standing, I could see there was a deep groove. He lifted his gaze, looked at me with a thin smile.

'Or maybe,' he said, 'you'd better pray that somewhere on the blank pages at the back of this *Stanley Gibbons Commonwealth & Empire Stamp Catalogue* – going back, like you said, to the year dot; in stamp terms, 1840 – we find Barnaby Rieff's name.'

And he tossed it to me, a gentle underhand lob that saw the thick volume execute a shallow parabola before dropping heavily into my waiting hands. It was almost, I thought abstractedly, as if someone had thrown it through the window.

'Oh, God,' I said. 'Billy, I've just had a brilliant thought. Actually, it's more than brilliant, I think I've just solved the locked-room mystery.'

I was holding the heavy book, at once suffused with excitement and awed by my powers of deduction and observation. Dancer took one look at my face, groaned, and leaned back against the bookshelves.

'Go on,' he said, 'let's have it.'

'It was the way you threw the book at me,' I said, 'no pun intended. I watched it and all these wild thoughts fluttered off in different directions then came together to roost – is that right? – and I remembered something and what had been a weird notion that didn't make sense suddenly did and I could see how it was done. Unintentionally. Moneydie said it was pure accident, and of course he was right.'

'What, pulling the trigger?'

'Not that exactly. Indeed, that's what I said to him: a revolver doesn't fire itself. But on Wednesday, I went to see Kirsty Tremayne. She's the young woman who was engaged to—'

'Andy Galleywood, yeah.'

'Right, and when I went to her flat in Chester, she had an old sash window propped open with a book. You see these marks, impressions, here, and here' – I lifted the book and rubbed my finger along the top and bottom of the big stamp catalogue – 'well, that's what Galleywood had done, wasn't it? He propped open his window because he'd just been to see his doctor and Moneydie knew he had angina and wanted him dead and he'd told him to get plenty of exercise and fresh air. And then, later that day, when Moneydie went strolling down that track behind the Galleywood house—'

'Strolling, in the pouring rain?'

'With a purpose, Billy. He was obsessed, he couldn't let Galleywood get away with stealing that coin from under his nose and when he saw him standing there, still alive, he flipped and pulled out that old revolver and took a pot shot.'

'It was a wild shot, the bullet hit the book, drove it into the room, the window banged down and the bullet flew on, deflected into Galleywood's eye – and he was a goner. Yeah,' Dancer said, 'we'd sort of worked that out, Penny. That's why a few moments ago I said it'd be nice to hear Moneydie *confirm* how it was done.'

'You *sort of* worked it out?'

'Well, actually, it was Josh. I told you I got something off him. He talked it over with me when you were in the shower the night that scally's body turned up. Like, he queried how the puny crack of a .38 revolver up there in the study could not only be heard in the kitchen but had sounded, in your words, like someone dropping a heavy book. And that set him thinking about the window. If a sash window won't stay open, you prop it open. If the prop's whipped away, the window comes down with a bang – which is what you and Wigg heard. And if you want to move a prop when you're not actually in the room, you must use some other means, sort of like remote control – in this case, a bullet.'

'And it was pure accident. Moneydie didn't plan any of it.'

'Yeah, he conjured up a locked-room mystery out of nothing. Nevertheless, me asking a crime writer to assist worked out well. The only thing we didn't work out was who fired the fatal shot, then along comes the crime writer's wife and—'

'Lo and behold.' I nodded in disbelief, deflating as quickly as my success had sent me whirling into rosy clouds of euphoria. 'Josh had worked it out, and he didn't tell me. Oh, my goodness, you just wait till I see that man.'

'When you do, you might be armed with reprisals, so to speak,' Dancer said. 'Or to put it in lingo Ryan Sharkey would understand, if you find what you're looking for in that book you'll have backed an outsider and watched it romp home at a hundred to one.'

The search got easier after that, in the end very easy, but the easier it got the more difficult it became to swallow what we found. In my case, anyway, because some of what Billy Dancer and I found at the back of that big book began to make me look a complete fool. And dangerous to boot. Other carefully and cleverly anno-tated entries had, as expected, started out as Larry Galleywood's salvation. In the end, for one reason or another, they had killed him. I think the old saying is that you can run but you can't hide. Well, for success in his double-cross Galleywood would have had to work things in a topsy-turvy way, turn everything on its head; and while he was extremely clever at hiding details of where he'd put the money that never did belong to him, he either couldn't run, or left it far too late to make a successful getaway.

'At the back, as expected,' Dancer said.

He'd clicked on the green, banker's table-lamp and doused the study's main light and we were at Larry Galleywood's leather-inlaid desk. Dancer was in the swivel chair, I'd dragged over a wheel-back with a cushion. We were looking through Galleywood's stamp catalogue. Dancer had checked in the usual way for loose inserts such as torn sheets from notebooks by holding the book at each end of the spine, dangling it over the desk and giving it a good shake. Nothing dropped out. He placed it on the desk under the green light, riffled through the pages to make sure it was all catalogue stuff, then went straight to the back.

Blank pages. Lots of pencilled notes.

He looked sideways at me.

'He's been doing this for some time.'

'Ever since he bought it – and it's a very old edition. But the property scam started at the beginning of this year and the money disappeared from the Greek bank just a couple of months ago. Notes referring to those crimes will come at the end.'

'Maybe. Unless he squeezed them in somewhere so they'd be missed.'

'They wouldn't be. He was very neat. Squeezing them in would look untidy and draw attention.'

Dancer nodded. 'Just testing.' He grinned at me. 'OK, so we go to the last page of notes and see what we find.'

I watched him lick his finger, turn the pages from the top corner until he got to the last one with any writing. I leaned closer.

'Countries. And dates – I think. Yes, I'm sure those are dates. He'd have jotted down the date colourful commemoratives were issued or the year a country brought out a completely new design for all its stamps, then ticked them off when he'd acquired them for his collection. Mostly twentieth century, so he's used just the year number: '08, '16, '28, '51, and so on.'

'Fantastic,' Dancer said, 'but where does that get us?'

'Take your pick. Bechuanaland, Belgian Congo, Easter Island, Mozambique, Tanganyika, Turks and Caicos ...'

'Yeah, but—'

'Then there's Orange Free State, Transvaal, Basutoland, Swaziland, Natal—'

'Penny!'

'And here.' With my finger on the page I looked at the gaunt DI who was beginning to turn a dangerous shade of purple, and smiled sweetly. 'Vontobel Cayman, and Cayman Islands.'

'Cayman Islands? That's not a colony.'

'It was until 1962, along with Jamaica. Since then it's been a British Overseas Territory.'

'Yeah, right, and you know that because it just happens to be the setting for a crime book Josh has written.'

'No.' I smiled smugly. 'My Dad had a stamp shop on

Smithdown Road. If he specialized in anything, it was British Colonials.' I shook my head impatiently. 'The point is, on our trip to the Greek Islands Sharkey and I were discussing the Caymans, looking them up on the internet. It's a tax haven; you might say it's *the* tax haven. Lots of banks there – we looked those up too – and despite changing legislation they're still as secretive as the Masons. Galleywood had money to hide. What if the figures he's jotted down alongside Cayman Islands are not dates, but an account number. They're in pairs, but if you remove the semi-colons ...'

'OK,' Dancer said, leaning closer. 'So what's this "unprocurable" he's put in brackets underneath one of those pairs? Looks like it means he's unlikely to get his hands on that one, but is it just misdirection, making it look as if he's talking about stamps when he's not?'

'Could be an account password,' I said, and saw the DI smile, then nod in undisguised admiration.

'Two out of three,' he said, 'which still doesn't get us anywhere without the name of the bank. Got any ideas?'

I stood up straight, massaged the small of my back and walked around the desk. Dancer was still bent over the thick book, reading through Galleywood's recent notes, yawning, scratching his head. If I was right, if *we* were right, then we'd got an account number and password but more than 300 banks to choose from. Not promising. OK, what Sharkey and I had gleaned from the internet suggested individuals with offshore bank accounts had to be more open ... but even if Galleywood had used his own name, we still needed to know which bank he'd used.

I glanced towards the window as the wind moaned, then back to the desk where Dancer seemed to have frozen with his finger stuck to the page. Watching him, I ran through the names I'd read out, old British colonies, almost all of them now independent and with new names. Then the Cayman Islands and—

'Got it,' I said.

Dancer came to life and shook his head.

'Never mind that—'

'No, honestly, I told you Sharkey and I looked at the names of banks. Well, just as "unprocurable" is probably a password carefully chosen so it could have a perfectly logical but entirely different meaning, so is Vontobcl Cayman which Galleywood has paired with the Cayman Islands. The Cayman Islands comprise Grand Cayman, Cayman Brac and Little Cayman. Billy, Vontobel Cayman is a bank. The full name is *Bank* Vontobel Cayman, but Galleywood deliberately left off the word that would have given the game away.'

'Yeah, brilliant,' he said. 'You worked that out and I like it. But what I worked out is that, like the Caymans, Easter Island's not a British colony.'

I stared. 'What's that got to do with it?'

'Why's it here?'

'Because he put his notes all in one place. Billy, it doesn't matter, we've got the bank, the account number and the password—'

'If I'm right,' he said, 'we've also got a name *and* a phone number that shouldn't be here.'

I felt a sudden, crawling sense of dread.

'I'm not going to like this, am I?'

He still had his finger on the page. I moved closer to the desk. Edged might be a better word; suddenly I was terrified. I reached blindly for my chair, gripped the back until my knuckles turned as white as bone.

'Like you said,' Dancer went on, 'most of the numbers are years, twentieth century so he used just two digits – but take away the commas or whatever and after the Cayman Islands you've got, not a date, but an account number. What it amounts to is if it doesn't make sense, fiddle with it, rearrange – which is what I've done with those he's scribbled after Easter Island. The 01 and the 51 were easy: put those together and you've got the Merseyside area code. After that I've got seven numbers – and that set alarm bells ringing because everywhere else on the page you've got pairs and you can't divide two into seven. What d'you call it?'

'A prime number,' I said huskily.

'Yeah. But it splits neatly into blocks of three and four, and then it has the same pattern as most Liverpool phone numbers.' At last he lifted his hand from the page, flexed his fingers.

''Course, those seven could be mixed up too, but I'm not both-
ered because what do I need with the phone number if I've got
the bloke's name?'

I sat down heavily.

'Let me see.'

He slid the book towards me. I ignored the 0151 and looked at
the other numbers. Stared at them until they began to waver,
blur. I looked up at Dancer, rubbed my eyes, let my hands slip
down to my mouth and kept them there, pressed together in an
attitude of prayer.

'Yes,' I said, 'that's Steve Easter's phone number. And now I
know why I felt sick when I was leaving Dr Moneydie's house. He
got angry with me, slammed his hand on the desk. I went cold.
Because at that moment at the back of my mind I must have
sensed I'd got it wrong; pointed the finger at the wrong man.'

'Rieff,' Dancer said. 'Not Steve Easter. But how did you get it
wrong?'

'Because the man who attacked me had not one mannerism
that I vaguely recognized, but two – and I focused on remembering the wrong one to the exclusion of the other. When I was
with Rieff in his office he slammed his hands on the nearest thing
– his desk – and I imagine he does it all the time when he's angry.
It's a violent act that can be quite shocking. It sticks in the mind.'

'And Easter?'

'He has a stray lock of hair that falls over his forehead, and he's
always pushing it back with his hand – it's a gentle tic he's
unaware of and that in the end goes unnoticed by anyone because
it's, well, it's just Steve. The man who attacked me was doing that
all the time. Unfortunately, the significance of it didn't hit home
because he was wearing a balaclava. I thought that horrible black
woollen helmet was irritating him, and he was making it more
comfortable. I was wrong. It was Steve Easter, and he had
marbles in his mouth so I wouldn't recognize his voice and ...'

I trailed off. My mouth had gone dry. My hands were trembling. I took them from my mouth and clasped them together in
my lap.

Dancer was nodding abstractedly. I saw no accusation in his
narrowed eyes. He was a detective inspector, doing his job, thinking

hard. He slipped a hand into his pocket, took out his mobile, then changed his mind and reached across for the phone on Galleywood's desk. He kept his hand resting on it, looked at me.

'If Easter's the man behind the property scam and the killings, why's he going to see Rieff?'

'I don't know.'

'Who suggested Josh went with him?'

'I did.'

'Not Easter? And he didn't lead you by the nose by saying exactly the things he knew would drag the offer of Josh's help out of you?'

'I ... I think he probably did. I told him about Rieff attacking me. Steve said something about needing powerful backup.'

'OK, so he's not going to see Rieff, and he's worked it so Josh is with him. Why? What else did you tell him?'

And then he looked at my face, and drew in a deep, deep breath.

'You told him you were coming here didn't you?' he said, letting the breath out explosively and shaking his head. 'You told him you were coming here to Galleywood's house; you told him why, and you told him I'd be with you.'

'Yes,' I said in a very small voice.

'Then Easter's expecting you to succeed,' Dancer said flatly. 'You're setting out to do something he failed to do with brutality and torture: find the missing millions Galleywood squirrelled away. He's got his hands on Josh, Penny, and he'll use every vicious threat he can think of to force you to hand over the location of that missing cash.'

I quickly told Dancer where Steve Easter and Josh had gone and he picked up the phone and keyed in numbers then paced up and down the stained Chinese rug with the cordless pressed to his ear, snapping out instructions and every so often flicking a searching glance in my direction. He probably thought I was about to collapse in a bout of hysterical sobbing, or fall swooning across the desk, wrist pressed to clammy brow, but I had just one thing in mind and, like so much that evening, it was a name.

Sharkey.

My mobile was in my tote bag. I was desperate to phone my staunch colleague, but what I wanted Sharkey to do would be hotly disputed by Dancer if he heard me, so I waited until the DI's restless pacing took him over to the window with his back towards me and I simply walked out of the room.

Of course he'd been watching my reflection in the window. By the time I reached the stairs he was out of the office and damn near snapping at my heels, but mine had wings and I was still ahead of him when I flung open the heavy front door and ran down the steps into the wild wind and rain.

'Penny!'

He was calling after me from the front door. I couldn't suppress a wintry smile at the thought that he was desperate to stop me but wouldn't risk yet again soaking that expensive alpaca suit. I slid into the Ka, clinging to the door as it was caught by the wind, and as I slammed it and drove away with a little shimmy of the Ka's tail end I could see him in the doorway, hands on hips, shaking his head.

It was almost eight o'clock. The wild weather had thinned the traffic and I quickly put half-a-mile between me and the furious DI then drew to a halt at the side of the road and reached for my mobile.

It rang so suddenly I dropped it, scrabbled for it between my wet feet, picked it up and said a breathless, 'Hello?'

'Penny, it's Steve.'

Mind suddenly numb, I swallowed, closed my eyes.

'Hi, Steve. Has Josh reached you yet?'

'Yes, he's here.'

'Right, well, something's come up at this end and I need his advice, would you put him on?'

'Did you find what you were looking for? Did you find the money?'

'No. No, we didn't—'

He chuckled. 'I don't believe you.'

'Dancer was with me. Ask him. We didn't find *any* money.'

'Of course you didn't. But you *did* find Larry's notes, you know exactly where he moved that money to and you're going to tell me.'

'Steve, I really need to talk to Josh.'

'Well, when I say he's here, he's not actually with me.'

'So where is he?'

He chuckled again, and I went cold.

'He's in the lamp room.'

A car's headlights flashed in the rear-view mirror and, now praying it was Dancer, I watched in despair as it drew level then raced on by in a hiss of fine spray.

'The *lamp* room? What—?'

'A lamp room's at the top of a lighthouse. This particular lighthouse is on the point of land jutting into the sea to the west of the golf course. Royal Liverpool, Hoylake. You must have been close to it a couple of months ago when you stumbled on that body. It's a very old lighthouse, so old it's got a big kerosene lamp or lantern—'

'Never mind that,' I cut in. 'What's Josh doing up there?'

'Not a lot. He's got other things on his mind – you might say that he's likely to be tied up for some time,' Steve said, and now his chuckle was a full-blown laugh and for a moment he couldn't speak. Then he said, 'You can help him out, of course. I'm there now, in the room just below, listening to the wind and rain and trying to ignore the stink of kerosene. All you've got to do is come and talk to me – choosing your words carefully, of course, telling me exactly what I want to hear.'

'I might not be able to.' My heart was thumping. One hand was holding the phone tight against my ear. The other was gripping the steering wheel. 'All we found were the names of British colonies, some dates—'

'Bullshit. They mean more than that, you know they do, so bring them,' Steve said. 'Josh is all right – for the moment. The trouble is, I was careless when I filled that old lamp, and kerosene got splashed everywhere. All over the floor, all over Josh. And now I don't trust myself. I might get careless again before you get here, this time with a naked flame.'

'Don't. Please. Steve, I'm on my way.'

I pulled away from the kerb without looking, my mind fluttering helplessly like a bird with injured wings. I recognized that chill feeling of panic that sets your scalp prickling. Easter had imagined I was still in Galleywood's house. He expected me to have the information he needed there at my fingertips. Instead I was rushing to meet the man who was holding my husband hostage, but would be unable to give him what he wanted because in Galleywood's study I had taken no notes, photographed nothing, and hadn't even thought about memorizing the Cayman Islands' account number.

I had to go back to Galleywood's house. My foot moved to the brake. I slowed, began looking for a side road. Then I remembered Dancer, and knew at once that one escape had been lucky, getting away from him twice would be impossible – especially if I rushed out clutching that heavy catalogue.

I lifted my foot from the brake and picked up speed again. Vaguely I was aware that the headlights that shortly afterwards appeared in my mirror remained constant both in intensity and in their distance from me, but I was much too preoccupied to start worrying about a tail – as we PIs say. Like Josh, I had something much more serious on my mind. I was a trader going to market with an empty wallet and, with nothing to bargain with, the best I could hope for was to come away with badly damaged goods.

Sharkey answered the illegal call I made on my mobile while exceeding the speed limit through Heswall, picked me up at the bungalow less than an hour later and we left the Ka in the drive and headed for Hoylake in his Lexus. Broke he might be, but he'd managed to hang on to that flashy car and by the look on his face I knew that being asked to come to the aid of the woman who was *the best thing that had happened to him* in a long time was just the fillip he'd needed. He'd told me he was subtle, but subtle can only take you so far and I guessed that in some men violent action is needed to release tension and frustrations and if Steve Easter was on the receiving end …

'Nearly there.'

I nodded. 'We need a plan A, and a plan B. But first, to give us something to work with, what do you know about lighthouses?'

'Glassed-in lantern room at the top of the tower, glass storm panes reinforced by metal Astragal bars, service room below that for stores and so on – often called the watch room because that's where some of the keepers used to stand watch some of the time.' He took his eyes off the road and grinned across at me. 'Need any more?'

'Why *used* to?'

'Because all lighthouses have been automated for years. The last one with a keeper was the North Foreland in Kent. He left in 1998.'

'What's access like?'

'I've no idea. My hazy recollection is that the older lighthouses are tall, circular stone towers with just one door at the base. I know there's often an open gallery around the watch room – the main gallery – sometimes another one round the lantern room. The keepers used them to go out and clean the lamp-room windows.'

We were on Telegraph Road – the A540 – and the tyres were hissing through enough surface water to cause dangerous aquaplaning and Sharkey was driving too fast but his hands on the wheel looked strong and capable and as I watched him and the ribbon of slick black road unwinding beneath the wheels my persistent feeling of optimism was transformed into a rush of excitement that was like, well, I've never done drugs but the brain produces its own, doesn't it? What are they called, endorphins? Doesn't matter. I just knew everything was going to be OK provided the speeding silver Lexus became invisible or the rain and wind kept DI Dancer's traffic cops in the station canteen or parked in some side road with cups of coffee steaming up the patrol cars' windows.

And if bloody Steve Easter didn't strike a match.

Through the wet windscreen the lights of Hoylake appeared ahead of us like blurred jewels sparkling against a backdrop of velvet. Sharkey slowed, took the first exit from the roundabout into The King's Gap, the next left into the long straight of Stanley Road at the end of which, I knew, we'd have to get out and walk with the wind and rain driving straight at us off the Irish Sea.

'We've got a tail,' Sharkey said.

'Thanks a bunch.'

I flipped the visor down and looked in the vanity mirror – and suddenly remembered the lights that had slipped in behind me as I left Galleywood's house and, for all I knew, had followed me home then picked up the Lexus and been behind us ever since.

'How d'you know they're following us?'

'Been behind us for miles.'

I grunted. 'I think it's Dancer. I told him Josh was going with Steve to see Barns Rieff. I know he phoned in. After that he must have considered his options, tossed a coin and decided to follow me. And by now he'll have got word from Old Hall Street that nobody's been near Rieff.'

'If it's Dancer, backup won't be far behind.'

'Is that good for Josh, or bad?'

'Good, if they bring fire extinguishers.'

I clenched my fist and banged him on the knee as he chuckled, then watched as he again slowed the Lexus, swung on to an area of rough ground and rocked and bounced through deep puddles until we were moving down a gentle sandy gradient and I could see in the bright halogen headlights a line of thin surf and beyond that the deep waters of Liverpool Bay, flattened by the rain.

On a spit of land poking out like a timid toe testing the waters, rising out of the darkness like a huge finger and weakly illuminated by Hoylake's street lighting that was being reflected from the low, scudding clouds, the pencil-thin white shape of the old Dee Bar Lighthouse seemed to be urging extreme caution.

And something else. There was a second car parked alongside Steve Easter's BMW on the rough land near the lighthouse's crumbling outbuildings. It was the silver Vauxhall Corsa I'd seen drive away from Larry Galleywood's house. Melanie Wigg was here, and suddenly a lot of things I had heard or seen began to make sense.

chapter twenty-six

The wind was buffeting the Lexus. Sharp sand and salt spray driven by the wind was threatening to strip the gloss from its metallic paintwork. Inside the car the heater was off, the windows steaming up. I leaned forward to scrub at the windscreen with the side of my hand. High up at the top of that ghostly tower the lantern room was in darkness. Beyond it, thick cloud was being torn ragged to allow fleeting glimpses of a cold full moon.

I sat back and shivered.

'Steve Easter was having it off with another woman; Vince Keevil's wife as good as told me who she was,' I said. 'I really should have worked it out sooner, because the liaison stopped about eight months ago.'

Sharkey nodded. 'When a property scam was born out of Steve Easter's previous experience. He had Galleywood, the man who'd sell the houses for him, but he wanted someone there, on the spot, start to finish. Easy. Get attractive mature girlfriend Melanie Wigg to come up with a plausible excuse to move into the Galleywood residence.'

'She was desperate for a place to stay, he had rooms to spare – and of course, they were friends – or at least business associates – because she worked for him in his office.' I nodded, seeing how easy it must have been. 'Remember what she said when we found Galleywood? Did I tell you?'

'Verbatim. She said, *Christ almighty, he's bloody well gone and died on me.*'

'The meaning of which is now clear: he'd squirrelled the

money away somewhere, she'd been trying to worm the information out of him without letting him know she was a mole, and
suddenly he was dead. She couldn't understand it. Steve
wouldn't have shot him like that, from a distance, because she
knew he'd questioned the son and got nothing and was coming
after the father. And now they had to face the possibility that the
secret of the money's location had died with Galleywood.'

'Squirrels and moles,' Sharkey said, grinning at me. 'Josh
would love that.'

'Yes, and a few minutes ago I was thinking in terms of fingers
and toes and pencils. One of the reasons Josh loves me is because
quite often I think and talk in mixed metaphors. But he can't love
me from up there where he is now, can he…?'

I trailed off, swallowing hard. 'Christ, what can we do,
Sharkey? We've been sitting here half the night already and my
hunk's tied up in that lantern room, probably going all funny
from sniffing those horrible fumes—'

Sharkey's gentle hand on my arm stopped me in full flow.

'They heard us arrive,' he said. 'The door's open.'

Without another word we left the warmth of the Lexus and
stepped out into the storm. The rain had stopped but the wind
plucked at our clothes, pushed me back against the car as I
slammed the door. Sharkey came around to me. He took my arm.
Like a tired old couple struggling home from an evening at the
bingo we fought our way across rough ground to the lighthouse.

Melanie Wigg was holding the door open. Her black cloak was
flapping, her short grey hair a damp skullcap.

'Up the stairs,' she said, stepping back to let us past. 'If you're
thinking of grabbing me, remember the man up there with the
lantern and think of flames and naked flesh and silent screams
behind armoured glass.'

In a stone structure as strong as the rock it stood on I was
amazed to find rickety wooden stairs clinging to the walls. I went
ahead of Sharkey, feeling my way in the darkness. Timber creaked
beneath my feet. I climbed until effort and anxiety reduced my
breathing to painful gasps. Then suddenly there was a landing of
sorts and another door in front of me. I walked through it into a
circular room. A square window was set into damp stone walls.

Light from a single hurricane lamp hanging from a beam cast yellow light on massive gears. Glistening with grease, a vertical shaft rose to a dark hole in the ceiling.

So this, I thought leadenly, is what a watch room looks like.

'Rotates the big lamp up in the lantern room,' Steve Easter said, as he saw me looking at the shaft. 'Driven by clockwork, would you believe. I thought of lots of uses for it, like putting a rope around Josh's neck and using the rotation to tighten it slowly until he choked, or you coughed up.' He chuckled. 'Too complicated. Keep it simple, right? And everyone's scared of fire.'

He was sitting on a wooden bench up against the damp, curved wall, looking much as he had been when I watched him step out of the car that was carrying Andy Galleywood's battered body: jeans, dark fleece over a rugby shirt. I looked at him with open contempt. He smiled almost shyly and, without realizing he was doing it, raised his hand to his forehead to brush back the errant lock of hair.

'This is daft,' Sharkey said. He'd come into the room behind me, closely followed by Melanie Wigg. He was looking at Easter with obvious perplexity. 'Josh is upstairs, you two are down here. I could overpower both of you, end of story – so what is it we're not seeing?'

'Jimmy Rake.'

Sharkey frowned. 'Rake's locked up.'

'No, he's out on bail. And now he's here, and upstairs.'

'Doing what?' I said.

Easter grinned. 'He's got his instructions.'

'Let me guess. If I don't hand over the information, Rake drops a lighted match.'

'Something like that. He'd be in no danger. Kerosene burns slowly enough for Rake to get out, plenty hot enough to make Josh's eyes water.'

'While he's still alive,' Melanie Wigg said. 'Come on, Lane. You and your friend can't help him. Give us what you've got and bow out gracefully.'

'Unfortunately,' I said, 'I haven't got anything.'

'Rubbish.' Easter's face had darkened. 'You went to Galleywood's study and you found what you were looking for.'

'Of course I did. It was easy. The information was in the heavy book that deflected a bullet into Galleywood's brain.'

I glanced at Wigg. She was biting her lip in chagrin, her eyes registering dismay. She'd stabbed a young woman to death in Galleywood's kitchen. Now she was being told she'd several times over the weeks since their return from Greece been no more than six feet away from the key to three million quid.

'The trouble is,' I went on, as Easter glowered and his lips tightened in anger, 'I've got a terrible memory, and I didn't make notes or take photographs. I couldn't walk out with the catalogue because DI Dancer was there, watching me, and I was already some distance from Galleywood's house when you phoned.'

'You knew your husband's life was at stake. Why didn't you go back?'

'I've just told you why.'

He grimaced. 'Dancer?'

'Yes. He was still there.'

He looked at Wigg. She was nervously pacing the worn boards. The black cloak was clutched about her trim frame. I caught glimpses of a white blouse and a dark crimson skirt as she whirled to face me.

'When you left, did you tell Dancer where you were going?'

'No. But he believes Josh was going to Liverpool with Steve to confront Rieff.'

'And Dancer phoned that in.' It was a statement. She was nodding slowly, thinking hard. 'Had Dancer finished at the house?'

'I left him at the front door. He was there with me, searching the study for my benefit. Off duty. With me gone there's nothing to keep him there.'

She looked at Steve. 'She's right. Dancer will assume she's gone to Liverpool. He'll go chasing after her. And although she said she doesn't remember details, she's given us what we need: we now know the information's in Lex's stamp catalogue—'

'Ah, but it's well hidden,' I said. 'Admit it, Steve, this is slipping away from you.' I smiled. 'I couldn't take the catalogue because Dancer was watching me, but I'm sure he'd want it for evidence and, if he's taken it with him, that puts it out of your reach for good.'

'We'll see.' Easter stood up. 'You found it, you'll go with us, and if it's still there you'll show us what you discovered and explain every last detail.'

'Or maybe not,' Sharkey said.

He'd drifted to the small square window. Suddenly he was bathed in bright light. There was a heavy silence in the watch room. Then I heard the hum of a car's engine, the whisper of tyres on the rough ground.

'Black Volvo station wagon,' Sharkey said. 'Tinted windows. Two men, big as houses.'

'A black volvo was outside Galleywood's house on Monday,' I said.

Wigg was looking at Steve Easter. Her face was white.

'You're in trouble,' she said, and she walked across the watch room as if deliberately putting distance between them.

Heavy footsteps thudded on the stairs. Easter flung a worried glance towards the open door, then swept the room with his eyes searching for another way out.

There was no escape.

The first man into the room was the man from the car-park, the man who had stumbled against Sharkey at the bar in SCENE SOUTH. Big enough to block the doorway, he was wearing jeans and navy reefer jacket. Shaven head, scarred eyebrows, a nose that had been broken several times. His colourless eyes glanced sardonically at Sharkey, then switched to Easter.

Behind him came the man who was also in the car-park photographs and had been sitting at the table in SCENE SOUTH. Standing up, he was even bigger than I remembered. He was wearing the same tight dark suit. He'd been sweating then, and he was sweating now.

'You're Ellis Barnes,' I said softly. 'And you,' I said to the man with the broken nose, 'are Jimmy Rake.'

'Got it in two,' he said, and his chest swelled at his wit. He moved away from the door and pointed at Steve Easter. 'An' he's a dead man unless he's got some good news for me.'

'Don't be so bloody hasty,' Easter said. 'You'll get what's coming to you.'

'It'd better be quick, because what I've got comin' is a life sentence for murder,' Rake said. Then he grinned. 'We all have. We could end up as cell mates, you, me an' Ellis, fifteen years sharin' the same bedroom.'

Easter shook his head, horror in his eyes. He'd been backing away. Now he hit the bench with the back of his knees and sat down suddenly. Ellis Barnes grinned. He crossed the room, sat down by Easter and put a big arm around his shoulders. As a pairing, it looked grotesque. Easter seemed to shrivel.

Melanie Wigg edged towards the door.

I looked at Easter. 'You told me Rake was upstairs. That was a lie, so who's up there with Josh?'

'Nobody,' Sharkey said, his back to the window. 'Because Josh isn't up there.'

I felt a sudden, heady thrill of excitement as I realized what he meant.

'No, they didn't meet in the car-park, did they? They were never intended to. Easter concocted a story so he could split us up: Josh on a wild goose chase to Liverpool; me in Galleywood's house finding the money for him. Then, when he decided he'd given me enough time, he phoned to tell me he was holding Josh.'

'Nice, that is,' Rake said. 'If you've found the money, you've found it for me. That's the good news I've been waiting for, and Stevie there's a very lucky boy.' He leered at me. 'So where is it, darling?'

'It's in Larry Galleywood's study.'

'Really? Yeah, well, we've been watching you ever since dumpin' poor Loxy in your garden. Figured if anyone could find the dough it'd be you.' He shook his head at Barnes. 'If we'd known what she was doin' there with Dancer we could've saved ourselves a long drive, couldn't we? Never mind. What we do now is we all toddle down to the car and go for another drive.' He grinned. 'You included, Lucky,' he said, and he winked at Easter.

Easter was looking at me. His face was a greenish-white, glistening with sweat. But behind the fear in his eyes, there was confusion. He knew the money wasn't in Galleywood's office, knew that would very soon become apparent and draw Rake's wrath, and he couldn't understand what I was up to. Neither could I. All I knew was that out in the open air under *any* circum-stances I'd feel freer than I did in that lamp-lit watch room. Also, something was telling me that Josh wouldn't have been idle. Once he realized Steve had set him up he'd have taken the obvious step. If he had—

The sound of a car engine starting cut through my thoughts.

'Oh dear,' Rake said, 'Lucky's girlfriend's buggered off and left him. Never mind, more room in the car, bigger slice of the money for us – right, Ell?'

'Absolutely,' Barnes said. He squeezed Easter. 'Didn't tell you, did we? You bein' late payin' means we've had to change the terms. An' not in your favour. Come on, let's go get it.'

He stood up, pulled Easter with him and walked him to the door. Rake jerked a head at Sharkey, waited for him to follow the other two then fell in behind me as I did the same.

We clattered down the stairs and across the windswept rough ground to the Volvo. It was a big car, three seats wide. Barnes pushed Easter into the front and climbed after him into the passenger seat. Rake held the rear door open, waited for Sharkey and me to slide in then slammed the door. He got in, started up, then splashed his way over bumps and flooded ruts and turned on to Stanley Road. Less than a minute later we were back on Telegraph Road and speeding towards Heswall.

Galleywood's house was in darkness. The rain had started again and was dancing on the roof of Melanie Wigg's silver Vauxhall Corsa. Rake pulled up behind it.

He said, 'Nice. Her bein' here saves us the trouble of breaking in.'

'Her bein' here means the *money's* still here,' Barnes said. 'I was facing the door with dick-head here when she walked out of the lighthouse. She slipped away when she heard Lane say it was in the study. If she gets hold of it she'll be away on her toes.'

'Well, let's make sure she doesn't do that,' Rake said, and he opened the door and stepped out of the car into the rain.

We all got out. Barnes took up the rear. Heavy rain swept in through the trees, slashing at us as we ran for the steps. Wigg must have been in a hurry. She'd put the snip on the lock and the door was ajar and banging in the wind. Rake stepped inside, flicked on the light. It lit up the hall, the shiny wet footprints on the floor.

I heard the front door click shut, Barnes breathing hoarsely through his mouth.

'Upstairs,' I said. 'Turn right on the landing.'

Rake tried another switch, then another. The landing remained dark. He banged the banisters angrily with his fist, then started up the stairs. Steve Easter followed. I went next, felt Sharkey move up protectively behind me. Barnes was last. On those cold linoleumed stairs our ascent sounded like an army on the march. We reached the landing. The light from downstairs was weaker. Rake stopped, looking uncertainly left and right, and we closed up.

'Right, past the bathroom,' I said. 'The door with the splintered lock.'

I felt like a tour guide in a shabby stately home. My heart was thumping. I reached for Sharkey's hand, grabbed it. He squeezed, bent to whisper in my ear.

Very softly he said, 'There's a police car parked at the side of the house.'

I shot him a startled glance. Then he released my hand, and moved away.

A little light was reaching the landing from the frosted glass skylight. I was watching Jimmy Rake.

He had reached the study. He stretched out an arm and pushed the door with the tips of his fingers. It swung a little way open. Rake stood with his head turned, listening. Then he pushed the door harder. It began to swing open. In one smooth movement Rake turned, grabbed Steve Easter and flung him at the door. Easter crashed into the hard timber. The door banged open. It rebounded from the wall. Easter crashed into it for a second time. He yelled in pain, stumbled, then fell over the threshold.

Suddenly the study blazed with light. Rake backed away, his shadow falling long across the floor. He growled something unintelligible, and his hand dipped to his pocket.

From inside the study Josh roared, 'Penny, get away from them.'

I moved, but I was too late, Rake and Barnes much too fast.

Again a muscular arm whipped around my throat from behind. I was pulled hard against Barnes. I choked, grabbed at his arm and tried to turn. Holding me effortlessly, he lashed backwards with his free arm. His elbow slammed into the advancing Sharkey's face with a crackling crunch. Sharkey went down with a hard thump, his nose and mouth gushing blood.

Metal glittered as Rake lifted a pistol. Then he was pounding back along the landing. Barnes went after him, half carrying me, keeping my body between him and the study. My feet scraped along the floor. I saw DI Dancer and Josh walk out of the brightly lit room, then stop as they caught the glint of metal in Rake's big fist. Josh went down on one knee by Sharkey, eased him up, sat him with his back against the wall. Dancer walked past them, then stopped, waited.

Rake reached the stairwell. He grabbed the banisters, took the first step down then yelled in frustration and anger. Still with one foot on the stairs he twisted to snap a glance along the landing at Dancer and Josh. Then he cursed again, stepped back off the stairs and walked without haste towards the other end of the landing.

Barnes, breathing hard, went after him. He dragged me backwards. My feet scrabbled on the slippery lino as I tried to take the weight off my neck.

There were two doors on the other side of the stairs. Barnes let me get my feet under me, and I watched Rake try them both. Both were locked. The landing was a dead end, just a wall and a high naked window running with condensation.

'Keep hold of her,' Rake told Barnes.

'Yeah, an' then what?'

'Wait.'

Dancer and Josh had followed cautiously as Rake and Barnes moved away with me. They stopped at the stairs.

'It's over,' Dancer said. 'Easter's in handcuffs. Galleywood moved the money to where it can't be reached. Put the gun down. Let Lane go and we'll all walk out of here nice and easy.'

Rake sneered. 'Or else?'

'Armed police officers will be called in. There's nowhere for you to go, and you cannot win a hostage situation.'

A sudden crack made me flinch. Rake had fired the gun. He'd aimed high. White flakes floated down from the ceiling. He grinned, held the gun up and waggled it, then stepped forward and put the muzzle against my head.

'There is no hostage situation. We walk away now, or Lane dies.'

Behind Dancer, Josh actually smiled. I squirmed in Barnes's wicked embrace, squinted at my husband in disbelief, thought *wait until I get you home, you cocky, army barmy—*

'You won't do it,' Josh said. 'You kill Penny now and you're still trapped, but without a hostage.'

'Oh yeah?' Barnes said, tightening his arm with a jerk, his breath hot on my scalp. 'Well maybe that works in books—'

'A book he probably wrote,' Dancer said, 'and if he did, he's right. Killing your hostage makes no sense, so it's time to make up your minds.'

'Done,' Rake said. 'Right now here's as good as anywhere and you're not wanted. So this is what we *do* want. We'll hold Lane. You pick up that sorry-looking tosser and piss off – you *and* that copper down there. Before you leave the house, find the keys to these rooms and throw 'em up the stairs. Short of burnin' the house down, you're going to have a hard time shifting us.' He grinned. 'And forget bed and breakfast. Terms are half-board, or human rights'll be hearin' from us.'

For a few tense moments it seemed as if Dancer was about to stand and argue. Then he turned away. Josh, staring hard at Rake, gave me a quick, encouraging nod. Then he and Dancer went to Sharkey, lifted him to his feet and helped him towards the stairs.

I watched them descend, watched them struggle downwards holding Sharkey between them; watched them until all I could see were three heads, one looking at the stairs ahead, one wobbling on a powerful neck that had lost all strength; one turned towards me as if a last lingering glance could capture an image that would be stored in memory and treasured, if necessary forever.

Not a pretty picture to have in a mental album, me slowly being throttled by an evil swine who was sweating like a pig. There I go, I thought, despite the situation almost giggling as my words tripped over each other. Well, let's change that. What did this bastard use on Sharkey? He used his elbow. Right, then ...

As if easing my shoulders, I wriggled and strained inside the restraining arm. That brought my right arm forward without it looking suspicious. With my left hand I gripped the arm clamped across my throat and tried to pull it away as if the better to breathe. A diversion, get it? Then I took a huge deep breath and rammed my elbow into Barnes's solar plexus. Or is it celiac plexus? Doesn't matter. It worked a treat.

I hit him just under the ribs with the point of my elbow, trying – as Josh had advised many times – to drive my arm through and hit a spot six inches behind the man. Barnes's breath left him in a whoosh. His head snapped forward. I felt his nose and teeth hit the top of my head, a stabbing pain, a sudden liquid warmth. Then his arm slipped away. Suddenly unrestrained, I stumbled forward. I heard Barnes hit the floor, heard Rake's angry roar, and ran.

I almost made it.

My hand hit the smooth wooden ball on the newel post. I hung on and let momentum swing me towards the stairs. Almost at the bottom, silhouetted against the hall light, I could see Josh and Dancer clinging on to Sharkey's dead weight. Rake's yell of rage was still echoing around the stairwell. Josh twisted his head, and looked back.

I cried out, 'Josh, I—'

Then Rake's foot hooked around my ankle and I took off. It was an Olympic standard belly flop without the water. My teeth clicked together as I hit hard and slid on my squashy bits, tried to save myself with my arms and managed to turn the belly flop into a forward roll I hadn't executed since school days. Not a good idea at 58 and on steep stairs. They told me later that when I came out of the roll and my head bounced off most of the banister's spindles it sounded like someone playing the xylophone.

Not very well, either, but I wouldn't know. I was unconscious. I don't even remember slamming into Josh at the end of my spectacular dive and breaking his right leg.

Sunday

'There's several things I don't understand,' I said. 'One is why Easter arranged for Andy's body to be put in the luggage box on top of his own car.'

'He was being clever,' Josh said. 'He figured if he put himself under suspicion and was then cleared by the estimable Barns Rieff, the police wouldn't look at him again.'

'Right, so the second thing is why didn't Dancer have armed officers at Galleywood's house *before* I arrived?'

'Not enough time,' Josh said. 'You left the house, and Dancer thought you were making for Liverpool to save me from a terrible fate. He covered that end by phone. I knew where he was, so shortly after that I reached him on the Galleywood land line and told him Steve Easter hadn't turned up. Dancer stayed put. When I got there, we put our heads together. Easter knew you were at the Galleywood house searching for clues to the money's location. We worked out what was likely to happen, and knew we were running out of time. All Dancer could do was alert the nearest patrol car and get minimum backup. By then, of course, you were on your way back from the lighthouse.'

It was Sunday morning. We were in the conservatory. Josh was on the wicker settee with his plastered right leg stretched out, Sharkey on the stool by the open door, elbows on knees, hands clasped together under his chin supporting his heavily bandaged face. I'd just come in from the garden; danced in, you might say, so good did I feel. The rain had stopped but the dry pond was now half full, and two murder cases had been solved.

'More by good luck than judgment,' Josh said, watching me and accurately interpreting the signs.

'Er, no, I don't think so. Easter's in clink because I recognized the man who attacked me.'

'Which means he gave himself away.'

'Nonsense.' I shook my head. 'All right, who was it who worked out where Galleywood had hidden the loot?'

'You and Sharkey. But the writing in the book led you to the money, not a killer.'

'Easter's name was there too.'

'Yes, but he'd already given himself away with that familiar mannerism when he attacked you.'

'Ah, but I hadn't realized that until I saw his name in the book. I thought it was Rieff.'

Sharkey chuckled, the sound decidedly weird coming as it did through a broken nose and two missing front teeth.

'And from what you've already told us,' he said thickly, 'the police had already worked out how the locked-room killing was done.'

'Yes,' I said triumphantly, 'but it was me who forced Moneydie into confessing by finding a witness who could prove he was lying.'

'So let's recap,' Josh said. 'Steve Easter gave himself away. The police worked out the locked-room mystery. Moneydie confessed. So what exactly was it you did, my sweet?'

'She got us a holiday in Greece,' Sharkey said.

'A working holiday,' I said ruefully. 'One day, and we never stopped.'

'Luxury suite, dinner at Plaka,' Sharkey said, and winked at Josh. 'Nice work if you can get it, but I don't mean that holiday. I'm talking about the one the three of us are going on when wounds have healed.'

'I haven't got any wounds,' I said loftily. 'A slight headache perhaps from a minor fall down a few stairs and a collision with a brittle obstacle, but other than that—'

I stopped, looked at Josh. He looked at me, wide-eyed. We both looked at the dark eyes sparkling at us from swollen and bruised flesh above white bandages.

'Care to explain?' I said.

'I phoned the manager of the Rhodes National Bank.'

'Impossible, it's Sunday.'

'When we visited him he gave me his card with his home number. I told him about your remarkable discovery. With the location – Grand Cayman – and the account number, he's convinced they'll recover the money. He's very grateful, because that goes some way to restoring the bank's reputation.'

'But not all the way?'

'No. Which means we've been offered a holiday, but there is a slight catch.'

I rolled my eyes. 'Go on.'

'Can't you work it out? Thanks to you the Rhodes' bank gets its money back, but there are still a lot of losers—'

'Cut to the chase, Sharkey.'

So he did. At length. And suddenly clever little me had another case to work on.